Sweet wife in the 1970s

Chapter 1The sky is clear outside the window.Lu Zhi got up and washed his face, still a little shocked.She had a very magical experience. She lived in the future world in her dream for more than 20 years. She accidentally saw a chronicle and found that this chronicle was about her life before time travel. Then she woke up. .Lu Zhi couldn't tell whether he had had a dream for a long time, or whether he had really experienced those things in the future and then returned to them.In this period novel, Lu Zhi is the infatuated heroine in the novel who is fair-skinned and beautiful, and likes the hero. After the hero and heroine get married, she still likes the hero, and finally becomes the comparison group of the heroine in the courtyard.Maybe she really has lived in the future for more than 20 years. Now she is no longer infatuated with the male protagonist, and even doubts why she likes him.After finding a light blue skirt and putting it on, Lu Zhi tied her braids into a high ponytail.Outside, Li Lan was already urging.Lu Zhi: It'll be ready soon.Seeing Lu Zhi come out, Li Lan looked satisfied.This is no better looking than the new daughter-in-law of Lao Li's family next doorLi Lan said with a straight face again, "Let me tell you, if you are acting like a monster during this blind date, don't even eat when you come back today."Lu Zhi said nothing.She really didn't know how to answer this question. After all, she had messed up more than a dozen blind dates before this.If it weren't for her good looks, probably no one would be willing to introduce her.Li Lan: Did you hear that? Looking at the faces of the old Li family, I don＇t think there is anything to like about the second son of the Li family. Isn＇t it just that he is better at studying?If Lu Zhi married not as well as the second child of the Li family next door, their family would probably be proud.Li Lan: Do you know?Lu Zhi: I understand.

Lu Zhi and Li Lan went out, and people from the courtyard greeted them.Aunt Zhou stopped them and talked to them a few more words.What are you doing?Blind date, you don＇t know, our Lu Zhi is good-looking and has graduated from high school. If it weren＇t for her high vision, by now, the threshold would have been crossed by those who propose marriage.Yes, I think Lu Zhi looks better than before.I don＇t know who this girl looks like anymore.Aunt Zhou also felt strange.Aunt Zhou: Why does your Lu Zhi look more handsome?Li Lan's eyes and brows are always smiling, and you will say nice things. This isn't always the case.Inside the room, He Li stretched her neck and muttered a few words. No matter how good-looking she is, my son will look down on her. He can't even do housework. What's the use of looking good.

teahouseLu Zhi's blind date this time was quite special. Both families had proposed blind dates several times, hoping very much to become in-laws, but none of them succeeded.Grandpa Zhou contacted the Lu family again a few days ago and learned that Lu Zhi was still single and proposed that he wanted the two children to meet.Lu Zhi remembered that it was written in the novel that her blind date was particularly good, and after being rejected by her, Li Lan lost her temper.Because he came in advance, Lu Zhi waited in the teahouse for a while.There were so many people going on a blind date in the teahouse, which made Lu Zhi a little bit happy.Interesting.For example, at the table next to Lu Zhi, the man's narcissism had already said that the girl should do her housework well, and the forbearing expression on the girl's face could no longer be obvious.I am usually busy at work, so I have to leave all the things at home to you.I am a frugal person, so when you buy groceries, you have to keep an account.

The introducer said that his mouth was dry and he drank a large glass of water. Xiao Li is a good person. He has a good job and a decent appearance. He has a house at home. You and Xiao Li are alone in a room. This is a rare blind date. , I don't know how many people are rushing to have a blind date with him.Lu Zhi couldn't help but take a sip of water, a rare blind date.Is her blind date round or flat?The content of the novel mainly describes the affairs of the male and female protagonists. When Lu Zhi appears, he is just a tool, either to set off the female protagonist or to be infatuated with the male protagonist to promote the relationship between the male and female protagonists.Lu Zhi's blind date was also brushed aside.If this blind date was this so-called rare blind date, even if she went back and was scolded by her whole family, she wouldn't do it.The introduction was still going on, but the girl couldn't help it anymore and stood up. We are not suitable. I am also a regular worker and I have to go to work. We are all the same. Why should I do all the housework?Lu Zhi gave this girl a thumbs up in his heart.That's right, this is the idea of finding a partner. Why are girls doing all the housework?Lu Zhi nodded.A cold and magnetic voice sounded, Hello, are you Comrade Lu Zhi?Lu Zhi looked up and then froze.The man is tall, has long legs, and has sharp eyebrows. He looks a bit serious, but with this face, it is no exaggeration to say that if it were in Lu Zhi's dream, some people would believe him even if he was a popular figure.They agreed on the phone that Lu Zhi was wearing a blue dress today and would meet at the teahouse at ten in the morning.Lu Zhi: Hello, you are Comrade Zhou ChenganZhou Chengan nodded, yes, I am Zhou Chengan.The two people looked at each other.Zhou Chengan sat down, and he brought with him a chubby, white little boy. The little boy sat next to Zhou Chengan, looking a little reserved.Zhou Chengan didn't think too much about this blind date, and just came to meet him as his grandfather said.Zhou Chengan: Let me introduce my situation. I am stationed on an island. If we are together, you may have to accompany me to the island, or you may have to live separately in two places for a long time.The island is great, oysters, lobsters, swimming crabsZhou Chengan: This child is my younger brother. His name is Zhou Jun. He will live with me.Zhou Jun's chubby fingers clenched his sleeves and looked at Lu Zhi.I have a younger brother who looks chubby and is very funny.Lu Zhi smiled, and it looked like even his hair was sweet.Zhou Chengan clenched his fist slightly, the tips of his ears were slightly red, but his expression remained calm.Recalling what he heard when he just came in, Zhou Chengan continued: I can wash clothes and cook. Although I have a younger brother who will live with me, he is very sensible and will not cause you any trouble. He will also hand over all salary and allowances.Zhou Jun looked pitiful, as if he knew that he was a loser, and I could pour you water to wash your feet.This is no better than the male protagonistLook at Zhou Chengan's face again.Must rushIn the novel, after Li Lan knew that she rejected Zhou Chengan, he scolded her, not without reason.Lu Zhi still has one question that concerns him. Is the island far from here?Zhou Cheng'an: It's not far. It takes about an hour by car to get to the pier, and it takes about two hours by boat to reach the island.That's about three hours away.This island is the island where the second sister Lu Zhi is accompanying the army.Lu Zhi: I agree, Comrade Zhou Chengan, what about you?Zhou Chengan seemed to want to see something from Lu Zhi's eyes, but there was only a bright smile in her eyes, without any regret or hesitation because of her impulsiveness.Zhou

Chengan and Lu Zhi looked at each other for a few seconds, and I now went back to write the wedding report.Lu Zhi: Okay.Zhou Jun seemed to be in disbelief that his sister-in-law agreed to marry his eldest brother even though she didn't dislike him as a dragster.Zhou Chengan: Comrade Lu Zhi, I have finished typing the marriage report and will propose marriage to you next Monday.To propose marriage, you need to prepare gifts. During this period, after finishing the wedding report, he went to prepare these.Lu Zhi's smile became even brighter, okay.

Lu Zhi arrived home just in time for lunch.Today is the weekend, and the Lu family are all at home.Lu Zhi took a look at the food on the table, a dish of cabbage vermicelli, a dish of fried green vegetables, and a dish of fried pork with chili.The five members of the family all looked at Lu Zhi, Lu Zhi's parents, Lu Zhi's eldest brother, sister-in-law, and Lu Zhi's little niece.The Lu family's conditions are pretty good. Lu Zhi's parents, Li Lan and Lu Xiangde, are a worker in the logistics department of a garment factory and the other is a level six fitter in a steel factory.Lu Zhi's eldest brother and sister-in-law, one works as an apprentice in a steel factory, and the other works as a temporary worker in a sugar factory.Lu Zhi graduated from high school and failed to find a job.My niece is in kindergarten.Lu Zhi was a little hungry and sat down, first taking a coarse-grain steamed bun with Erhe noodles.Li Lan: Don't eat it. How's it going?Lu Zhi: He went back to file a wedding report.The family looked at each other.Li Lan even twitched the corner of her mouth. This daughter of hers really doesn't do ordinary things.We were on a blind date a few days ago, so today I just filed a wedding report.Lu Xiangde: You guys, this is too fast.Lu Zhi: I think he's pretty good.It's not bad.The condition is good and the appearance is good. Although he has a younger brother, he seems to be very obedient.Lu Zhi told the story again, and Li Lan almost clapped her hands.Li Lan: What is this called? It's called meeting each other thousands of miles away. You two are so suitable. You don't like to do housework, but he can do housework. You don't have a job, but he can make money. You like children, right? He also has Your younger brother was transferred to the island where your second sister is serving in the army. Your second sister can still take care of you, which is perfect.Of course, the premise is that it is not far away, about three hours away, otherwise the Lu family would not agree.The Lu family had no objection to what Li Lan said.No, this wedding report is well done, wonderfully done.Li Lan: He didn't say when he would come to propose marriage.Lu Zhi: After finishing the marriage report, I will come over to propose marriage on Monday.Li Lan: Okay, okay, if he comes to propose marriage, we also need to prepare your dowry. Also, we need to make a call to your second sister first.Lu Zhi nodded and had no objection.Lu Xiangde: Okay, everyone, stop being stunned and eat quickly.Li Lan took a few mouthfuls of rice, stopped eating, and went out.Sister-in-law Lu watched her mother-in-law go out, took a few bites, and quickly followed her out, looking at her majestic and high-spirited appearance.Lu Xiangde laughed accordingly.Now, they, Lu Zhi, finally don't have to be talked about by those in the courtyard. He doesn't like to hear it.Li Lan brought Sister Lu back again. Our little son-in-law is the deputy leader, right?Lu Xiangde: Yes, he is young and promising.Li Lan: Yes, he is young and promising, otherwise he would be a son-in-law.Lu Zhi's cheeks felt slightly hot, and he was still a little embarrassed.

chapter 2Lu Xiangde picked up some food for Lu Zhi and asked him to eat more.Lu Zhi ate the smooth vermicelli in the cabbage stewed vermicelli. It was made by her sister-in-law and was delicious.Brother Lu: Your second sister will be happy if she finds out.After talking about it, Brother Lu was still a little disappointed. When Lu Zhi was born, Brother Lu was in junior high school and could help take care of the child.During the winter and summer vacations, he basically took Lu Zhi with him.But you can't help but get married.Looking at Lu Zhi, Brother Lu just felt that Zhou Chengan was simply making money.Lu Zhi ate a lot of food, but she didn't finish the steamed buns of Erhe Noodles. She found some spicy food, put it in the steamed buns, and ate the rest of the steamed buns.Mmm, it smells so good, spicy and spicy.After returning to the house, Lu Zhi was able to hear more clearly what was going on outside the courtyard.Aunt Zhou has relatives who work in department stores.Li Lan: There are sewing machines over there in the department store. Aunt Zhou, please help me find out.Aunt Zhou: Sewing machine, don't you have a sewing machine at home?Li Lan: Yes, our family has a sewing machine, but when our daughter gets married, we don't want to give her a sewing machine as a gift. When our second son gets married, our family also gives a sewing machine as a gift.Sister-in-law Lu: That's okay. When Lu Zhi gets married, we, as elder brothers and sisters-in-law, will definitely need some subsidies. Then I'll ask her whether to give her money or buy her things. After saying that, he smiled, "Aunt Zhou, I'll treat you to some wedding candy in a few days."Li Lan: She just found a job in a sugar factory. Although she is a temporary worker, she finally has a job.Aunt Zhou: Really, I won't be polite to you anymore.He Li listened hard to the noise outside. The more she listened, the more she frowned.The daughter-in-law of the old Lu family has found a jobLu Zhi is also on a blind date and is getting married.As expected, Lu Zhi was being hypocritical towards her son, and she said she liked her son. It was not a blind date, and they were going to get married.Probably because she felt that she could not marry her son, so she thought of making do with it.Aunt Zhou: I haven't asked you yet, what does your partner Lu Zhi do?Li Lan: He is the deputy leader. He is young, promising and good-looking. This is also true. He fell in love with us, Lu Zhi, at first sight, and he would not marry us unless we, Lu Zhi, would marry him.At this moment, Aunt Zhou seemed to remember something. I remember, you said that, and later you said that arranged marriages were not popular.Li Lan: Arranged marriages are not popular. This is not my son-in-law's grandfather. He said he wanted two people to meet, and then it became aAunt Zhou laughed along with her, good thing, this is a good thing, I will ask you about the sewing machine now.Sister-in-law Lu quickly said: Aunt Zhou, thank you.Aunt Zhou: Thank you for what.Mother-in-law and daughter-in-law are very satisfied.People in the courtyard knew that Lu Zhi's marriage was settled and he was getting married, so they all said a few words of congratulations to Li Lan and Sister Lu.He Li listened to the commotion outside, threw the rag on the table, and sneered. With such a good condition, she would like Lu Zhi. Maybe she is older and ugly.

In the afternoon, Li Lan took Lu Zhi to the post office to make a phone call.Lu Zhi seemed to have experienced another life, and it was a pity that he could not use a smartphone.There were a lot of people calling the post office on weekends, so Li Lan and Lu Zhi had to wait for a while, standing in line.Li Lan: Your second sister must be very happy. I would like to ask him by the way whether she recognizes my son-in-law and his character.She believed that Zhou Chengan had a very good character. Zhou Chengan's grandfather had a very good character and was good at teaching children, so Zhou Chengan could not be wrong.If you ask around, it's definitely true.Li Lan thought of this and said a lot, "Grandpa Zhou, when you were young, you were very kind, capable, and devoted to your wife. Later, when you became the captain of the brigade, you, Grandpa Zhou, were also capable and afraid of his wife."Carefully recalling the events of that year, Li Lan finally remembered the intersection between Lu Zhi and Zhou Chengan.Li Lan: Once, when we went back to the countryside, we met your grandfather Zhou's family. Zhou Chengan gave you candy when you were about four years old.Li Lan: Yes, this is the case. At that time, our family's life was not as good as it is now. I was a temporary worker and your father was an apprentice. This candy was much more expensive than it is now. Zhou Chengan even gave it to you.Lu Zhi must not remember clearly what happened when he was four years old, and Zhou Chengan must not remember it either.But the more Li Lan thought about it, the more she felt that these two were a perfect match. She only regretted that she had listened to Lu Zhi and directly rejected this blind date.When Lu Zhi and Li Lan arrived, Li Lan said the number that he knew by heart.After waiting for a while, Lu Yue called back.Li Lan takes the microphone, Lu Yue, let me tell you something.Lu Yue:

Is it the Li family's business? Why don't I go back in a while and give Lu Zhi some advice? There are a lot of singles on our island. We are having a social gathering recently. I'll bring Lu Zhi to join. Maybe we'll fall in love with each other. Who is it?Li Lan: Good thing, good thing. Your little sister thought about it and went on a blind date with his blind date. The two of them became her blind date and they were also transferred to the island. I am not just asking you to see if you know. Zhou Chengan.Lu Yue: Who are you talking about?Li Lan: Zhou Chengan.Li Lan couldn't help but recall a few days ago. Li Lan went back to her parents' home a few days ago and met the newly transferred deputy captain Zhou on the ship.He has a cold temperament and looks really nice.Some of the unmarried girls blushed when they looked at her.But this person's character is really too cold.Later, Lu Yue heard her man say how serious and meticulous Zhou Chengan was, and even his younger brother had a cold face.Such a man, with them Lu ZhiLu Yue: Was this matter forced by Grandpa Zhou?Grandpa Zhou hopes that Zhou Chengan and Lu Zhi can be together, and Lu Yue knows that.Li Lan: Why did Grandpa Zhou force you to do this? It was because he fell in love with Lu Zhi at first sight.Lu Yue slapped his thigh and said happily: "This makes sense. I know that our Lu Zhi is so good, that is, the second son of the Li family. His bad eyesight makes Zhou Chengan's character good, but his temper is a bit cold." .Li Lan: It's okay, just be cool with Lu Zhi.There were people around who were looking at Lu Zhi, but Lu Zhi was still able to remain calm about this kind of thing, and how many layers of filters her family had on her.Lu Zhi got the phone, second sister.Lu Yue: Make a call before you come. Your brother-in-law and I will pick you up at the pier. Do you knowLu Zhi: Yes, I know.Thinking that Lu Zhi would also accompany the army to the island, Lu Yue couldn't help but smile.Lu Zhi was brought up by Lu Yue. She had a busy family and she often took care of Lu Zhi when she was a child. They had an eldest brother, but Lu Yue always felt that she had a better relationship with Lu Zhi.Their elder brother can understand a girl's thoughts

In the evening, everyone in the courtyard had finished their meal, some were working in the courtyard, and some were enjoying the shade.Lu Zhi's marriage has obviously become something that everyone in the courtyard will talk about after dinner.I heard that Lu Zhi's partner is the deputy captain.I know, it's because she looks particularly good-looking.Stop talking, stop talking, He Li is here.Everyone, say hello to He Li. Your second son and daughter-in-law haven't come back yet.He Li: When the new daughter-in-law comes home, as a mother-in-law, I can understand and tell them to stay at her parents' house for one day.He Li, who had been a good mother-in-law, returned to the house, obviously not wanting to continue talking to them.The Lu family is discussing Lu Zhi's dowry.I definitely need to buy a sewing machine.Brother Lu and Sister Lu discussed it and planned to give Lu Zhi 150 yuan as a bottom line.Li Lan and Lu Xiangde took out two hundred yuan.The total is three hundred and fifty yuan.Among other things, there were wedding clothes. They planned to make two sets for Lu Zhi. Li Lan and Lu Xiangde also prepared other items such as enamel basins and kettles.The Zhou family must have been very considerate of the betrothal gifts. They knew Grandpa Zhou's character.Li Lan still felt that it was not enough. Zhou Chengan's family was in good condition, and since we were marrying into a wealthy family, the dowry must be high.Lu Xiangde: This month's salary will be paid, which is sixty-five yuan, and the bonus will be about seventy yuan. Let's add more, and the dowry will be added to the one hundred yuan. Lu Yue, let's save some money and then give her some dowry.Brother Lu and Sister Lu looked at each other, and they also added next month's salary. They were adding fifty yuan.Lu Zhi's dowry money totaled five hundred yuan.Brother Lu and Sister-in-law Lu grew up together as childhood sweethearts. Sister-in-law Lu also felt that she had watched Lu Zhi grow up since she was a child, and she had liked the look of Sister Lu Zhi since she was a child.The two got married, and she became Lu Zhi's sister-in-law, and she treated Lu Zhi even better.

When Lu Zhi was resting, he was lying on the bed unable to sleep, tossing and turning.Thinking about his marriage, Lu Zhi couldn't help but think of Zhou

Chengan's appearance, pursed his lips and smiled.I made a profit, I really made a profit.At the same time, Zhou Chengan and Zhou Jun did not fall asleep.Zhou Jun was sleepy and wilting, but thinking about Lu Zhi, he stayed awake and looked at Zhou Chengan eagerly, "Brother, sister-in-law is so beautiful."Zhou Chengan was folding his clothes and said nothing.The little fat guy Zhou Jun ran over, brother, don't you think my sister-in-law is pretty?Zhou Chengan's Adam's apple moved slightly, thinking about how amazing he was when he saw Lu Zhi today, he nodded, "Well, your sister-in-law is pretty." After a pause, he added: Very good-looking and good-tempered.

Chapter 3The garment factory has been a little busy recently. After Li Lan worked overtime to finish the work assigned to him by the logistics department, he took a day off and took Lu Zhi to the mall.Li Lan first took Lu Zhi to the counter selling sewing machines and found Aunt Zhou's relatives.Li Lan: I'm here to buy a sewing machine.The salesperson smiled. My aunt told me to keep it for you. If you give me the ticket, just give me another hundred and thirty yuan.After receiving the money, the salesperson issued the invoice and said: We will deliver it to you in the afternoon. I know the address.Li Lan: OK, I'll trouble you then.With that said, Li Lan took the wedding candy and gave it to the salesperson.The sewing machine side is a little better, but when it comes to the fabric and ready-to-wear counter, it's simply spectacular.This lesbian, please don't squeeze.I won't squeeze, so don't squeeze either.You stepped on my foot.Everyone, line up, line upLu Zhi stood on tiptoe and took a look. It seemed that a new batch of fabric had been put on.Li Lan had already rushed over.Lu Zhi also hurried over. She stood outside and finally kept up with Li Lan.Li Lan bought three feet of blue plaid cloth, six feet of red cloth, and three feet of red polka-dot cloth.After that, I went to buy porcelain basins, soap, toothbrushes, kettles, towels, and even enamel cups for brushing my teeth. These were all dowries.When they came out, both of them carried a lot of things.Li Lan: The quilts have been prepared for you at home a long time ago. There are two quilts in total. They are made of cotton and cloth stamps saved over the years. They are the same as your second sister's. I will look for a cotton player to play them again. , and then make the quilt cover.Li Lan continued, "There is also a summer quilt. I have also prepared a bed for you. This does not cost any cotton."After returning to the courtyard, everyone looked at him sideways.The dowry prepared by the Lu family for Lu Zhi is quite a lot.Some people were red-eyed, but it was a pity that Lu Zhi had high vision and good looks, otherwise he would have let his son try it.Aunt Zhou: I'm backLu Zhi: Well, I'm back.Lu Zhi and Li Lan returned to the house, and only a few people outside started talking.Sister-in-law Lu Zhi, she didn't go to work at the sugar factory. She was buying candies at the sugar factory today. She didn't buy the defective ones at the cheapest price. She said that her sister-in-law was getting married and she couldn't use defective wedding candies.I just hate that my son is not worthy of marrying Lu Zhi.Hahahaha, I think so too.Okay, okay, let's cook quickly.Lu Zhi washed his hands, then his face, and went back to his room to rest.Li Lan: Let's have noodles for lunch.Lu Zhi: I want to add a poached egg.Li Lan: OK, add a poached egg.Dinner is served at noon.Lu Zhi sat down at the table with a steaming bowl of white noodles, vegetables and a poached egg in it.The smooth and chewy noodles were delicious. Lu Zhi took a bite of the noodles, picked up the poached eggs, and finished the meal in several bites.Li Lan: In the past few days, you can learn some simple meals from me. After you get married and your son-in-law is on a mission, you can make some food yourself.Lu Zhi raised his head, then smiled and said, "Okay."In the magical experience of time travel, Lu Zhi is a food blogger.Cooking is easy for her.It just so happens that this is an opportunity to learn it, otherwise there would be no way to explain it.Li Lan thought about what else she had not prepared for the dowry, and what else she needed to tell Lu Zhi.I should also give some of the tickets at home to Lu Zhi.There is also a box to bring with you.Thinking of something, Li Lan looked a little embarrassed when she looked at her sweet-looking daughter who was eating noodles.

In the evening, Sister Lu came back.This is what a large courtyard is like. When you come back from shopping and pass by someone's house, everyone can see it.Sister Lu was carrying a quilt and bacon.At noon, Lu Zhi and Li Lan bought a lot of things, and a sewing machine was delivered in the afternoon. Now Mrs. Lu brought these things up again.Aunt Zhou saw her and asked with a smile: What are you doing?Sister-in-law Lu: My parents both like my sister-in-law. That's right. Knowing that she was getting married, they bought a quilt for my sister-in-law as a dowry. This bacon was given to them by a friend. They gave it to me, saying it was a treat. My sister-in-law's partner used it.Under the eyes of everyone, Mrs. Lu returned with her things.Sister-in-law Lu sent the bacon to the kitchen, the quilt to Lu Zhi's house, and said a few words to Lu Zhi.After going out, Li Lan looked at Sister Lu without hesitating to speak.Li Lan whispered: "Sister-in-law, there's something you want to say. I'm afraid she will be embarrassed. I'm embarrassed too."Sister-in-law Lu met Li Lan's gaze and understood.Sister-in-law Lu blushed, and then said: I will live with her today.In the evening, Lu Zhi was called to the kitchen.Lu Zhi steamed rice.Li Lan: My daughter is smart and can learn how to do it as soon as she is taught.Sister-in-law Lu was smiling on the side, but that's not the case. Our Lu Zhi has been smart since she was a child. She is still in kindergarten. When I read the text, she sits next to me obediently and can read along with me.Lu Zhi raised his head and smiled at them.She herself felt that she seemed to be something great.Under the guidance of Sister Lu and Li Lan, Lu Zhi not only steamed the rice, but also made a portion of spicy and sour potato shreds.The Lu family had dinner in the evening.The taste of spicy and sour potato shreds is really overpowering.Lu Xiangde took a bite. Today's spicy and sour potato shreds are so delicious.Lu Zhi's five-year-old niece, Lu Anan, is holding a bowl of rice. It's the best time. My aunt's cooking is the best.Li Lan smiled, and I said, my daughter is smart, look, this is the first time she makes it, and it tastes so delicious.Lu Anan nodded seriously, her aunt is smart

At night, Sister Lu and Lu Zhi sleep together.Two people were lying on the same bed, one person and one quilt.It was a little quiet at night, and the two people spoke in whispers.Sister-in-law Lu: You are getting married, are you nervous?Lu Zhi turned over and lay on his side, not nervous.I'm really not nervous.After all, Lu Zhi is different now.Sister-in-law Lu smiled, you know, when I got married, my sister-in-law also asked me such a question, and I said I wasn't nervous. Then she told me that on the wedding night after we got married, I turned red with embarrassment.Lu Zhi said for a long time, coyly, sister-in-law, you have to teach me thisSister-in-law Lu: You are not allowed to cover your ears.Sister-in-law Lu talked for more than ten minutes, and Lu Zhi blushed.Finally going to bed, Lu Zhi pulled the quilt. Sister-in-law Lu was already asleep, but she was not asleep yet.Zhou Chengan has a good figure and good looks, but she has never been in love.If Sister Lu asked her again now if she was nervous, Lu Zhi would probably answer that she was nervous.

The day was agreed upon for Zhou Chengan to propose marriage.Early in the morning, the Lu family became busy.For this matter, everyone took leave, even Lu Zhi's five-year-old niece did not go to school.The fabrics bought in the department store have been made into clothes for Lu Zhi by Sister Lu.Sister-in-law Lu came over specially to tell Lu Zhi to wear new clothes when she was not busy.Lu Zhi wore a red polka-dot shirt and jeans, with his hair hanging down, with the hair on both sides tucked behind his ears.Lu Anan looked at Lu Zhi with her chin in her hands, blinking her big eyes, "Aunt, you are so beautiful. I will be as beautiful as my aunt in the future. I will be like my aunt, right?"As he spoke, he clenched his fist, making Lu Zhi laugh.Lu Zhi didn't have any cosmetics at this time. She looked at herself in the mirror and felt that she could do without makeup.After waiting for a while, Lu Zhi heard the movement outside.Excuse me, where is the Lu family?Lu Zhi remembered that this voice was Zhou Chengan's.Zhou Chengan's voice is very nice, clear and magnetic.When Chen Xiangde came out, he looked at the people carrying large and small bags, and his eyes first fell on Zhou Chengan.At this moment, Chen Xiangde smiled more sincerely.Okay, okay, what a talent.Those in the large courtyard who were not working at home, some came out, and some were quietly looking outside the house.good guyLu Zhi was just as good-looking as her.Looking at what they were carrying, it seemed like they were sincere.Chen Xiangde looked at Zhou Chengan's grandfather again, took a few steps forward, and held his hand. Uncle, it's been a long time since we last seen him.Zhou Chengan didn't come here to propose the marriage on his own. After filing the marriage report, he returned home, found his grandparents, and prepared the bride price, and then officially came to propose the marriage.Lu Zhi went out, and Lu Anan followed Lu Zhi.Lu Zhi's eyes met with Zhou Cheng'an's. She thought she would be embarrassed, but in the end she was not only embarrassed, but also showed a bright smile to Zhou Cheng'an.Zhou Chengan walked over, Comrade Lu Zhi, we met again.Lu Anan laughed, and Zhou Chengan looked down.Lu Anan: You are my uncle, right?Lu Anan is very cute, chubby, and looks somewhat similar to Lu Zhi.Zhou Chengan knelt down and looked at her level, um, I am uncle.Lu Anan tilted her little head. You are so stupid. You are my uncle. Why do you call my aunt Comrade Lu Zhi?Da da da da, Lu Anan ran to the opposite side of Lu Zhi, imitating Zhou Chengan, Comrade Lu Zhi, I am Lu Anan.Lu Zhi couldn't hold back and almost laughed.Li Lan had just wiped her hands and came out when she saw their scene. Chengan, right? What do you call Comrade? Just call her Zhizhi.He looked at Lu Zhi again, don't call him Comrade Zhou Cheng'an, just brother Cheng'an. When you were a child, I remember you called him brother Cheng'an.Two people stood facing each other.Everyone was busy chatting, and Zhou Jun was hugged by Brother Lu. Only Lu Anan stood among them, looking at Zhou Chengan and Lu Zhi.Lu Anan: Aunt, uncle, are you sorry?Zhou Chengan's hand hanging on one side tightened slightly, and his voice was a little tight and childish.Lu Zhi's voice has a slight tail tone, which is nice and sweet, sincere.Lu Zhi didn't say the word "brother".When everyone went back to the house, Li Lan gave Lu Zhi another task and gave him money to buy a bottle of soy sauce.Zhou Chengan: Let me go.Li Lan was very satisfied with Zhou Chengan, but there was no need for Lu Zhi to do the soy sauce thing. She smiled and said: You guys go together.

Chapter 4Lu Zhi and Zhou Chengan went out to make soy sauce together.The Supply and Marketing Cooperative is just outside the alley, turn left two to three hundred meters away.When we arrived at the supply and marketing cooperative, two people stood there. The stranger looked at them and subconsciously looked at them a few more times, while the stranger said hello.Lu Zhi, this is your partner.Your partner is here to propose marriage, right?Lu Zhi: Well, my partner is coming over today to propose marriage.Another person who came to queue asked. Lu Zhi smiled and wanted to answer. Zhou Chengan on the side replied before Lu Zhi: Well, I am her partner.The summer breeze gently blew through Lu Zhi's hair. She turned around with her hands behind her back and looked at the front of the team, smiling softly.

The engagement between the two families went very smoothly.Grandpa Zhou: We plan to make a three-turn and one-ring call. Since you have all bought a sewing machine, the tickets and money for the sewing machine will be used as a betrothal gift for Lu Zhi.After finishing speaking, Grandpa Zhou sighed, "You don't know, last week, when I received a call from Cheng'an, I scolded him directly. After scolding him, he told me that he was getting married. The marriage report has been filed.Li Lan: When Lu Zhi came back from our blind date, I also planned to scold her, but I didn't expect it to happen.Lu Zhi and Zhou Chengan stood at the door, listening to the sounds inside before going in.Lu Zhi thought it was really amazing. He didn't expect that the two of them were going on a blind date and faced somewhat similar situations.Zhou Chengan: The marriage report will be approved in a few days. I will go to the island next week.Lu Zhi: Are you in a hurry to get married?Zhou Chengan stood up straight. I want to ask your opinion. If we get married as soon as possible, we will get the marriage certificate and hold the wedding. If you want to wait, you can wait until my next vacation.Lu Zhi stood in the shade and looked up at him. Do you want to get married as soon as possible, or do you want to wait a little longer?Zhou Chengan's voice was tight, I listen to your opinion, but if you want to ask my opinion, I hope to get married as soon as possible.Lu Zhi: The marriage report has been approved. Come and see me. We will go to the Civil Affairs Bureau to get the certificate. She paused and her eyes sparkled, "Comrade Zhou Chengan, don't be embarrassed all the time, we will be husband and wife from now on."This was what Lu Zhi said to himself.Zhou Chengan said seriously, okay, I understand.It was almost lunchtime, and Li Lan came over to ask Lu Zhi and Zhou Chengan to go back to eat.The family was extremely lively.Sister-in-law Lu sat on Lu Zhi's side and gave her some bacon that she hadn't eaten enough.Today's bacon is stir-fried with chili peppers. It has a spicy and rich flavor with the unique flavor of bacon. It is fragrant but not greasy, and the meat is firm.Zhou Chengan: Do you like bacon?Lu Zhi: Yes, bacon is delicious.Grandpa Zhou asked: What are your plans for the wedding?Everyone looked at Zhou Chengan and Lu Zhi.Zhou Chengan: Once the marriage report is approved, we will get married.Grandpa Zhou: Hey, didn't you say you shouldn't be anxious about getting married? How do I see you, you are quite anxious.Everyone laughed out loud.Since Lu Zhi and Zhou Chengan were getting married, the two families discussed their marriage together.

In the afternoon, the Zhou family went back.Grandpa Zhou and the others have to go back to help Lu Zhi prepare for the wedding and return to Hongxing Commune.The Lu family came out and sent them to the door.Zhou Chengan: Are you free tomorrow?Lu Zhi nodded, free.Zhou Chengan asked again: I will come to you at ten o'clock tomorrow morning. We can buy watches, radios, and bicycles, okay?Lu Zhi nodded, I'll wait for you.Zhou Jun's chubby hands were still tugging on Lu Zhi's sleeves. He was reluctantly picked up by Zhou Chengan, and he said, "Sister-in-law, I won't come over tomorrow."Lu Zhi: Why?Zhou Jun was actually a little proud, as if he had done something great and right. Grandpa said, "You can't delay your relationship."Lu Zhi:When the Lu family went back, the yard was as usual, with people working and people chatting.When they saw Lu Zhi, they all started to praise him, and some even asked about the bride price openly and secretly.Only those with poor conditions had to cover it up. She was so satisfied with Li Lan's son-in-law that there was no need to cover it up.Li Lan: After three rings and one ring, our family bought a sewing machine. They said they would give the sewing ticket and money directly to us, Lu Zhi.Aunt Zhou: You have really found a good son-in-law. You don't know it. When he came in today, I felt that standing with Lu Zhi, they looked like a perfect couple.He Li went out early in the morning to watch the excitement, but she saw Zhou Chengan. He was still hiding in the house, and he didn't come out.As you can imagine, it's really good.Otherwise, given He Li's temperament, she would definitely not be so quiet now.Aunt Zhou said in a low voice: He Li is probably going crazy. He deliberately put on airs in front of you before. Those who didn't know it thought his son was so good.Under everyone's attention, Lu Zhi returned to the house.As soon as he entered the house, Lu Zhi went to the kitchen.There was still some bacon left at noon, everyone was talking about the marriage, and there were so many people, Lu Zhi was too embarrassed to just eat the plate of bacon in front of him.Sister-in-law Lu came over and made an appointment to go out together tomorrow.As he said that, he served Lu Zhi some rice and sat down to eat it. I looked at you and found that you weren't full at lunch either.Lu Zhi: Thank you, sister-in-law.Lu Zhi sat down at the dining table. Tomorrow, he was going to buy a watch, radio and bicycle.As he said that, he sat up a little straighter and asked, "Do I want to buy him a watch too?"Sister-in-law Lu: He is wearing a watch. If you really want to express your feelings, why not knit a scarf?Lu Zhi looked at the wilted leaves outside and shook his head.Materials are really scarce now, and the only thing Sister Lu can think of is a scarf.Lu Zhi also racked his brains and thought for a while, then lay down.Forget it, I won't buy it.Sister-in-law Lu joked, she is indeed satisfied with him, as long as you are satisfied.Satisfied, definitely satisfied.Zhou Chengan's conditions are not easy to find. The most important thing is that he has the courage to be conscious.

Zhou Chengan and Lu Zhi made an appointment to meet at ten in the morning.Entering the courtyard, he went to find Lu Zhi.The Lu family all went to work, and Lu Zhi was the only one at home. When she heard the noise, she opened the door and was a little surprised when she saw Zhou Chengan still carrying bacon.After putting away the bacon, Lu Zhi locked the door again, and then went out with Zhou Chengan.It's a nice day today, sunny and windy.It's still quite a distance from the supply and marketing cooperative, so you need to take a bus.While waiting for the bus at the bus stop, Lu Zhi subconsciously glanced at Zhou Chengan's wrist, which had a watch on it.Lu Zhi didn't pay attention yesterday. It is estimated that his family, Lu Zhi, looked at Zhou Chengan slightly less than his niece.There were not many people on the bus at this time. After getting on the bus, Zhou Chengan handed over the bus ticket.Zhou Chengan glanced at the empty seat and sat in the back.Lu Zhi is fine.After Lu Zhi sat down, Zhou Chengan sat down next to Lu Zhi.The two of them were close, and Lu Zhi smelled the clean and refreshing scent of soap locust on Zhou Chengan's body, which smelled very good.Sitting next to Zhou Chengan, Lu Zhi had a feeling that he wanted to sit upright, so he subconsciously sat very upright.Lu Zhi: Are you from Hongxing Commune?Zhou Chengan: Well, I went back with my grandfather yesterday and came by car in the morning.When they arrived at the mall, the two of them were about to get out of the car. Lu Zhi followed Zhou Chengan out of the car. She found that going out with Zhou Chengan not only straightened her back, but also made her feel very safe, which was also an advantage.The two of them arrived at the mall. Lu Zhi went to buy a watch first. She chose one of the same brand as Zhou Chengan, and then a radio.When buying a bicycle, Lu Zhi said: I don't know how to ride a bicycle, so buy a men's model. You can just take me on the bicycle.Zhou Chengan: Buy the women's model, which is lighter. You can learn it if you want, and I can use it too.Aunt Zhou's relatives were at the counter next to her. She remembered Lu Zhi. After all, with Lu Zhi's appearance, it would be strange that she couldn't remember him.At this moment, she looked at Lu Zhi with a look of envy.Lu Zhi, who had three turns and one ring, planned to go back.Zhou Chengan asked: Is there anything else I need to buy? How about we go look at other things?Lu Zhi: No, I＇ve bought them all.At noon, the two of them went to a state-owned restaurant near the shopping mall for dinner.The state-owned restaurant served dumplings for lunch today, and there was not much to choose from.Lu Zhi was sitting at the table waiting for Zhou Cheng to arrange the team. Unexpectedly, he met the girl who had a blind date in the teahouse that day.This girl also came for a blind date. Obviously, the blind date this time was very reliable.When Zhou Chengan came back, Lu Zhi put his chin on his hands and looked at a table not far away with a smile.can you do housework togetherYes, I often do housework at home.I spend money without keeping accountsno, I'm fine.Zhou Chengan followed and looked over. Apparently Zhou Chengan also remembered it.Lu Zhi: If, on the day we went on a blind date, you saw me and didn't see what they said during the blind date, what would you say to me?Zhou Chengan didn't speak for a long time, as if he was thinking about it.Zhou Chengan: I will introduce my situation and then ask you what your requirements are.Lu Zhi: Then I have many demands, much more than this.She frowned slightly as she spoke, but she looked a little cute.Lu Zhi: You don't think I have too many things to do, do you?Zhou Chengan met Lu Zhi's eyes, was silent for a moment, and then shook his head, no.Dumplings should still be eaten while they are hot.Lu Zhi took a bite. The dumplings in the state-owned restaurant were very delicious.Lu Zhi: After a while, after dinner, are you going back?Zhou Chengan replied: I will send you back and then go back.After sending Lu Zhi back, he was going to the post office to ask about the marriage application. It would take a few days to get it approved.

Chapter 5When Lu Zhi returned home, the sun outside was still quite strong.Lu Zhi: You should go back early. Grandpa Zhou and the others are still waiting for you.Li

Lan and Chen Xiangde would definitely ask about this kind of gift when they came back from get off work, and Grandpa Zhou would probably do the same.Zhou Chengan: Okay, then I'll go back first.As expected, he was a very steady man, and he could keep his expression calm even when he was anxious. He must have planned everything, and he knew which bus to take back to Hongxing Commune.

Zhou Chengan arrived at the post office and queued up to make a phone call.When Political Commissar Li received Zhou Chengan's call, he was stunned for a few seconds.Zhou Chengan: Political Commissar Li, when will my marriage application be approved?Political Commissar Li was shocked when he received a call from Zhou Chengan last time about getting married. Unexpectedly, Zhou Chengan called again and asked.Political Commissar Li laughed hahaha, why, this is because your family is pressingAfter making a joke, I started talking about business directly. The phone bill is expensive now.Political Commissar Li: It has been approved today. Someone happens to be going out for a meeting. I asked them to send the things to you. They will definitely arrive before the day after tomorrow.Zhou Chengan: OK, thank you, political commissar.Political Commissar Li asked some more about Zhou Chengan. Actually, there was no need to ask. Zhou Chengan's second daughter-in-law was on the island, and Political Commissar Li knew his man. He really wanted to ask Zhou Chengan, who cherishes words like gold. He really wanted to know. , might as well ask his future brother-in-law.The phone bill is also expensive.Political Commissar Li: I wish you a happy marriage in advance.After ending the call, Political Commissar Li shook his head. Zhou Chengan's cold temper is really unacceptable. When I get back, I want to tell him that I can't be cold to my wife.

These days, under the guidance of Li Lan and Sister Lu, Lu Zhi's cooking skills have improved by leaps and bounds.In the evening, no one came back from get off work. Lu Zhi washed the dishes and cooked in the kitchen at home.The bacon sent by Zhou Chengan is just right for dinner.This time, Lu Zhi didn't want to eat fried bacon with chili peppers, and planned to make a pot of bacon rice directly.The processed bacon is fried in oil in the pot, and the potatoes are added and stir-fried together. Add salt and soy sauce, and the flavor is rich and fragrant. Finally, it is simmered with rice.Lu Zhi also found a reason why he knew how to make bacon rice. He had heard it from others before.Thinking about the seafood on the island, Lu Zhi felt that it was necessary to buy a few cookbook books. After all, her second sister was also on the island, so it made sense.When cooking in a large courtyard, sometimes everyone knows who cooks well and can smell it.Li Lan and Lu Xiangde came back together. As soon as they entered the courtyard, they smelled the fragrance.Li Lan, who was anxious to come back and ask Lu Zhi about the betrothal gift, slowed down when he smelled the smell.Li Lan: Whose cooking is this? It's so delicious.The people who were busy looked at Li Lan and Chen Xiangde.Aunt Zhou is doing laundry at your house.Li Lan and Chen Xiangde looked at each other and hurried back.When they saw Lu Zhi in the kitchen, Li Lan and Chen Xiangde couldn't be happier.Li Lan's voice was a little higher. My daughter is amazing. She has only learned to cook for a few days, and her cooking is so delicious. What did you do today?Lu Zhi: Bacon braised rice with potatoes and beans added to it.Lu Xiangde: Aren't we finished eating the bacon at home?Lu Zhi replied: Zhou Chengan brought it to me when he came here today.Li Lan on the side smiled and said: Yes, he is attentive. I can see that you like to eat bacon. You don't know, he has high vision. He wants to marry you after meeting you. He must like you.Chen Xiangde nodded in agreement, yes, Chengan had a high vision.When Brother Lu and Sister Lu came back, they also brought back Lu Anan, who was in kindergarten.The family has dinner.The rice in the bacon braised rice has the aroma of bacon, the potatoes inside are soft and glutinous, and the beans are also soft and tasty.Take one bite and your lips and teeth will be fragrant.A lot of ground rice and potatoes were added, but it didn't affect the taste at all, and everyone was very full.Lu Anan was so full.At night, Lu Zhi and Sister Lu were talking in the room.Sister-in-law Lu looked at the watch Lu Zhi was wearing and said with a smile: This watch looks good, not bad.After finishing speaking, the two of them looked at the radio together.The Lu family has a radio, which was bought when Sister-in-law Lu and Brother Lu got married.Mrs. Lu listened to the sound on the radio and asked: Do you want to send your sewing machines and bicycles over first?Lu Zhi: Well, I have to send it over first.It's as lively and lively outside as usual. After all, it's hot and everyone likes to enjoy the cool air.When Lu Zhi and Sister-in-law Lu were talking, they could also hear people talking outside.I think your son-in-law is really good, but Lu Zhi is also good, right?No, the rice I cooked today was so delicious.What's the name of the meal?Bacon braised rice.Yes, yes, bacon stewed rice.He Li's smile was a bit forced, and she was unwilling to come out to enjoy the cool air. Her refusal to come out seemed a bit deliberate.Seeing that his second son and his daughter-in-law were back, He Li's voice was loud, "The second son is back."Everyone looked not far away and their voices became softer.Sister Lu heard the movement outside and looked at Lu Zhi subconsciously.

Lu Zhi couldn't sleep at night.Because Li Yu is the male protagonist in this novel.Lu Zhi didn't know whether he liked him because of the content of the original article or because of something else.But now Lu Zhi is sure that she doesn't like Li Yu anymore.Li Yu is married and will be very affectionate with the heroine in the future, and she will wake up.Sister-in-law Lu: Zhizhi, are you asleep?Lu Zhi: Sister-in-law, I'm not asleep yet.Sister-in-law Lu came in with a quilt in her arms and slept with Lu Zhi. The two of them lay on the same bed.This kind of quiet time at night is particularly suitable for heart-to-heart conversations.Sister-in-law Lu: Li Yu is back. This time he and his wife returned home and stayed at his wife's house for a few days.Lu Zhi couldn't help but smile, "Sister-in-law, it's not that I couldn't sleep because he came back, I was thinking about why I liked him before."Not to mention Sister-in-law Lu, the rest of the Lu family are probably worried that Lu Zhi still wants to marry Li Yu.陆大嫂：我记得，是小时候，咱们一起去乡下玩，你被人欺负了，李裕把人揍了，之后你就喜欢和他一起玩，年纪大了，情窦初开，就说喜欢他。Lu Zhi remembered it. That experience was really amazing. Lu Zhi woke up after reading the novel again and felt it was outrageous. He had never thought about why he liked Li Yu before.Maybe it's because of what her sister-in-law said, or maybe it's because she's been playing with Li Yu and just started falling in love, so she felt that she liked him.Lu Zhi nodded, that's it.Sister-in-law Lu: I really don't like it anymoreLu Zhi: Well, I don't like it anymore, sister-in-law, let's sleep.Sister-in-law Lu: OK.At this moment, Lu Zhi fell asleep quickly.

He Li was talking about her grievances with her son, daughter-in-law, and you don't know that Lu Zhi next door just found a partner to make them proud.Li Yu: We should congratulate her for finding a good partner.As I spoke, I felt a little awkward.How could Li Yu be dissatisfied when a beauty like Lu Zhi chased after

Li Yu? Now that she had found someone who was much better than him, Li Yu had an indescribable feeling.Chu Tong gently persuaded He Li, but actually felt a little uncomfortable.Chu Tong and Lu Zhi were classmates. She was not as good looking as Lu Zhi, and her conditions were not as good as Lu Zhi's. She married a man that Lu Zhi liked. As a result, Lu Zhi is now married to a better man.He Li: That's right. Lu Zhi got married on a blind date. Maybe it was just a matter of makeshift. I heard that the man also brought a younger brother with him. Lu Zhi's second sister is on the island again. Maybe it's because she's getting married and wants to Lu Zhi helped take care of his younger brother, and her second sister could also help since she lived close by, so she married Lu Zhi.Chu Tong is a little embarrassed, don't say that.Li Yu: We have a good relationship.When Chu Tong and Li Yu lay down to rest, neither of them mentioned this matter.

After Zhou Chengan obtained various documents, he came to the courtyard again.When Lu Zhi saw Zhou Chengan, he smiled and asked: Has it been approved?Zhou Chengan: Well, after the approval, you can now get your marriage certificate.The Lu family had already helped Lu Zhi with all the materials she needed for her wedding.The two men stood facing each other, one with a serious face and the other with pursed lips.Zhou Chengan suddenly saluted, his voice was clear and serious, Comrade Lu Zhi, I apply to go to the Civil Affairs Bureau to get married with you.Lu Zhi couldn't help laughing, and I agreed.This is also considered a proposal.Li Yu and Chu Tong came back. They went out today. Li Yu bought Chu Tong floral cloth from the supply and marketing cooperative.Because of this incident, Chu Tong was envied by others and found a good partner.The two of them returned to the courtyard, and Chu Tong was thinking about how she would answer when someone asked her. She had already thought about making this floral cloth into a doll collar skirt.Seeing Lu Zhi and the man standing opposite him, Li Yu and Chu Tong were stunned.I just heard that the person Lu Zhi was looking for was good-looking, but I didn't expect that the person Lu Zhi was looking for was so good-looking.Lu Zhi locked the door and went to the Civil Affairs Bureau with Zhou Chengan to get a marriage certificate. Zhou Chengan stretched out his hand and handed Lu Zhi a ring.gold ringZhou Chengan: My grandma told me to give this to you. It's for my grandson-in-law.Lu Zhi smiled brightly, please help me wear the ring.Zhou Chengan held the ring on his slender fingers and helped Lu Zhi put it on.Lu Zhi looked at the ring in the sun and said with a smile: After getting the marriage certificate, let's go buy a ring.

Chapter 6It's a little far to the Civil Affairs Bureau.Lu Zhi had already made plans to get married, and felt that he had made a profit by marrying Zhou Chengan, but he was inevitably a little nervous.After all, she has lived two lifetimes without ever falling in love.On the bus, Lu Zhi held the documents for his marriage certificate. The gold ring on his hand shone lightly in the sun.Lu Zhi is serious, Comrade Zhou Chengan, you must be nice to me in the future.After all, it's different from before.If in the future, Lu Zhi feels that their life cannot go on, or if both of them are uncomfortable, he will file for divorce from Zhou Chengan.Zhou Chengan turned his head and looked at Lu Zhi, his voice firm like a promise, don't worry.Lu Zhi raised his chin and smiled brightly, "I will also be kind to you."Zhou Chengan: OK.Lu Zhi: And your brother, I will also treat him well.Zhou Chengan looked at him with a smile on his serious face.Lu Zhi tilted his head. You smiled. You look better when you smile than when you don't smile. Smile more in the future.Zhou Chengan nodded after a while and said: OK.After arriving at the Civil Affairs Bureau for a while, Zhou Chengan took the red-wrapped wedding candy and handed it to Lu Zhi.Lu Zhi ate the wedding candy and felt it was very sweet. It was really sweet.Lu Zhi: Do you want to eat one?Zhou Chengan took out another piece of wedding candy with the same red packaging as Lu Zhi's, opened the packaging and ate the candy.When he arrived at the Civil Affairs Bureau, Lu Zhi discovered that there were a lot of people getting marriage certificates from the Civil Affairs Bureau today, and everyone was queuing up.After hearing from several newlyweds, Lu Zhi knew that today was a good day to get married.The weather outside is also very sunny.When Lu Zhi and Zhou Chengan arrived, they sat down on the two chairs in front of them.Zhou Chengan took the wedding candies to the staff.The staff asked them questions and checked the identity information of the two people according to the procedures. Lu Zhi and Zhou Chengan were also very cooperative.The staff handed over the marriage certificate. Okay, here is your marriage certificate. There is also this, the newlyweds handbook. You can take a look at it when you go back.The marriage certificate at this time is different from the marriage certificate in the future. It is paper.Lu Zhi and Zhou Chengan left the Civil Affairs Bureau, and several staff members smiled and talked.This couple is so beautiful. Novel reading public account: Jiuju tweetsYes, I'm so envious.Get to work quickly.knew.Once two people receive their marriage certificate, they are officially husband and wife.Lu Zhi knew before that this was his marriage partner, but he felt a little different with and without a marriage certificate.Of course, now they still have to go back to their respective homes.Their wedding will be this weekend as discussed when they proposed marriage.Lu Zhi took Zhou Chengan to the mall.Now, Lu Zhi's five hundred yuan dowry money is with her. She can still buy gold rings, but not expensive ones.Lu Zhi looked at the gold ring in front of the counter, his long and thick eyelashes trembling as he blinked.Unexpectedly, I saw the plain hoop style that became very popular later.Lu Zhi pointed to the gold ring on the counter. Does it look good?The current price of gold is more than 120 yuan, and the price of this ring is 260 yuan.But since Zhou Chengan gave her a ring, she must buy a wedding ring.The ring on Lu Zhi's hand, Lu Zhi estimated, would cost more than seven hundred yuan based on this price.The salesperson took out the ring, and Lu Zhi took it and put it on Zhou Chengan's finger.Such a simple style is very suitable for Zhou Chengan. It has more design than the style and is more suitable.Lu Zhi looked at Zhou Chengan's slender fingers with clear joints, and then looked away for a while. Doesn't it look good?Zhou Chengan clasped his fingers, nodded and said: It looks good.Lu Zhi: We want this.Salesperson: Okay, this needs to be settled first.Zhou Chengan paid before Lu Zhi.Lu Zhi:Lu Zhi didn't want to discuss such things as who would pay in front of the salesperson, otherwise it would definitely be extreme pulling.When he came out, Lu Zhi looked at Zhou Chengan and said: I want to buy you a ring.Zhou Chengan took out an envelope and handed it over. Almost all the salary allowances and bonuses earned before are here. Take it and I will hand over your monthly salary in the future.In recent years, Zhou Chengan has not spent much money.Lu Zhi wasn't pretentious either.There seems to be no differenceLu Zhi accepted Zhou Chengan's salary and allowance. I will give you twenty yuan of pocket money every month.Zhou Chengan raised his eyebrows and still had pocket moneyLu Zhi: Of course, there must be pocket money.With that said, he gave Zhou Chengan twenty yuan, which is for this month.I took out five more unity cards. We are going to get married and go to the island recently. We need money for something. You can't use it once and ask me for it once. Take these and be richer.

Lu Zhi was in his room counting the money Zhou Chengan gave him. In addition to cash, there was also salary in the envelope.Probably Zhou Chengan doesn't spend much money at ordinary times, so he saves a lot from his salary. It's also possible that he also has a lot of bonuses.There are a total of 1,300 yuan in cash and a total of 3,300 yuan in the passbook. These are 4,700 yuan.For now, it's a huge sum of money.Lu Zhi gave Zhou Chengan one hundred yuan of his five hundred yuan. The twenty yuan pocket money was not taken from the five hundred yuan in the dowry, but it was five thousand one hundred yuan.Lu Zhi still had thirty-one and twenty-six cents left.In addition to this, there are various tickets.This man really wanted to marry her and live a happy life.Lu Zhi did not hide this matter from the Lu family. They were very pleased when they found out. They did not ask about the specific amount.After packing up the money, Lu Zhi felt that his life would be better in the future.Sister Lu knocked on the door and came in. Her parents wanted to see the marriage certificate.Lu Zhi sat up and found the marriage certificate and gave it to Sister-in-law Lu. Sister-in-law Lu took the marriage certificate and went out.Lu Zhi stood up and followed him out.Chen Xiangde looked at the marriage certificate and said several good words in succession.He is satisfied with this son-in-law.

Zhou Chengan returned to the 10th Brigade of Hongxin Commune.Before they even returned home, everyone enthusiastically told Zhou Chengan that his parents were back.This is amazing.To put it bluntly, the captain of their team is great. For them to do practical things, their conditions are obviously better than those of other teams.Teach your son well, and your son will teach your grandson well.Last time, when Zhou Chengan came back, so many girls were thinking about Zhou Chengan. The matchmaker almost broke the threshold of the Zhou family.Zhou Chengan nodded his head after saying something shamelessly, saying that the girl he wanted to marry could go from the beginning of the village to the end of the village.I heard that I was getting married, and I didn't know what kind of girl she was, but I knew without thinking that the girl Zhou Cheng'an could like would definitely be good.When Zhou Jun saw Zhou Chengan, he ran over and said, "Brother, my parents are back."Zhou Chengan touched Zhou Jun's hair before going in, grandparents, parents.Zhou Chengan's parents are very busy. Zhou Chengan's father and mother sometimes live in separate places, both of them in the capital.None of them could help take care of Zhou Jun, which is why Zhou Jun followed Zhou Chengan.Originally, Zhou Jun planned to follow Grandpa Zhou and Grandma Zhou, but these two were old, and Zhou Chengan's second uncle's daughter had no choice but to be sent back.Zhou Chengan's second uncle's daughter is younger than Zhou Jun. She doesn't speak much now. She is young and has many things to take care of.Zhou Jun hopes that he can follow Zhou Chengan.Chen Jiaojiao stood up and looked at her son and hugged him. My son is getting married. Is he marrying Lu Zhi? This little girl, I liked her when I saw her when I was a child.She continued: When you proposed the marriage, your grandparents went with you. If we don't show up, we can't. Wait until you take us there again. I still have a lot of things here that I want to give to my daughter-in-law. Woolen cloth. And your second uncle and second aunt, they also wanted to come back, but they were really busy, so they asked us to help and brought some things.Chen Jiaojiao asked again: "Where is the marriage certificate? I got the marriage certificate today, right? Let me take a look."Looking at his wife, Zhou Ang looked a little gentler.Zhou Chengan took out the marriage certificate, and everyone gathered around to look at Lu Zhi and Zhou Chengan's marriage certificate.Chen Jiaojiao couldn't help but laugh. She didn't expect that my son could actually get a wife. Your father did it because of his good-looking face, and you should be the same. Fortunately, he looks good.Looking at Zhou Jun, Chen Jiaojiao said: In the future, your personality should be more like me.Zhou Jun is a little confused, because am I not good-looking?Everyone laughed.Good-looking, how could Zhou Jun not be good-looking.Chen Jiaojiao and Zhou Ang are both easy to watch.

At night, when Lu Zhi went to bed, he was still a little excited about the fact that he was getting married.Early the next morning, when she woke up, the Lu family had all gone to work, and breakfast was left for her at home, including egg porridge and pickles made by herself.The porridge is still hot.Lu Zhi finished his meal and waited for Zhou Chengan to come over.Today, Zhou Chengan wants to find someone to help bring some of the things they want to bring to the island.Mainly large sewing machines and bicycles.Lu Zhi didn't have too many things to pack, so he had packed them all now.After lunch, the courtyard was busy.He Li and Chu Tong were talking to everyone in the yard.What can He Li do about Lu Zhi finding a good partner? She still feels a little unwilling to give up on her previous sense of superiority.Today I specially bought new clothes for Chu Tong and gave Chu Tong's parents a lot of things, which she was reluctant to eat.He Li: My son is married to my daughter-in-law. I must be nice to my daughter-in-law. This is all the result of the daughter-in-law becoming a mother-in-law. Do you think this is right?Chu Tong felt a little embarrassed sitting next to He Li.While everyone was talking, a child from the courtyard ran in.A car is comingYes, the car entered the alley.Just as he was talking, the car stopped outside their compound.Zhou Chengan got out of the car, opened the door, and Grandpa Zhou and Grandma

Zhou also got out of the car.Zhou Ang got out of the car and opened the door, and Chen Jiaojiao also got out of the car.Zhou Chengan said: I'll go in and talk to Zhizhi.

Chapter 7Lu Zhi was stunned when he heard that his father-in-law and mother-in-law were coming.During that magical experience, Lu Zhi's friends also got married one after another. During regular gatherings, Lu Zhi learned something about life after marriage from them.Romantic love has many more things to face after marriage than before marriage. Almost most people cannot make one plus one equal two. One of the problems is the relationship between mother-in-law and daughter-in-law.Lu Zhi has a good friend who complained to Lu Zhi many times because of his mother-in-law.It's almost like I haven't had a fight these days. Every time my husband and I quarrel lately, it's almost always because of my mother-in-law.My husband and I went on a trip, and she actually wanted to go tooMy husband and I had a quarrel, and she got involved. Then our original quarrel turned into a quarrel, and the two of us had a cold war for several days.His son and I both earn wages, and I think I look good, but she actually thinks I'm not good enough for his son.The fact that Lu Zhi, a good friend, and her husband did not divorce was also due to the fact that their relationship was really good.Zhou Chengan noticed that Lu Zhi was a little nervous.Lu Zhi: Your mother, no, what kind of daughter-in-law does my mother-in-law like?Fortunately, Lu Zhi was going to the island with Zhou Chengan, so there was no big problem.Zhou Chengan: My mother may be a little enthusiastic.Lu Zhi: PassionateZhou Cheng'an: She thought I couldn't get a wife. After a while, he looked at Lu Zhi and thought he couldn't get a wife.When he met Chen Jiaojiao and Zhou Ang, Lu Zhi realized that Zhou Chengan's enthusiasm was not an exaggeration at all.Chen Jiaojiao was followed by Zhou Ang, who was carrying large and small bags. The couple looked very young, especially Chen Jiaojiao.Chen Jiaojiao: This is my daughter-in-law. I know that my son is blessed.Chen Jiaojiao held Lu Zhi's hand, "Your father-in-law and I knew you were getting married, so we started preparing various things for them. We also asked for leave, so we came here. Don't be surprised." If you hadn't gone to get your marriage certificate yesterday, we would have come back from the capital yesterday.She looks cheerful and gentle.What a surprise.Grandma Zhou was smiling on the side, and I knew that Jiaojiao must like this daughter-in-law.Lu Zhi invited them in.Chen Jiaojiao was so enthusiastic that she kept holding Lu Zhi's hand.Lu Zhi: I'm going to make some tea.Chen Jiaojiao raised her head and winked at Zhou Chengan, "You kid, why are you so ignorant?"Zhou Chengan: I'll go to the kitchen to make tea.Lu Zhi stood up quickly. He didn't know where the tea leaves were. I told him.In the kitchen, Lu Zhi found some tea and handed it to Zhou

Chengan. He said in a low voice, "Go to the steel factory and ask for my dad. He is not busy today and can ask for leave."Everyone is very considerate of Chen Xiangde. He is conscientious, hard-working and capable, and he is very attentive in taking care of his apprentices. In these years, he only asked for leave for the sake of his children.

Chen Xiangde finished his work in the factory and taught his apprentice seriously.Another apprentice hurried in, sweating, master, your son-in-law is here.Chen Xiangde pointed out several problems of his apprentice before going out.Chen Xiangde: Your parents are here. I need to take a leave of absence. Please wait for me for a while while I go to the clothing factory again.I want to call Li Lan together.When preparing to go to the clothing factory, Chen Xiangde watched Zhou Chengan open the car door.The clothing factory is not far away, so I just looked for Li Lan. It took me some time to ask for leave.The car stopped outside the courtyard.Li Lan got out of the car. This car was so fast.Sitting there is much more comfortable than taking a bus.Not forgetting the business, Li Lan went back quickly.Zhou Chengan and Chen Xiangde followed behind.I see that Lu Zhi's parents-in-law bought a lot of things for them.I saw two roast ducks, which seemed to be the roast ducks from the capital.Li Lan and Chen Xiangde came back by car.He Li felt her face was hot and she was so embarrassed.Chu Tong's face didn't look good either. If she had known she would marry Li Yu and Lu Zhi could marry so well, she wouldn't have married Li Yu.Maybe, she can also marry someone like Zhou ChenganUncomfortable panic.Looking at the people around me, I feel like their eyes are mocking.

Chen Jiaojiao: This snack is delicious, and this, the White Rabbit toffee, this is the cloth I bought for you to make a skirt for you to wear, and these are all the cloth tickets I saved, and you take them.There are simply too many.Chen Jiaojiao took out three more envelopes. This one is from your father-in-law and I. This is from Cheng'an's grandparents. This is from Cheng'an's second uncle and second aunt. This is from Cheng'an's cousin. Take what my brother gives you.Zhou Chengan's second uncle's family really had no way to ask for leave and come back.Chen Jiaojiao took out another red envelope, and this one is from Uncle Chengan, and it is also your uncle's wish.Chen Jiaojiao: Regarding Zhou Jun, he is Cheng'an's younger brother and my son. Logically speaking, his father and I should take him with him, but we really don't have time. Your father has been busy with the machinery of the steel plant recently. I'm also busy at the food factory.Thinking of the little fat boy Zhou Jun, Lu Zhi really didn't think this kid was a drag, and living together was lively.Lu Zhi lived a lonely life after his parents divorced.The two of them remarried each other, and their thoughts were on the children they had later. Fortunately, they were given a lot of money.After coming back, Lu Zhi felt that his family was kind to him, but they also liked the excitement.After all, he has experienced something, and his temperament is different.For example, if she felt unhappy, she could file for divorce from Zhou Chengan, which Lu Zhi would not have thought of before.Chen Jiaojiao: I am really grateful to you. We originally planned to pay Zhou Jun's living expenses to your grandparents. Now every month, I will remit his living expenses to you.Things should be looked at individually and should not be interfered with too much. Zhou Chengan and Lu Zhi had no obligation to raise their younger brother. They took care of it and they could not be asked to pay for it.The two families get together and are very harmonious.At noon, Li Lan and Sister Lu went to cook and brought the roast duck they had brought.Fat but not greasy, crispy on the outside and tender on the inside, with a rich sauce flavor.Lu Zhi was even more happy that he hadn't finished eating the bacon yet.After one meal, Lu Zhi was very full.In the afternoon, Zhou Chengan asked someone to help deliver the things they wanted to bring to the island. After all this work, the Zhou family wanted to go back.The Lu family sent them to the door and watched the car drive out of the alley.Lu Zhi took Li Lan's arm and went in.Li Lan: Your parents-in-law are really good.

After returning to the house, Lu Zhi sat on the bed and unpacked all the things Chen Jiaojiao gave him.Chen Jiaojiao and Zhou Ang gave them a thousand yuan and some tickets.Zhou Chengan's second uncle gave him five hundred.Zhou Chengan's cousin gave him two hundred.Zhou Chengan's uncle gave him five hundred.Grandpa Zhou and Grandma Zhou gave another sewing ticket and one hundred yuan.Two thousand three hundred quick bucks plus five thousand one hundred yuan, Lu Zhi now has a total of seven thousand four hundred yuan.It's really a huge sum of moneyThese include remittance orders and cash, as well as passbooks.After collecting the money, Lu Zhi said something to Li Lan and went out.Lu Zhi plans to keep only 400 yuan of this money and take it with him. Zhou Chengan's salary and allowance are more than 100 yuan a month. Zhou Jun has his own living expenses, so they don't need to take this money.At the post office, Lu Zhi deposited a total of 7,000 yuan.If you say you are not excited, you are lying. If this were Lu Zhi before, he would probably not be able to sleep.After leaving the post office, it was still early, so Lu Zhi took the bus to the bookstore.Buy a few cookbooks, this one is a must.Buy a few books that you usually read for leisure.This is college entrance examination review materialLu Zhi moved quickly and bought all the college entrance examination review materials he could buy, including paper and pens.Lu Zhi's eldest brother is good at studying. Lu Zhi helped his eldest brother buy a set of books. When the news of the resumption of the college entrance examination came out, these books were not easy to buy.Thinking that maybe her sister-in-law could also give it a try, and there would be no worries about not passing the exam, she bought another set, making a total of three sets.These things are just too heavy.While Lu Zhi was carrying these things, he still kept an eye on the bankbook hidden in his arms.The bus was too crowded, and Lu Zhi didn't want to squeeze in. Finally, she found a bus that was somewhat empty, and she sat down at the back of the bus.After these things were done and the things were delivered to the island, they were waiting to get married and then set off to the island with Zhou Chengan.

In the evening, the Zhou family ate the leftover dishes from lunch and a separate plate of scrambled pepper eggs.Chen Xiangde drank some wine for himself today, and Brother Lu drank a few sips with him.My parents-in-law have also met. Lu Zhi is getting married this weekend.They were still a little sad.Apart from the initial shock and confusion about these books, no one mentioned them at the moment.Li Lan and Sister Lu also recalled Lu Zhi's childhood together.The little one is particularly cute.Yes, in the blink of an eye, I will get married.Zhou Chengan is really discerning.Yes, why not get married? I fell in love with Zhizhi as soon as I went on a blind date.

Lu Zhi returned to the house after dinner, and Sister-in-law Lu went there with her.It was Lu Zhi who called.Lu Zhi: Sister-in-law, it's always good for us to be a little educated. Those books I bought, you and your elder brother can read and learn more in your free time, even if it's to teach An An in the future.Sister-in-law Lu was very pleased. We all knew how to worry about this.Lu Zhi: Sister-in-law.Sister-in-law Lu: Okay, okay, don't worry, I will study hard. I'll ask your elder brother to study with me.And Li Lan.Li Lan listened to what the two people said and learned, and I watched them learn.Of course, it doesn't matter if they fail the exam in the future. When they can go into business, Lu Zhi can give them another push.These are opportunities that belong to the times.

Chapter 8The third day of the sixth lunar month is a good time to get married.Lu Zhi was woken up by Li Lan before he woke up. He got up and cleaned up. After a while, Chengan came over to pick up the bride.I glanced at the opened curtains. There were red words of joy on the windows. It looked festive, but it was not yet dawn outside.On your wedding day, get up early, just get up early.Lu Zhi went to brush his teeth and wash his face.Compared with the complexity of future weddings, today's weddings can be said to be very simple.Lu Anan sat next to Lu Zhi, her big grape-like eyes unblinking.Seeing Sister Lu coming over, Lu Anan said: "Auntie is so beautiful."She has thick black hair and skin as white as snow. Today she is wearing a wedding dress, which makes her look even more graceful.Sister-in-law Lu: Yes, my aunt is pretty.After giving the boiled eggs to Lu Zhi, Sister-in-law Lu said: Eat an egg first.Originally, she wanted to say that after finishing eating, she pursed her lips with red paper and looked at Lu Zhi's pretty lips.

Sister-in-law Lu swallowed her words back.Well, Lu Zhi probably doesn't have to, that's good.

Zhou Chengan came over to get married. He drove the car from yesterday. Several members of the Zhou family also came.Lu Zhi didn't know many of them, they were all relatives of Zhou Chengan in Hongxing Commune.Everyone was busy for a while, and then Lu Zhi and Zhou Chengan went back.It was Brother Lu who carried Lu Zhi out. Zhou Chengan opened the car door and Lu Zhi got in the car.Sister-in-law Lu patted Lu Zhi on the shoulder and said nothing. He would always be the big brother who loved Lu Zhi and doted on her.Everyone's blessings were still ringing in my ears, and there were many people watching the excitement around.Lu Zhi showed a bright smile to Brother Lu, Sister Lu, Li Lan and Lu Xiangde.Lu Zhi and Zhou Chengan sat in the back, and the car drove smoothly.The scenery outside the car window is fleeting.Zhou Chengan held Lu Zhi's hand, and Lu Zhi responded, with their fingers clasped tightly.Lu Zhi: How long will it take to arrive?Zhou Chengan: About half an hour.

The 10th Brigade of Hongxing Commune was even more lively than that in Luzhi Hutong. Because there were so many people, many people who joined in the fun ran over and watched.Lu Zhi got off the car and Zhou Chengan carried Lu Zhi inside.bride, brideThe bride is so beautiful, better looking than any movie star.I want to see the brideMany children were jumping around.Fatty Zhou Jun was very proud, with his hands on his hips, my sister-in-law looks good, right?Seeing Zhou Jun, Lu Zhi waved his arm towards him.Zhou Jun: Sister-in-lawThe little fat man was so excited that he almost jumped up.Lu Zhi lay on Zhou Chengan's broad shoulders, smelling the faint scent of soap on his body.Her wedding was incomparable to some of the weddings Lu Zhi had attended, but she liked it very much.When we entered the courtyard, tables were already set up and many people were seated.Lu Zhi also saw people following the gifts, and Grandpa Zhou was sitting there taking notes.Lu Zhi followed Zhou Chengan closely, followed their procedures, and then made a toast.Fortunately, it was just water mixed with a little bit of wine, so it had no taste.

The Zhou family has set aside a house specifically for Zhou Chengan. There are many happy words posted in the house, and the quilts and mattresses are all red.It's not a bed, it's a coiled Kang.While Lu Zhi was resting in the house, many relatives came over and introduced themselves to Lu Zhi one by one.Except for one of the fatter ones, Lu Zhi was said to be Lu Zhi's cousin. There was a boy who looked very cute and said that he wanted to call Lu Zhi his cousin.Others are a bit messy.It's hard to tell who it is at first glance.Chen Jiaojiao came over and greeted everyone out, and Zhou Chengan came over with food.They were all dishes that Lu Zhi had seen at the banquet, as well as a large bowl of rice.It's a big bowl.Zhou Chengan: Grandma asked people to keep this in advance. You should eat some first.Lu Zhi: I can᾽t finish eating. Why don᾽t you find me a bowl and I᾽ll just scoop out some.Zhou Cheng settled down for a meal, you eat and I'll eat the rest.Lu Zhi looked up at him, pursed his lips and picked up the chopsticks.Stir-fried cabbage, beans stewed with potatoes, lard residue, and a braised pork stew with potatoes.There weren't many vegetables or meat on the tables outside, most of them were potatoes, so it was already a particularly good banquet.Lu Zhi's bowl of braised pork and potatoes is different, there is a lot of meat in it.Lu Zhi had half a bowl of rice left and a lot of vegetables left. The braised pork was specially reserved for Zhou Chengan.Zhou Chengan sat down to eat with his dinner. He ate quickly, but it was not ugly and had a clean and neat feeling.Lu Zhi looked at him quietly. There was no disgust in his eyes, and there was no disgust in his eating movements.A piece of braised pork was handed to Lu Zhi's mouth.Lu Zhi was stunned and took a small bite. She realized that she should finish it in one bite. She gripped her skirt, finished eating, and finished the remaining half of the fat and thin pork belly.When she was eating it, she felt that this was not as delicious as the one made by her sister-in-law, but now she felt that it seemed quite delicious.Zhou Jun stood at the door, and Lu Zhi called him, come here.Fatty Zhou Jun ran in, raising his head and looking at Lu Zhi with bright eyes, sister-in-law.Lu Zhi gave him a handful of peanuts to eat, and also took some for himself.Zhou Junke was proud, raising his little head, I know, this is called having a child early, which means to have a child early.Lu Zhi:While eating peanuts, Lu Zhi gave some to Zhou Jun.Woo woo woo wooMy sister-in-law is so kind. She peels peanuts for him to eat. The peanuts are so fragrant.Zhou Jun stood there and Lu Zhi fed him peanuts. Zhou Jun stopped eating after eating a few.Zhou Jun: Sister-in-law, you eat, I am a man, you can't give me all the peanutsHe said and ran out.Lu Zhi held the freshly peeled peanuts in his hand and ate them slowly.Now that you are married, you will definitely have children.At this time, many people will have many children.Lu Zhi opened his mouth, Zhou Chengan.Zhou Chengan had finished eating and was about to go out and wash the dishes when he heard Lu Zhi calling him.Lu Zhi: Can you close the door first?After closing the door, there were only two people in the room, and the noise outside seemed to be much quieter.Lu Zhi: I don't want to have children for the time being. If I do, I just want to have one.As she spoke, she also felt a little uneasy.During the blind date, Lu Zhi was so satisfied with Zhou Chengan's conditions that he forgot about it.At this time, everyone generally has a lot of children at home.Lu Zhi waited for Zhou Chengan's answer.Still thinking about what to do if Zhou Chengan is unwilling, what to do if they can't reach an agreement on this matterZhou Chengan: OK.Lu Zhi was slightly surprised, did you agree?Zhou Chengan nodded and agreed.After his blind date with Lu Zhi, Zhou

Chengan had no plans to get married, let alone how many children he wanted.It is already a surprise to have a child in the future.

After the banquet was over, everyone started to clean up.Lu Zhi wanted to help but was stopped by Chen Jiaojiao. He just got married. How can he do any work? Go back and count the gifts. They will be given to you. There are also some things given to you. These things can be used by both you and Cheng'an. Let's go together. Take it to the island.Lu Zhi looked at several new kettles next to him. Our kettles have been delivered to the island, so let's keep this one.Chen Jiaojiao: Okay, take whatever you need with you, and leave whatever you don't need. He said, patting Lu Zhi's hand, "Your dad and I still have some things to do. We have finished attending your wedding and will go back. Then you can call or write to us."After saying that, he gave Lu Zhi a piece of paper with his address and phone number written on it.Chen Jiaojiao: Keep this away. If you have time, come to the capital to play.Lu Zhi: You have to go back nowChen Jiaojiao looked at Zhou Ang, who was holding Zhou Jun, and nodded.Chen Jiaojiao and Zhou Ang were going back. Everyone went out to see them off and watched them get into the car.Lu Zhi and Zhou Chengan stood together, and Lu Zhi was still holding Zhou Jun's hand.After watching the car drive far away, everyone went back.Grandma Zhou said, okay, let's pack up quickly. Zhizhi, you go back to the house, count the gifts and everything, and put them away.Lu Zhi took Zhou Jun back to the house, while Zhou Chengan helped with the work outside.Lu Zhi looked at the chubby Zhou Jun sitting opposite him and wondered if he could count money.Zhou Jun: I can do it within a hundredLu Zhi was pleasantly surprised, you are so awesome.This was already known in kindergarten, so Lu Zhi thought he could help count some dollars, dimes, etc.There were many people attending the banquet, and although some of the gifts were not large, there were still some after counting.After cleaning up outside, Zhou Chengan came back and brought an apple to Lu Zhi and Zhou Jun. Looking at the two of them, Zhou Chengan gave the big apple to Lu Zhi and the small apple to Zhou Jun.Lu Zhi took the apple and asked: Who paid for the banquet?Zhou Chengan: It came from my parents.Lu Zhi nodded.If the money for the banquet came from Grandpa Zhou and Grandma Zhou, Lu Zhi planned to give the money to Grandpa Zhou and Grandma Zhou.However, many of these courtesy are due to Grandpa Zhou and Grandma Zhou's courtesy.Zhou Chengan: Take it, your grandparents also told you to give it to you. You don't have to worry about your grandparents, parents, and uncles and aunts. They will give them money every month. If you tell them no, they will be unhappy.Lu Zhi: We won't take that thing.Zhou Chengan: Okay, I'll listen to you.With that said, Lu Zhi talked about buying books for himself. Before we set off, we had to go back to my house. I bought some books to take with me.Zhou Chengan: We will come back in three days. We will go back and stay one night. Then we will set off to the island the next day. When we go back, we will take it with us.Zhou Chengan has arranged all this.Even if Lu Zhi didn't say anything, they still had to go back to the Lu family before going to the island.Lu Zhi nodded. I wanted to eat the dumplings we had at a state-owned restaurant last time.Zhou Chengan remembered, but he didn't know whether the dumplings were available or not. He nodded, I'll go out for a while and come back later.Lu Zhi nodded, and Zhou Jun on the side also nodded.One big and one small, each holding an apple and eating the apple seriously.Lu Zhi: It's quite sweet.Zhou Jun nodded in agreement, delicious

Chapter 9Zhou Chengan went out to look around and went to Li's house next door.Li Zhiqiang was lying in the house when he heard his son outside saying that Uncle Zhou was here. He glanced outside and swallowed.Inside the house.Li Zhiqiang was busy pouring cold water for Zhou Chengan, but Zhou Chengan took the water without drinking it.I felt anxious and nervous.Li Zhiqiang: Brother Cheng'an, tell me, I didn't know at the beginning that you would marry that Lu Zhi in the future. If I knew, I would definitely not bully her or pull her pigtails.Besides, didn't we all beat him up in the first place?What did he come here for?Has Lu Zhi remembered this?At that time, he just saw Lu Zhi's cuteness, so he couldn't help but pull Lu Zhi's braid. Lu Zhi didn't play with him, so he deliberately bullied Lu Zhi and wanted Lu Zhi to play with him.Zhou Chengan: You often go to the county seatChen Zhiqiang thought for a long time and said: Yes, I often travel to the county town. But when I go to the county seat, I go to the county seat. I do all the serious work and nothing else. Sometimes I run for our brigade, and sometimes I go to my wife's parents' house.By the way, I seem to have met Lu Zhi when I went to the county town, but neither of us spoke.Chen Zhiqiang is still thinking about what he has done recently. He has done nothing.Zhou Chengan talked about the state-owned restaurant where he and Lu Zhi ate. Do you know when their restaurant will serve dumplings?Chen Zhiqiang:No, Zhou Chengan is getting married today. Instead of getting bored with his wife, he came to see him just to ask him when the state-owned restaurants in the county will serve dumplings.Zhou Chengan: Do you know?Chen Zhiqiang: I know, I know, let me see what day it is today.After reading the calendar, Chen Zhiqiang said, on the day your wife comes home, their state-owned restaurant will serve dumplings.Zhou Chengan nodded, okay, thank you.Chen Zhiqiang went out with Zhou Chengan, and he followed Zhou Chengan. Lu Zhi and I have known each other since we were children. I happened to go over to say hello to her. You were so busy getting married today that I didn't even talk to her.Not many people spoke to Lu Zhi, but he called his sister-in-law, and Lu Zhi responded.

Zhou Chengan took Chen Zhiqiang back. Lu Zhi saw Chen Zhiqiang and thought for a while, you called me sister-in-law, right?Chen Zhiqiang: Congratulations, sister-in-law, you and Brother Cheng'an are happily married. They have been together for a hundred years.Lu Zhi: Thank you.Chen Zhiqiang sighed: It was many years ago before you came to our Red Star Commune. I bullied you when I was young and ignorant, but I was beaten by Brother Cheng'an. You two are really a match made in heaven.Lu Zhi was stunned for a moment.Chen Zhiqiang: You won't forget that I also wanted to play with you, so I pulled your pigtails and pushed you.红星公社，欺负她，男主揍了欺负她的人，她开始喜欢和男主不一起玩，后来情窦初开喜欢男主。Lu Zhi: I was young at the time and don't remember much. Did I come to Red Star Commune later?Li Zhiqiang thought about everything he had done again. He was a man of many minds and had many things on his mind.He racked his brains and almost thought about what he had done when he was a child. He only remembered that he met Lu Zhi once in the Red Star Commune.What is this?What does Lu Zhi want to know? What does he want to say?Chen Zhiqiang: I only met you once in Red Star Commune.Lu Zhi: So, you bullied me onceAt this moment, Chen Zhiqiang was almost sweating. I wanted to play with you, but I was ignorant and brother Cheng An also beat me up. Later I went home and was educated again, and I never did this again. This kind of thing, I didn't mean to push you, really.It's true that Lu Zhi was so cute when she was a child.Chen Zhiqiang's mouth went dry when he explained, and he still thought that it was so beautiful. He was cute when he was a child, and he is also so beautiful when he grows up.Lu Zhi had no intention of talking to Chen Zhiqiang. She suspected that it was Zhou Chengan who helped her beat up the person, not the male protagonist Li Yu.But if this is the case, why is it misunderstood again?Lu Zhi: Do you still remember what exactly happened?Chen Zhiqiang regretted that he shouldn't have come here, or he should have waited until Lu Zhi and Zhou Chengan were about to go back.Probably because Lu Zhi's expression was too clear, Chen Zhiqiang, a man with eight hundred thoughts, actually felt that Lu Zhi really didn't mean anything else and just wanted to ask about the original situation.Chen Zhiqiang recalled carefully.Chen Zhiqiang: When you came over that day, you were wearing a small skirt, leather shoes, and two pigtails.Zhou Chengan raised his eyes and looked away, and Chen Zhiqiang was sweating again.Unexpectedly, Zhou Chengan was quite jealous.Chen Zhiqiang: We were playing outside my yard. I pulled your pigtails and accidentally pushed you down. You cried, and Brother Chengan beat me when I got home. When I saw you later, I even apologized to you.The memories of my childhood seem to be getting clearer little by little.Lu Zhi watched Chen Zhiqiang apologize to herself. Chen Zhiqiang and Li Yu were both dirty and looked as if they had fought, so she misunderstood that it was Li Yu who beat Chen Zhiqiang.When Chen Zhiqiang went back, his speed was like a trot.

In the evening, everyone ate the leftover food from lunch, which was ready to be heated up.I can still eat it tomorrow morning, and maybe another meal at noon.Everyone was sitting around the table. Lu Zhi couldn't help but laugh when he listened to Grandpa Zhou and Grandma Zhou talking about Chen Zhiqiang next door.Chen Zhiqiang was really educated.Chen Zhiqiang also had his pigtails tied up. A girl's pigtails were not particularly long. His parents pulled his pigtails and asked him if it hurt.This Chen Zhiqiang is a grown man, so he probably felt embarrassed and didn't say anything.Grandma Zhou: Zhiqiang, he's pretty good now, but he's a little too narrow-minded, but he doesn't do bad things either, he's pretty good.Zhou Chengan picks up vegetables for Lu Zhi.Grandma Zhou: You know why your grandfather wanted you two to go on a blind date, right? Back then, Chengan had a stable personality and never fought. He rarely went out to play with others. When he saw you being bullied at home, he went out. .Lu Zhi served Zhou Chengan with braised pork and had dinner.Then, Lu Zhi gave Grandma Zhou, Grandpa Zhou, and Zhou Jun a piece of braised pork.Duan Shui Master, greatGrandpa Zhou and

Grandma Zhou went out for a walk after dinner, and Zhou Jun also ran out to join them.It's hot now and everyone likes to enjoy the cool air.Lu Zhi was too lazy to move. If he went out for a walk on the first day of his wedding, he would definitely be greeted by many people.After washing up, Lu Zhi returned to the house.Today she will live in the same room as Zhou Chengan.Hearing the sound of Zhou Chengan washing outside, Lu Zhi curled his fingers slightly, and then spread the quilt on the kang.This is the first time Lu Zhi has slept on such a kang since he grew up.It was a bit hard, and it would be a little softer if there was a mattress on top. Lu Zhi simply spread it on two layers, which seemed to make it more comfortable.When Zhou Cheng'an came back, Lu Zhi was tugging on the quilt. She raised her head and met Zhou Cheng'an's eyes without saying anything. Lu Zhi's ears were already a little red.From here, they could hear the voices of people enjoying the cool air outside, and Lu Zhi seemed to hear Grandma Zhou's voice.It's not quiet at this time, so it's not too embarrassing.Lu Zhi thought this was amazing.For example, Lu Zhi met his friend's friend at his friend's house before. Neither of them knew what to say or do. They all watched TV together and listened to other voices, which made them feel less awkward.Later, Lu Zhi's friends still laughed at her.When her husband went to her house for the first time, her inarticulate husband and her inarticulate father were both grateful for the TV in their home.Lu

Zhi: Are you sleepy?Zhou Chengan: Not sleepy yet.Lu Zhi nodded. Let's wait until our grandparents come back before we go to sleep.Don't know what to say.Zhou Chengan: You are too toughLooking down at the two-layered mattress he had laid out, Lu Zhi nodded. It was a bit, okay now, quite soft.Soon, Zhou Chengan took out another quilt and spread it on the mattress.Lu Zhi helped to stay with him.Zhou Chengan: This can make it softer.Lu Zhi pressed it and said with a smile: Well, it's a little softer again.

Lu family.The Lu family is still a little worried about Lu Zhi getting married.Brother Lu: Tell me, will you get used to being naive?Hearing this, Sister-in-law Lu also nodded, and then said: Probably not, they all like Zhizhi, and Zhizhi has a good personality, so it may be a bit uncomfortable to live there, but it will only be a few days. There are many kangs in Hongxing Commune, so I was a little worried that she wouldn't be used to sleeping there.Li Lan nodded, a little worried about his daughter.It would be great if the daughter could be married nearby, and they wouldn't be so worried.But in this neighborhood, there is no one as good as Zhou Chengan, who looks good, has good conditions, and treats Lu Zhi well.The key is that Lu Zhi's second sister on the island can take care of her, otherwise they will not agree.Thinking about it this way, these two people really meet many conditions at the same time.

Grandpa Zhou and Grandma Zhou came back with

Zhou Jun.Zhou Jun: Sister-in-law, good night, I'm going back to sleepHe came here after washing up. Fatty Zhou Jun looked refreshed. Lu Zhi smiled and said good night to him.When it was time to go to bed, Lu Zhi wore his pajamas and lay down under the quilt.Lu Zhi felt that his heartbeat was a little fast.Zhou Chengan closed the curtains and turned off the lights. The room became dark, and Lu Zhi felt his heart beating faster.Thinking of Zhou Cheng'an's thin waist, I no longer felt nervous.Zhou Chengan lay down next to Lu Zhi. He held Lu Zhi's hand. I didn't buy contraceptives. Let's sleep first.Since Lu Zhi doesn't want children for the time being, if they are together on their wedding night and Lu Zhi gets pregnant, this may disrupt Lu Zhi's plan.Lu Zhi turned around and was very close to Zhou Chengan. Her voice was very low, Zhou Chengan.Zhou Chengan: Yeah.Lu Zhi: I think I chose the right husband.Somewhat relaxed, the smell of Zhou Chengan's body was really good, but it was a bit hot being close to Zhou Chengan.Soon, Lu Zhi fell asleep.As soon as he reached out, Lu Zhi hugged Zhou Cheng's waist.Zhou Chengan's hand on one side clenched and unclenched tightly, unable to sleep at all.

a new day.When Lu Zhi woke up, Zhou Chengan had already gotten up to help with the work.Zhou Chengan: I've prepared the water. You can just wash up. Breakfast is hot. You wash up first. I'll take it out for you after washing.Zhou Jun is also helping with the work.Thinking that Grandpa Zhou and Grandma Zhou would live together, and Zhou Chengan's second uncle had to send their children over, Lu Zhi became worried about these two old people.Lu Zhi: Are grandparents usually doing all this work?Zhou Chengan didn't say anything. Grandma Zhou came out and smiled happily because of Lu Zhi's remarks.Just know she is a good girl.Grandma Zhou: Your grandfather and eldest brother's family live near us, and they usually help with some work.Grandpa Zhou is already busy now, it is a double grab.Grandma Zhou will go to deliver food soon.Zhou Chengan was waiting for Lu Zhi to wake up, and he would also go to help later.Lu Zhi sat at the dinner table and found that what he ate had yesterday's leftovers, but there was also egg custard, and the porridge was freshly cooked.Zhou Chengan: I made egg custard separately. You can try it.Lu Zhi took a bite and nodded to Zhou Cheng'an. It was delicious. The chicken cake was very smooth and tender.Zhou Chengan: I'm going to help. I'll be back in a while. Can you and Zhou Jun stay at home?Lu Zhi: No problem for me. I will deliver food to you at noon.Zhou Chengan smiled: Okay, tell Zhou Jun, he knows, and let him take you there.It was left to Lu Zhi to deliver meals at noon, and it was Grandma Zhou who cooked.Lu Zhi and Zhou Jun were playing in the house.When Lu Zhi smelled the aroma, he went to the kitchen. Because it was a double grab, he had to eat enough at noon. Dry food was essential. Grandma Zhou was steaming Erhe noodles.Lu Zhi saw mung beans in the kitchen and asked: Grandma, do you want to make mung bean soup? I'll do it.Grandma Zhou: We are so childish that we can make mung bean soup. It's amazing.Lu Zhi smiled and just made mung bean soup.Grandma Zhou: You may think this is a small thing, but if you can do it, you are already very powerful. Today you will make the mung bean soup and I will deliver it to Chengan later.The mung beans have been processed.Lu Zhi only needs to boil some mung beans and add sugar.Lu Zhi was busy in the kitchen, and Zhou Jun followed Lu Zhi to help. Although he was a little chubby, he could help Lu Zhi with a lot of work.At noon, Lu Zhi looked like it was almost done, so he filled the mung bean soup and went out with Zhou Jun to deliver the food.Seeing the golden ears of wheat rustling in the wind, Lu Zhi carried something and led Zhou Jun.From a distance, Lu Zhi saw Zhou Chengan.Zhou Jun: It's the eldest brotherLu Zhi: Yes, it's your eldest brother.Zhou Jun: Brother, brother, sister-in-law is here to deliver food.Hearing Zhou Jun's voice, Zhou Chengan stood up straight. He put down what he was doing and walked over. He was tall and strong, with very long legs.Grandpa Zhou was busy working, directing everyone and leading everyone to shout slogans. Some people had already started eating.Zhou Chengan found a cool place to sit down with Lu Zhi.Zhou Jun: Brother, my sister-in-law made mung bean soup for you to drink.Zhou Chengan looked over.They were already a couple who had received their marriage certificate and had their wedding ceremony.They slept together yesterday.Lu Zhi had nothing to be embarrassed about.Lu Zhi: Grandpa drank it for you. Grandma soaked the mung beans yesterday.When Lu Zhi took out the mung bean soup and handed it to Zhou Chengan, he was washing his hands with water because of work.After Zhou Chengan washed his hands, Lu Zhi handed him a spoon and said to him, "Try it."Zhou Chengan took a sip of mung bean soup, which was refreshing and relieving the heat.Lu Zhi: Does it taste good?Zhou Chengan: It tastes delicious and very sweet.very sweetLu Zhi remembered that she didn't add much sugar. The mung bean soup was too sweet, and she felt that the refreshing feeling was a little weak.

In the evening, Zhou Chengan took a clean bath and went back.Today they are still the same as yesterday.Probably because the weather was a bit hot today, Lu Zhi felt that sleeping with Zhou Chengan was much hotter than yesterday.Lu Zhi: Zhou Chengan.Zhou Chengan: YeahLu Zhi: I'm a little hot. I'm going to get a summer quilt out.Soon, Zhou Cheng settled down. Without turning on the light, he found a summer quilt in the cabinet nearby and gave the quilt to Lu Zhi.Zhou Chengan: Is it still hot?One more thing, Lu Zhi covered her with a little quilt, and she said softly: It's not hot anymore, good night.Zhou Chengan went out again. When he came back, he took a cattail leaf fan and gently fanned Lu Zhi.Lu Zhi turned around to face him, and could hear each other's breathing.Zhou Chengan:

Let's buy another fan when we go back.After mentioning these, Lu Zhi was interested, okay, buy a fan.After a long time, Lu Zhi felt very sleepy and fell asleep leaning on Zhou Chengan's arms.Zhou Chengan fanned Lu Zhi for a long time before falling asleep.Early the next morning, Zhou Chengan woke up early as yesterday. Grandpa Zhou and Grandma Zhou got up, and Zhou Chengan woke up.When he woke up today, Lu Zhi was still in his arms, almost holding him.Zhou Chengan lay down without getting up, and he didn't call Lu Zhi.After waiting for about half an hour, Lu Zhi turned over and continued to sleep on the other side. Only then did Zhou Chengan get up and go out.Grandma Zhou: Keep your voice down, don't wake up Zhizhi. You and Zhizhi are both good-looking, and the children you will have in the future will also be good-looking.Zhou Chengan lowered his eyes and said nothing.

On the day they returned home, Grandpa Zhou and Grandma Zhou prepared many things for Lu Zhi.There are mushrooms that Grandpa and Grandma Zhou dried themselves, fresh wild vegetables and fruits, and sour beans that Grandpa and Grandma Zhou pickled.For the rest, Zhou Chengan and Lu Zhi had to buy them themselves when they arrived at the county town.Lu Zhi: Grandpa and grandma, we will go back to the island for a day this time. When Chengan is free, we will come back to see you.Grandma Zhou nodded, "Okay, okay, come back and have a look when you are free. Take one portion of these sour beans back for your family to eat, and keep the other portion for you to take to the island to eat." If it tastes good, you call grandma, and grandma will ask someone to help deliver it to the dock, and you can go get it yourself.Lu Zhi: Okay, thank you grandma.Grandpa Zhou looked at them and then at Zhou Jun, "You have to be obedient. Do you know that you are a little man now and you have to take care of your sister-in-law."The little man Zhou Jun nodded seriously, knowing that I am a little man now. I have to be obedient and sensible. Like my elder brother, I also have to take care of my sister-in-law.Lu Zhi looked at Zhou Jun, who was still in kindergarten, and smiled softly.

When the three of them got on the bus, they sat in the back. Lu Zhi sat by the window, then Zhou Chengan, and next to Zhou Chengan was Zhou Jun.Grandpa Zhou and Grandma Zhou didn't come over. They were busy. Grandpa Zhou was still the captain, so it must be important to double grab. Grandma Zhou also had to cook.When they arrived at the county, Lu Zhi, Zhou Chengan and Zhou Jun got off the car at the state-owned shopping mall. They wanted to see the electric fan first.Among the tickets Zhou Ang and Chen Jiaojiao gave them, there were tickets for electric fans.When he arrived at the electric fan counter, Lu Zhi asked: Is there an electric fan?Salesperson: Yes.They bought an electric fan and continued shopping.Zhou Chengan bought some more pastries and candies, and then some spare ribs and pork belly before they went back.Zhou Chengan was carrying everything, looking very relaxed.Zhou Jun looked at Zhou Chengan and then at himself. He clenched his fists and said, "Sister-in-law, I can also help you carry your things in the future."Lu Zhi: But you are still in kindergarten.Zhou Jun: Soon, I will be able to go to primary school.Lu Zhi couldn't help but smile, "That's it, you will be a primary school student from now on."Zhou Jun looks very proud, yes, I will be a primary school student from now onLu Zhi: Okay, future primary school students.Zhou Jun is even more proud.When I become a primary school student, I will be able to help my sister-in-law with work and carry things.When passing by the supply and marketing cooperative, Lu Zhi took Zhou Jun in to buy soda, and they drank soda again.Then we took the bus back.Finally arrived at the courtyard.Brother Lu was waiting outside the courtyard. He quickly strode forward and saw that Zhizhi was back.Lu Zhi smiled, big brotherBrother Lu looked at Lu Zhi for a while, and then he saw Zhou Chengan and Zhou Jun. He wanted to help carry things, but Zhou Chengan was useless. Lu Zhi and Brother Lu went back while talking.When people in the courtyard saw Lu Zhi and the others coming back, many of them were saying hello.Zhizhi is backWell, back.Eat some watermelon, my aunt's watermelon is so sweet.Thank you, Aunt Zhou. I won't eat it. You can give it to the child. When I just came back, I drank a bottle of soda.When Lu Zhi arrived home, the house suddenly became more lively.Sister-in-law Lu: I'm just waiting for you to come back. Where is Chengan?Zhou Chengan: Sister-in-law.The family was cooking. Sister-in-law Lu and Li Lan came out and talked with Lu Zhi and Zhou Chengan for a long time before continuing their work.Brother Lu knew that Lu Zhi and the others drank soda, so he poured them some water.Brother Lu: Can I stay at home for a day?Lu Zhi: Well, I won't go to the island until tomorrow. After saying that, she smiled and said, Brother, he's not far away either.Lu Zhi is getting married this time. Originally, Lu Zhi's second sister could come back, but Lu Zhi's second brother-in-law is on a mission. Lu Zhi's second sister has to stay at home to take care of the child, who is still too young to take the boat.Zhou Chengan: Brother, I will come back often with Zhizhi. You can stay there for a while when you are free.Brother Lu is not polite to them either. If I have time, I will definitely stay there. After finishing speaking, he added: "Don't forget, you have to go to the post office to call the second sister later and tell the second sister that your second sister called yesterday to ask."Lu Zhi: Got it.Lu Zhi took out the things. This was something sent by his grandparents. This was sour beans. They looked delicious.Brother Lu nodded, yes, it looks delicious.After finishing speaking, he looked at Zhou Chengan: During the weekend break, we will visit your grandparents when we have time to see if we can help with anything.This was all for the good of their little sister. Besides, Zhou Chengan's grandparents also remembered to bring them these things to eat.Zhou Chengan: Thank you, brother.Just as he was talking, the family began to clear the table and prepare for dinner.Lu Zhi and the others stopped sitting and went over to help.Lu Zhi discovered that there was even bacon that he liked to eat.Sister-in-law Lu: You like to eat, but we didn't eat the rest, just waiting for you to come back.Lu Zhi hugged Sister Lu's arm and thanked her.

Chapter 10The lunch meal was very sumptuous.Sister Lu makes fried bacon with dried beans.Dried beans taste very different from fresh beans, with a bit of toughness and more flavor.In the afternoon, Sister Lu packed a lot of things for Lu Zhi and Zhou Chengan, including dried beans.Sister-in-law Lu: This dried beans does not necessarily have to be fried with bacon to taste good, it can be delicious with fried eggs, fried potatoes, or fried pork belly.The weight of Lu Zhi and Zhou Chengan's luggage has increased a lot.Dried beans, dried radish, and dried cabbage.These things can be kept for a longer time.Outside, Zhou Chengan was talking to Lu Xiangde, and Sister-in-law Lu quietly asked: Is it okay on the wedding night?Lu Zhi, who was covered in quilts with Zhou Chengan, lowered his eyes and blushed, looking good.Sister-in-law Lu: That's good.Li Lan quietly told Sister Lu about this matter and asked her to ask about it.Sister-in-law Lu took out some clothes again. I have made all the fabrics your mother-in-law sent you in the past few days. There are summer skirts, autumn coats, and winter cotton-padded jackets. I also made them for you. You take it first.Sister-in-law Lu compares the clothes one by one. She knows the size of Lu Zhi's clothes. Some clothes are even made larger. If Lu Zhi gets fat, she can take them apart and continue to wear them.Knowing that Lu Zhi couldn't do it, Sister-in-law Lu told Lu Zhi how to dismantle it.After saying a few words, he simply said: It's okay. If you want to take it apart, just ask your second sister.Lu Anan's little head was lying on the window sill outside. "Auntie, you are so beautiful."Lu Zhi, who was wearing a navy-style dress, turned around and Zhou Jun was lying on the window sill again.Okay, so, how did the two little cubs lie here.Lu Zhi walked over and took a look. There were two people standing on a small bench.Zhou Jun: My sister-in-law is good-looking, my sister-in-law is the most beautifulChu Tong next door curled his lips and held the cream, feeling unhappy.She put down the cream and leaned over to chat with Li Yu, feeling better now.This was a man that even Lu Zhi couldn't get in the past.When she was in high school, Lu Zhi was the prettiest in the class. When school just started, she and Lu Zhi were playing with a few other people, and she was sitting closer to Lu Zhi.The boys in the class asked her to help send love letters and notes to please her. Chu Tong was unhappy when she needed her help.Before Chu Tong went to high school, she was also a pretty girl in their courtyard.

Zhou Chengan stood in front of the bicycle and took a mat to cushion the back seat of the bicycle.The bicycle belongs to Brother Lu. Brother Lu will not use it for the time being. Zhou Chengan wants to use it.Seeing Zhou Chengan's actions, Brother Lu nodded, very satisfied.Yes, when he sent Lu Zhi to school in the past, he always had to put a cushion on the back of the bicycle, otherwise he would get upset.Lu Zhi came out followed by two Zaizai, Zhou Jun and Lu Anan.Brother Lu: Okay, let's go. As he said that, he turned around and looked at the two Zaizai, "I'll take you back to play."Lu Zhi sat on the back seat of the bicycle. Zhou Chengan was very strong. She sat on it. It was an exaggeration to say that the bicycle would not move at all, but it was indeed very stable.They were going to a state-owned restaurant to buy dumplings to eat.Lu Zhi had forgotten about this matter.It seems that he told Zhou Chengan on the first day of their wedding. Unexpectedly, he actually remembered it.At this moment, Lu Zhi also wanted to eat dumplings.It's really delicious after all.Zhou Chengan: Let's goLu Zhi nodded, okay.Zhou Chengan rode out of the alley, his speed getting faster and faster.Lu Zhi's hair, which was tugging at the corner of Zhou Chengan's clothes, was blown up by the breeze, with a faint smile on his fair face.When we arrived at the state-owned restaurant, the dumplings had not even started being served, and there was already a queue.Zhou Chengan found a table for Lu Zhi to sit down, and went to line up himself.Zhou Chengan packed some dumplings stuffed with cabbage and pork in a lunch box and took them back to the Lu family to eat. He also took some and placed them in front of Lu Zhi.Eat while hot.It tastes the same as last time, very delicious.Lu Zhi took a bite, and soup burst out of the dumpling. She subconsciously looked for a napkin but couldn't find it.Lu Zhi: Zhou Chengan.His slender fingers wiped Lu Zhi's lips with a handkerchief. Zhou Chengan looked serious, but his movements were very gentle.Lu Zhi ate the dumplings in his mouth and said softly, "Eat it."Zhou Chengan: Yeah.The two of them were eating dumplings facing each other, with a bowl of steaming dumpling soup next to them.Lu Zhi: Next time, when we come back, let's come here to eat dumplings.Zhou Chengan raised his eyes and looked at her, okay.When returning, Lu Zhi was still sitting behind Zhou Chengan's bicycle.They did not go back directly, but went to the post office again.Lu Zhi wanted to call his second sister Lu Yue.Lu Zhi and Zhou Cheng arranged for the team to wait for a while, and then waited for a while for Lu Yue to answer the call.Lu Zhi took the microphone, "Second sister, let's go to the island tomorrow."Lu Yue: Okay, okay, your brother-in-law and I will pick you up at the pier.

At night, Zhou Cheng and Lu Zhi lived in the same room.During the first few days of their wedding, the two of them slept on the kang at Grandpa Zhou and Grandma Zhou's place. The kang was very big, while Lu

Zhi's room had a bed measuring 1.5 meters.It might be a little cramped for two people to sleep.Lu Zhi thought so.At this moment, she felt that the kang was very good, and a few more layers of mattresses were also very soft.Zhou Jun slept with Lu Xiangde and Li Lan today, and he came over to say good night.Zhou Jun: Big brother and sister-in-law, I'm going to bed!After playing with Lu Anan all afternoon, Zhou Junchuan's eyes were slightly red.Li Lan: Let's go back to sleep.There were only two people in the room, Lu Zhi and Zhou Chengan. Lu Zhi lay down on the bed in his pajamas.When Zhou Chengan also lay down, Lu Zhi felt different from before, as if the two people were very close.There is actually no difference, it's just a psychological effect.Lu Zhi also fell asleep in Zhou Cheng's arms before.When Zhou Chengan fanned Lu Zhi with a cattail leaf fan, Lu Zhi felt extremely comfortable.All thoughts seemed to be thrown away.I was about to fall asleep when I heard a buzzing sound and there were mosquitoes in the room.Lu Zhi: Zhou Chengan, there are mosquitoes.Zhou Chengan: Close your eyes first, and I'll turn on the light.The light was still a bit dazzling, so Lu Zhi slowly opened his eyes, which made it feel better.Zhou Chengan wanted to swat the mosquitoes when he heard their cries, but Lu Zhi also kept quiet.Lu Zhi pointed at the flying mosquito, Zhou Chengan nodded and swatted it away.Lu Zhi sat on the bed and moved forward, but he missed the blow.When Zhou Chengan stretched out his palm, there was a mosquito inside.You can have a good sleep now.Zhou Chengan: I'm going to wash my hands.Lu Zhi nodded, okay.Lying down again, Lu Zhi felt no sleepiness at all this time.Lu Zhi didn't want to talk to him about Zhou Chengan's work, and Zhou Chengan wouldn't say anything.Lu Zhi asked a lot about the island.Lu Zhi: I went there with the army. Has the house been approved?Zhou Chengan: Well, it has been approved, but not everything has been sorted out yet.Lu Zhi: It's okay. We'll clean it up when we get there.Of course, this is being sorted out, and Zhou Chengan is probably doing most of the work.Lu Zhi discovered that Zhou Chengan was much more modest when they were on a blind date.As they talked, Lu Zhi quickly fell asleep as Zhou Chengan fanned him.

It takes two hours to set off to the pier. Lu Zhi and Zhou Chengan need to take a car to the city first, then take a car to the pier, and then take a boat.Zhou Chengan happened to have friends who wanted to go back. They could take a jeep back.It only takes less than two hours to take a jeep to the pier.Li Lan wanted to bring something more to Lu Zhi, but Lu Zhi stopped her.Lu Zhi: No, that's enough.Li Lan: Your dad said that he is going to take the seventh-level fitter exam. The salary of a seventh-level fitter is higher than that of a sixth-level fitter. You don't have to worry about us. Besides, everyone at home has a job.Lu Xiangde is now a sixth-level fitter and can support their family, but if this is the case, their life will definitely not be as good as it is now.Sister-in-law Lu: Yes, there are more. These are candies. Take them. You and Zhou Chengan have just gotten married. When you meet Zhou Chengan's friends, give them some wedding candies. Zhou Chengan's soldiers also give some.These are purchased directly from the sugar factory, and some are provided by the sugar factory as benefits.Lu Zhi's luggage was stuffed with some candies by Mrs. Lu.Li Lan: Just wait, I'm boiling eggs for you, take them with you.Lu Zhi looked at them busy and smiled, and said to Sister-in-law Lu: We have settled in and will come back when we have time.Unlike the second sister Lu Zhi, Lu Zhi and Zhou Chengan do not plan to have children for the time being, so they will not come back because the child is temporarily inconvenient.Sister-in-law Lu: Your elder brother has said that we will also visit you when we have time.Some people in the courtyard had watched Lu Zhi grow up, and they talked more with Lu Zhi.Aunt Zhou smiled and said: Lu Zhi has been delicate since he was a child. When we get to the island, you have to take more care of us, Lu Zhi.Zhou Chengan is by Lu Zhi's side, and I will take care of her.They stood together, looking like a match made in heaven.Chu Tong went over, Zongzhi, you can find your happiness, I am very happy for you, and so is Li Yu.Li Yu nodded, looking pleased, and so did I. I'm glad you found a good marriage partner.Lu Zhi:Everyone looked at it with somewhat subtle expressions.They knew that Lu Zhi was chasing Li Yu. Lu Zhi liked Li Yu. After Li Yu got married, she acted like a monster during every blind date. Fortunately, she later met Zhou Chengan and was willing to marry him.Lu Zhi had forgotten about this matter.Lu Zhi: Li Yu, I liked you before.Everyone looked at each other.Lu Zhi went to see Zhou Chengan, who was also looking at her sideways.Lu Zhi: However, this matter was a misunderstanding. I only found out about this matter when I went to Red Star Commune after I married Chengan.

Chapter 11Lu Zhi, we went to the Red Star Commune together when we were kids. After Chen Zhiqiang bullied me, I thought it was you who beat Chen Zhiqiang. Since then, I have been very attached to you and like to play with you.But that may not be the case. The person on that day was Zhou Chengan.Lu Zhi looked at him. He was naive when he was just in love. He didn't know what liking meant, so he might have done something that you misunderstood.The jeep pulled up outside.Lu Zhi glanced outside and nodded politely to the Li family.No wonder.When Lu Zhi was in high school, how many people liked her.Yes, I remember that there was a man from the capital who was chasing Lu Zhi almost crazy, but Lu Zhi didn't even nod. At that time, I also said that it was Li Yu and Lu Zhi's childhood sweethearts, otherwise Lu Zhi wouldn't like him.I said Li Yu, what you did in this matter was really unkind.Li Yu blushed, I don't know, I don't knowBrother Lu: You don't know, you don't know what you're feeling guilty about, I'll tell you, what's wrong with my sister? Our whole family dotes on her and treats her well, but she actually likes to chase you and play with her.It is no exaggeration to say that Brother Lu and Sister Lu were jealous because Lu Zhi always wanted to play with Li Yu.In the end, there was a misunderstanding. The more I thought about it, the more angry I became.Chu Tong was so embarrassed at this moment that he ran back directly and cried out.She thought she had won over Lu Zhi by marrying Li Yu, but she didn't expect that Lu Zhi would marry better. She liked Li Yu all because of a misunderstanding.

Everything Lu Zhi and Zhou Chengan wanted to bring were put on the jeep.Li Lan held Lu Zhi's hand and called home when she got there. If anything happens, I'll go see your second sister. Do you know?Zhou Chengan has a tall and straight figure, parents, elder brother and sister-in-law, don't worry, I will definitely take good care of her.Li Lan nodded. It was strange that Zhou Chengan didn't like her daughter who was so kind.Lu Zhi hugged Li Lan, then Sister-in-law Lu, then Brother Lu and Lu Xiangde.The little niece Lu Anan raised her head and hugged Lu Zhi's legs.Lu Zhi stroked Lu Anan's hair. When aunt is free, she will come back to see you, okay?Lu Anan nodded vigorously, okayZhou Chengan opened the door and the jeep was a bit high. Zhou Chengan helped Lu Zhi get into the car.Lu Zhi and Zhou Jun sat in the back, and Zhou Chengan sat in the front passenger seat.When the car started, the Lu family was still standing outside.Lu Zhi looked at them from the car window and waved his arms to them, "You go back."Li Lan couldn't hold it back, wiped her tears and smiled again.Li Lan: Okay, okay, we're going back.Save it, they, Lu Zhi, will also feel uncomfortable.

Lu Zhi was in a low mood.At this moment, I still feel a little sorry for my second sister, who is not far away, but has much more courage than her.When she found that her hand was held by Zhou Jun's chubby hand, she heard Zhou Jun whisper to herself: I will protect you.Zhou Chengan: Stop ahead.Zhou Chengan sat in the back. Three people were not as comfortable as two people, but it was okay. Lu Zhi occupied a seat by himself, and Zhou Jun and Zhou Chengan did not squeeze Lu Zhi at all.The car was driving smoothly.Zhou Chengan took a piece of candy and stuffed it into Lu Zhi's hand, and introduced the places he passed by with a straight face.The driver was Jiang Dong. He wanted to cry but had no tears. It was over. He had lost the bet and had to wash his socks.They really didn't expect Zhou Chengan to get married.Yesterday everyone made bets on whether Zhou Chengan also had a cold face when facing his wife.It was very lively.No need to think about it, he must have a cold face.But it's better than treating us.I don't know what kind of person our sister-in-law is.Everyone made bets.Whoever loses, help wash the smelly socks.The only one who was a bit honest scratched his head, but our deputy leader Zhou doesn't like his sister-in-law, and he won't marry her.Feng Jianshe may become the biggest winner in their dormitory.Their deputy leader Zhou handed his wife candies.Doesn't look serious at allAhhhhh, I don't want to wash my smelly socks.I really envy Feng Jianshe.

As the jeep approached the dock, Lu Zhi saw the sea.Open the car window, the sea breeze blows, and there are waves on the sea.Zhou Jun saw the sea for the first time and stared outside without blinking.Lu Zhi simply held Zhou Jun in his arms, one big and one small, and looked outside together.The boat is heading towards the shore.Zhou Jun: Sister-in-law, it's a boat, it's a boatYes, it's a boatLobster, oysters, swimming crab, shrimp, giant squidIsland life is about to beginWhen getting off the bus, Lu Zhi, who had been riding for more than two hours, felt that his legs were a little weak. After standing outside for a while, he felt more comfortable.Standing at the dock watching the ship dock.Wearing a blue and white navy dress, fair skin and waist-length hair, Lu Zhi smoothed her hair as the breeze blew by.Some people couldn't help but look over.Oh hahaThis girl is so beautifulAfter the people on the boat got off, everyone started to get on the boat.Lu Zhi was followed by Zhou Chengan, Zhou Jun, and Jiang Dong who came with them.Lu Zhi got on the boat first and felt that everyone around her was quietly sizing her up.Someone who knew Zhou Chengan couldn't help but ask after a while, Deputy Captain Zhou, is this your wife?Zhou Chengan looked over and answered, yes.Lu

Zhi smiled at them.There was a place to sit in the cabin, but Lu Zhi did not go in and stood on the deck looking at the sea. Zhou Chengan and the others accompanied Lu Zhi.When the boat started moving, Lu Zhi felt that the sea breeze was blowing harder.The sea breeze at this time is particularly comfortable.The boat didn't know how long it had been traveling. Zhou Chengan pointed to the island that seemed to be very far away from them and said: That's it.Lu Zhi looked over, turned to look at Zhou Chengan and smiled.For about an hour, Lu Zhi watched the island getting closer and closer to them.Lu Yue stood on the beach, waving his arms to Lu Zhi, looking very excited, and even took a few steps forward, Zhi ZhiLu Zhi also waved his arms, and the second sisterFinally the ship docked.When Lu Zhi got off the boat, Lu Yue strode over and hugged Lu Zhi.Lu Yue: Finally we're here. My second sister made a lot of delicious food and we went over to have dinner together.Zhou Chengan: Second sister.Zhou Jun is young, but when facing Lu Yue, he has to follow Zhou Chengan and call him second sister.Zhou Jun's little Douding seriously called her second sister, which was so cute.Lu Zhi: Second sister, I want to call home first.Lu Yue: Yes, yes, you have to call home. I will take you to make a call first. Everyone is probably waiting.At first glance, you can tell that the island is a very big island.Lu Zhi was not in a hurry. He wanted to familiarize himself with the terrain first, but it was more important to make a phone call first.When we arrived at the telephone service room on the island, we had to queue up and there were quite a few people making calls.Even if I call him, I have to wait for a while until Li Lan and the others call back.Soon, the call was connected, and Lu Zhi heard the voice on the other side.Childish, are you here?Have you seen your second sister?Are you used to life on the island?Look at you, this has just passed, what are you getting used to?Zhizhi, let me tell you, after you went back, we had a quarrel with the Li family next door, and Chu Tong went back to her parents' house.Lu Zhi listened to them carefully, but couldn't stay on the phone for too long.Lu Zhi: I'm here. The scenery here is very nice. You don't have to worry about me. I've also met my second sister.They said a few more words.Lu Zhi: Don't forget to write to me.Li Lan: I estimate that one person can write a letter to you for dozens of pages.Everyone is smiling.

The courtyard for the family members of the army was built on the same site. Zhou Chengan approved the house. It was not very far from where Lu Yue lived, about a few dozen meters away.Lu Zhi's brother-in-law was away on a mission, so Lu Yue went to pick up Lu Zhi. Their one-year-old daughter was taken care of by the neighbor next door.Lu Yue went to pick up the child first, and then took Lu Zhi and the others back.Lu Yue: This is your nephew Tuantuan. She teased Tuantuan, "This is my aunt, this is my uncle, and this is my uncle."Six-year-old uncle Zhou Jun stood up straight and seriously. At such a young age, he could already be an uncle.Tuantuan waved his arms and smiled at Lu Zhi.Lu Zhi poked Tuantuan's cheek, making Tuantuan smile even happier.Lu Zhi and Zhou Chengan said: It's so fun.Zhou Chengan smiled.In the evening, Lu Yue made steamed seafood and made a big bowl full of it.It's an island after allThere are also sauerkraut and pork belly vermicelli, shredded pork with green onions, and green pepper and potato shreds.Lu Yue: Why don't you stay here tonight? Over there, I helped clean the place, but I haven't bought many things yet.Lu Zhi: No need, we can just go back and live there.Still looking forward to where she will live next.Lu Yue: Okay, okay, if you say you want to go back and live there, go back and live there.The more Lu Yue looked at his sister, the more beautiful she felt.Lu Yue: My little sister has been very beautiful, well-behaved and sensible since she was a child. Later, when she grew up, everyone said that whoever went to my little sister would have made a profit.Lu Zhi was eating delicious oysters:Lu Yue: My little sister is good at studying, and the teachers always praise her.When I was about to go back, it was dark outside.Lu Yue carried Tuantuan and sent them out, and gave them a flashlight to use first.Lu Zhi kept walking forward and arrived at the place where they lived.Lu Zhi: Second sister, I will go back first.Lu Yuese gave Lu Zhi a red envelope and took it. This was the second sister's wish.It was also used to add makeup to Lu Zhi's face.

Chapter 12The new home is a two-story building with a large yard.After entering, there is a kitchen, living room, dining room and a bathroom on the first floor. There are three bedrooms on the second floor, one of which has a separate bathroom.The house was kept very clean.In the bedroom, Lu Zhi opened the window and looked outside. She could hear the sound of the waves and see the bright stars in the night sky.Zhou Chengan: There is also a large terrace upstairs.Lu Zhi was pleasantly surprised. It was a little dark. When she came in, she didn't know there was a large terrace upstairs.I usually enjoy the breeze on the terrace, drink tea, and just relax when I think about it.Zhou Chengan checked his watch and saw that there were still thirty minutes until lights out. They needed to tidy up and then go to bed.Lu Zhi: Let's go to the terrace and take a look.His eyes were bright and full of expectation.Zhou Chengan took the flashlight, okay.Standing on the terrace, the wind outside made Lu Zhi's skirt and hair seem to be flying in the air. She took a few steps forward and pointed in front, Zhou Chengan, you can see the sea from here.There are ships on the sea, and the lights are still on at the moment.They are some distance from the seaside, but the houses in front are not blocking it, so standing on the terrace, you can see the seaside in the distance.Now, Lu Zhi likes this terrace even moreLu Zhi: We need to put a set of tables and chairs here, and plant some flowers to make it look nice.After Zhou Chengan wrote it down, he nodded.Lu Zhi was confused when he heard the sound of the trumpet.Zhou Jun raised his little chubby hand and was very proud. Sister-in-law, I know, this is the lights-out signal. The lights-out signal means that there is a power outage and everyone has to go to bed.Zhou Chengan held up a flashlight and illuminated it for Lu Zhi. Sorry, I forgot.The two adults and one Zaizai all relied on a flashlight and took a simple shower before getting ready to rest.Lu Zhi hugged Zhou Jun: On the first day we move here, you sleep with us, okay?Zhou Jun shook his head firmly, sister-in-law, I am a little man, I want to sleep by myselfBack in the house, when Lu Zhi was lying on the bed, he realized that he was a little tired. He leaned on the pillow and fell asleep quickly.When Zhou Chengan came back, listening to Lu Zhi's even breathing, he put the fan aside and got into bed very lightly.

There is a lights-out signal at night and a wake-up signal in the morning.Lu Zhi almost woke up with Zhou Chengan.Lu Zhi: Good morning.Zhou Chengan: Morning, I'll go to the cafeteria to get some food. I'll be back soon. You wash up and we'll have breakfast.Because they don't have a complete range of cooking options, they can only choose to eat in the cafeteria.Their bicycles had been delivered a long time ago. Zhou Chengan rode his bicycle to the canteen to get food. Just as Lu Zhi packed up, Zhou Chengan came back.For breakfast, there was white porridge and vegetarian steamed buns. The steamed buns were stuffed with cabbage and vermicelli. Lu Zhi took out some of the sour beans that Grandma Zhou gave them and ate them.The pickled beans are particularly crispyLu Zhi ate sour beans, finished a bowl of porridge, and ate half of the steamed buns, leaving the remaining half for Zhou Chengan.After the meal, Zhou Chengan cleared the table and washed the aluminum lunch box.Today is a little busy. They have to pack things, take out their luggage, and buy whatever they need at home.The first thing to pack was Lu Zhi's clothes. Her clothes were hung in the closet in the bedroom. Her clothes were packed and they belonged to Zhou Chengan.Zhou Chengan doesn't have many clothes, and many of them are military uniforms.The clothes of two people are in the same wardrobe.Lu Zhi looked at Zhou Chengan's military uniform and couldn't help but think that she had never seen Zhou Chengan in military uniform.It will definitely look betterAfter packing their clothes, Lu Zhi and Zhou Chengan went to the supply and marketing cooperative together.Zhou Chengan took Lu Zhi on a bicycle, surrounded by lush trees, and the breeze carried a bit of the salty sea breeze.Lu Zhi: You need to buy some oil, salt, soy sauce, rice, white flour and whole grains.Thinking of spending money, Lu Zhi remembered the red envelope given by his second sister yesterday.The red envelope happened to be in Lu Zhi's pocket. She took it out and opened it. There were a total of twenty big unity cards in it.Another two hundred dollars came inLu Zhi: Zhou Chengan, my second sister gave me two hundred yuan.When speaking, Lu Zhi's voice was filled with joy.Zhou Chengan: Salaries and allowances will be paid today.Hearing this, Lu Zhi grabbed Zhou Chengan's coat and said he would pay wages and allowances today.Today seems to be her day to get rich too.Lu Zhi: In that case, we will buy some more things later.Zhou Chengan: OK.While riding his bicycle, Zhou Chengan introduced the island to Lu Zhi. Here is the canteen, and in front is the supply and marketing cooperative. Turn left in front of the supply and marketing cooperative and you will find a state-owned hotel. Turn right and you will find the elementary school. After the elementary school, you will find the junior high school.Lu Zhi: Where's the kindergarten?Zhou Chengan: Kindergarten is on the right after leaving home.Lu Zhi remembered these places.Very good, Zhou Chengan didn't say southeast, northwest, otherwise Lu Zhi probably wouldn't know.Lu Zhi was curious, why didn't you say, southeast, northwest?Zhou Chengan: My mother didn't know east, west, east, west, but my father just told her whether it was left or right, and she knew.Yes, Comrade Chen Jiaojiao cannot tell the difference between east, west and north.Unexpectedly, Zhou Chengan was quite attentive.Lu Zhi: I can't tell the difference either. If you tell me the north, south, east, and west, I probably don't know.As she spoke, she shook her legs slightly.Lu Zhi: After you turn right from home, you will find the kindergarten. Then what?Zhou Chengan: Next is the market. There are a lot of seafood there. In front of the market is a square. Many people usually play in the square.Lu Zhi took note of it and nodded.Remembering that she was sitting on the back of a bicycle, she said: I know.The bicycle stopped outside the supply and marketing cooperative.The supply and marketing cooperative on the island is very large.But the supplies are still the same.Rice, white flour, oil, soy sauce, salt, whole grains.Lu Zhi: And brown sugar.Zhou Chengan: Comrade, please help us weigh some more brown sugar. After he finished speaking, he asked again: There are wafer biscuits there, do you want them?Lu Zhi nodded: YesThere are really few snacks at this time, but you can still buy some.Lu Zhi: And red date cake.Zhou Chengan: OK.The salesperson at the supply and marketing cooperative watched the two people go out and couldn't help but start a discussion.So prettyShe is the daughter-in-law of Deputy Commander Zhou. I know. Yesterday when my sister came home, she said that Deputy Commander Zhou's daughter-in-law is very beautiful. I also laughed at how beautiful she could be. She is so beautiful.I heard that if Deputy Commander Zhou hadn't been standing next to her, many gay men would have rushed to her.

Zhou Chengan sent the things home, took Lu Zhi to collect his salary, and then the two of them went to the market, passing by the kindergarten on the way.The market is really lively, with a lot of seafood at first glance.Seafood is free of charge.Lu Zhi didn't eat enough steamed Pipi shrimps yesterday, so the two of them bought some Pipi shrimps and some swimming crabs, and went back to steam them together in the evening.I'm frying a piece of vinegar cabbage and add more spicy.Before the two of them got home, they saw Zhou Jun waiting for them at the door from a distance.Lu Zhi got out of the car and pinched Zhou Jun's cheek. The little man blushed, sister-in-law.Zhou Chengan: You two go back and rest, and I'll cook. After he finished speaking, he asked again: Steamed shrimps, swimming crabs, vinegared cabbage, is there anything else you want to eat?Lu Zhi: That's enough.Inside the house, Lu Zhi took out Zhou Chengan's salary. In addition, there was also the two hundred yuan given to her by her second sister.They spent some money on shopping today, and Lu Zhi counted the remaining money.The total was three hundred and three dollars and ninety-six cents, in addition to various tickets issued by Zhou Chengan.Zhou Jun looked at Lu Zhi eagerly from the side.Lu Zhi took out the wafer biscuits he bought for him to eat. After eating, we bought some more.Zhou Jun: Sister-in-lawLu Zhi: YeahZhou Jun looked very serious. You just laughed. When I grow up, I will make money for you.Ahhhhh, what kind of repayment is this?Lu Zhi felt so happy to be able to say this.Zhou Jun really gave it to Lu Zhi if he had money.Ta-ta-ta. He got off the bed and ran to his room. When he came back, he gave Lu Zhi a big unity. Sister-in-law, here it is for you.Lu Zhi: This is your lucky moneyZhou Jun: YesLu Zhi: I don't want it. When you grow up, you can make money for me. You can keep this new year's money yourself.The little fat guy's jiojio in slippers moved. My sister-in-law can help me keep it.At Zhou Jun's insistence, Lu Zhi helped Zhou Jun collect his new year's money.

Political Commissar Li Li Changyuan and his wife Chen Chunni went to Zhou Chengan with dumplings.Li Changyuan: You know Cheng'an's character. Let's talk about him together later. You can't be cold-faced towards your wife, otherwise you won't be able to live this life.Chen Chunni: Don't worry.Li Changyuan knew about it when Zhou Chengan approved the house, and even helped refer to the location.Soon, the two people arrived outside Zhou Cheng'an's courtyard.The aroma of vinegar is a bit spicy, which makes it quite appetizing.They moved to the island on the second day, and the family started cooking.Hearing that Zhou Chengan's daughter-in-law was beautiful, Li Changyuan thought that Zhou Chengan had married a coquettish daughter-in-law, but he didn't expect that coquettishness was coquettish and virtuous.In this way, Zhou Chengan can no longer live with others with a cold face.Lu Zhi and Zhou Jun came out together. Hello, are you looking for Zhou Chengan?good guyHow beautiful is this? It's so beautiful.Li Changyuan: Yes, we are here to see Zhou Chengan. Thinking that you have just moved here and cannot cook, we happened to make some dumplings at home and bring them to you, stuffed with fresh shrimps.Chen Chunni smelled the increasingly strong smell of vinegar and gently pushed Li Changyuan.Li Changyuan also reacted and was a little shocked.Zhou Chengan's wife is here, who is cooking?

Chapter 13Zhou Chengan put the vinegared cabbage on the plate and came out with a spatula in his hand, Political Commissar, sister-in-law, you are here.Li Changyuan didn't speak for a long time.Chen Chunni: Chengan, you know how to cook?Zhou Chengan nodded, yes.It seems like the relationship should be good.Lu Zhi: Political commissar, sister-in-law, Cheng'an is about to make dinner and steamed the seafood. Why don't we stay for dinner together.Zhou Chengan: It will be ready soon.Li Changyuan finally spoke, okay, okay.When he entered, Li Changyuan coughed lightly and whispered to Chen Chuni that Cheng'an had a cold face and could cook, which was considered an advantage. Bonus points, extra points.Chen Chunni nodded in agreement.Lu Zhi poured water for the two guests, which was cold and boiled, but he also brought them wedding candies.The red candy wrapper contains fruit-flavored sugar, which is very sweet.Before Lu Zhi left, Mrs. Lu gave Lu Zhi candy. It was also for Lu Zhi's sake. After she joined the army, she was not familiar with everyone, so having wedding candy could bring her closer to each other.Chen Chunni: I heard yesterday that the daughter-in-law of Deputy Commander Zhou is very beautiful. I didn't expect that when I saw her today, she was even more beautiful than I imagined. Everyone also said that Cheng'an has a cold temper, has high standards, and doesn't know when he will get married. If he had gone on a blind date with you earlier, he would have gotten married long ago.Lu Zhi wanted to be humble.Zhou Jun: My brother definitely likes my sister-in-law, and I also like my sister-in-law.This sentence made everyone laugh.Soon, dinner was ready.There was a large pot of steamed seafood on the table, a plate of vinegared cabbage, two boxes of shrimp dumplings, and steamed buns. Because Li Changyuan and Chen Chunni came over, Zhou Chengan was worried that it would not be enough, so he added another portion of hot and sour shredded potatoes.Chen Chunni: Seeing that your life is getting better, our family doesn't have to worry anymore.Zhou Chengan peeled off the shrimps and placed them on the plate in front of Lu Zhi.Chen Chunni looked at Li Changyuan, who was busy peeling shrimps for herself, and was speechless for a moment.The original Pipi shrimp is delicious, and the swimming crab is even more delicious. Although they both taste delicious, the texture is different.Not to mention the dumplings brought over by Li Changyuan and Chen Chunni. The main feature was a delicious one, filled with shrimp as expected. If it hadn't been for the dumpling wrapper, Lu Zhi would have thought he was eating shrimp paste.This was Lu Zhi's first time trying Zhou Chengan's cooking.It's not particularly delicious, but it tastes okay.After one meal, Lu Zhi was almost full.Zhou Chengan, who was talking to Li Changyuan, took the bowl in front of Lu Zhi naturally and ate the remaining dumplings.

Lu Zhi stood outside the yard. My sister-in-law often comes to play when she has time.Li Chuni nodded, okay, I'll come over to you when I have time. Cheng'an will also be working tomorrow, so I'll come over to talk to you. I just came here, don't get used to it.Lu Zhi paused for a moment, then smiled and said: Okay.Seeing Li Chuni and Li Changyuan walking forward, they looked back at them. Lu Zhi waved his arms to them, and Zhou Jun, who was standing next to Lu Zhi, did the same action.Lu Zhi looked at Zhou Chengan, you have to work tomorrowZhou Chengan: Well, you can go to bed tomorrow morning if you feel sleepy. I will get up and bring you breakfast. You can just eat it when you wake up.Zhou Jun's face lit up, as if he had found the direction of his life again. I can help my sister-in-law prepare food.Lu Zhi's reason for rejection was as perfunctory as ever, and he'll wait until you go to elementary school.The other side.Li Changyuan was still sighing that Chengan knew how to cook and clear the table.No matter how you think about this matter, you feel that it is a bit outrageous.Li Changyuan and Zhou Chengan have known each other for many years. How could Li Changyuan not know Zhou Chengan's character?Li Changyuan: Hahahaha, he actually has such a day. I thought that no one would look down on the flower of the high mountain.When he was almost home, he realized that Chen Chunni seemed to have been ignoring him.Li Changyuan looked at Chen Chunni in confusion.Chen Chunni: You said Cheng'an and his wife can't live together. I don't think it's you who can't live together. I've been married to you for so many years, but why haven't we seen each other or cooked for me?Li Changyuan touched his nose nonchalantly, while Chen Chunni snorted and walked forward.Zhou Chengan is the one who loves his wife.

Lu Zhi seemed to be in a particularly good mood today. She came out of the shower looking very bright.Lu Zhi: You must wake me up tomorrow morning.She didn't think she was someone who couldn't sleep in at all. She always slept in at home, with Grandpa Zhou and Grandma Zhou.I woke up early today simply because it was the first time I heard the reveille and I was not used to it.She had to get up early and watch Zhou Chengan wearing military uniform, but she didn't know which one he was going to wear.The white one looks good, the white one is really nice.Zhou Chengan: You don't have to get up early. After I get up, I will go to the cafeteria to get food. Zhou Jun will take care of himself.Lu Zhi shook his head like a rattle. You'd better wake me up tomorrow, and then we'll go to the cafeteria to eat together. I just happened to remember the way to the cafeteria. If I don't want to cook at noon, I will take Zhou Jun to the cafeteria to eat.After turning off the light, Zhou Chengan asked: Are you sure I will wake you up tomorrow?Lu Zhi: Yes, you must wake me up.The room became quiet.Zhou Chengan was a man of few desires, but the person lying next to him was Lu Zhi.Lu Zhi, who was about to go to bed, tugged on the sleeve of Zhou Chengan's pajamas.Lu Zhi called his name, his voice was very soft, but when he heard it, his ears felt itchy.Zhou Chengan's Adam's apple moved, huh.Lu Zhi: I also want to eat Pipi shrimpsIt's so deliciousShe feels that she can still show off a lotThere were many people in the evening, and there were also many shrimps. Li Changyuan and Chen Chunni spent a lot of time on the island. Compared with seafood, the two of them were more interested in the vinegar cabbage and spicy and sour potato shreds made by Zhou Chengan.Zhou Chengan: Let's go downstairs, or should I bring it up?Lu Zhi: Keep your voice down, can we go downstairs to eat?Zhou Chengan: OK.Zhou Chengan got up first and the lights were out. He found a flashlight and used it to illuminate Lu Zhi before getting off the bed.When they reached the door, Zhou Chengan held Lu Zhi's hand, and the two of them went downstairs one after another.Pipi shrimp is really deliciousZhou Chengan was responsible for peeling the shrimps for Lu Zhi, and Lu Zhi was responsible for eating them. In the process, he also ate a leftover swimming crab himself.When he returned, Lu Zhi was satisfied.Everything was fine, except that after eating, I had to brush my teeth before I could sleep.

Lu Zhi is a face-controller, but she is also voice-controller and hand-controller. She wakes up before the wake-up call sounds in the morning.Lying on his side, Lu Zhi looked at Zhou Chengan and just wanted to say, his eyelashes are really long.His skin is also great, but he doesn't seem to use anything.Now if she wants to use lotion, lotion, essence, and a whole set of skin care procedures, Lu Zhi obviously can't achieve it, but she will also use ice cream seriously.Zhou Chengan opened his eyes. He had just woken up. His voice was still a little hoarse. You woke up.Lu Zhi lifted the quilt, "Well, I'm awake. Let's get up. I'll go next door to see Zhou Jun."Lu Zhi got up to wash up. She had to have breakfast in the cafeteria today. She looked for her clothes and found a white skirt.The Lu family loved Lu Zhi and doted on her. Although she didn't have a job, she had a lot of pocket money. Before Lu's brother got married, almost all of the money was given to Lu Zhi. He had money and a lot of money. Therefore, Lu Zhi has the most clothes in the Lu family.For this wedding, Lu Zhi also made clothes.Wearing a skirt, Lu Zhi tucked her thick long hair behind her ears and went out. Zhou Chengan still had to wash up.The wake-up call just rang.After hearing the reveille, little boy Zhou Jun got up from the bed and went out wearing slippers.Zhou Jun: Sister-in-lawLu Zhi: Take the small stool to your elder brother, and let's wash up with you.Zhou Jun: YesNo comments at all.Zhou Jun went back to get the small bench and ran to find Zhou Chengan.Lu Zhi went downstairs to find his lunch box and waited for Zhou Chengan downstairs.Hearing the sound of footsteps, Lu Zhi, who was staring blankly outside the yard, raised his head and looked over, his expression full of surprise.He has a tall and straight posture and cold brows.It seemed that for a moment, Lu Zhi only had him in his eyes.Zhou Chengan: Let's go.Lu Zhi nodded, okay

In the morning, there are many people in the cafeteria.When Lu Zhi arrived at the canteen, he and Zhou Chengan stood in line at the back.Vice leader Zhou.Hello, Vice President ZhouHello sister-in-law.Hello sister-in-law.Lu Zhi also saw Jiang Dong and several others coming over for dinner. The people in Jiang Dong's dormitory were particularly enthusiastic, especially a man who looked very honest.As for Jiang Dong and the others, they seemed a little weird.It was almost time to reach Lu Zhi. Lu Zhi looked at this morning's breakfast, which was steamed buns, multi-grain porridge and some cold vegetables.Because it is by the sea, the salad dishes are all shredded kelp and asparagus.In the morning, these are the only things in the canteen.Lu Zhi felt that he could still occasionally eat it at home in the morning.The buns yesterday morning were delicious, but they are not available every day.The cold kelp shreds and asparagus are delicious, and she doesn't want to eat them every day.

Zhou Chengan went to work, while Lu Zhi and Zhou Jun were at home. Zhou Chengan had finished all the housework, and there was nothing left to do.Lu Zhi turned on the radio upstairs and listened to it with Zhou Jun.One big and one small lay on the bed.Chen Chunni came over and shouted outside the yard: Lu Zhi, Lu ZhiWhen Lu Zhi came out, Chen Chunni smiled at Lu Zhi and said: Let's go to the market together.Lu Zhi: Sister-in-law, wait for me for a while.After returning home, taking the money and tickets, and asking Zhou Jun's opinion on whether to go to the market with her or stay at home, she came out and set off to the market with Chen Chunni.Since she was going to buy groceries, Lu Zhi planned to cook something for her tonight.

Chapter 14Lu Zhi and Chen Chunni went to the market while walking.Chen Chunni: Tell me, why can＇t our Lao Li be like your Lao Zhou?Lao ZhouChen Chunni didn't think there was any problem with such a title, but she didn't notice the slight pause on Lu Zhi's expression.Chen Chunni: He also wants your old Zhou to learn from him. I think he and your old Zhou are more likely to learn from each other.After talking, Chen Chunni seemed to understand something.Yes, this is not a matter of everyone being positive, studying hard, and creating a harmonious family together.Li Changyuan must learn from Zhou ChenganHer men definitely don't know how to cook, but they can peel shrimps.Making progress step by step, one day their old Li will be able to help the family and be gentle and considerate.After figuring it out, Chen Chunni felt physically and mentally comfortable.Chen Chunni smiled a little more at Lu Zhi's performance, and then happily held Lu Zhi's arm, making the relationship between the two more harmonious.Chen Chunni: Why didn't you marry your old Zhou earlier, so that I could get to know you earlier?The two finally arrived at the market.There are many people in the market at this time, and the most popular items in the market are seafood.Lu Zhi wanted to eat Pipi shrimps today, but this time he didn't eat steamed ones, but pickled ones.As a food blogger, Lu Zhi still knows how to do this.Seeing the red dried chili peppers, Lu Zhi couldn't help but buy some.Chen Chunni is surprised, you also like spicy foodLu Zhi nodded, I also like spicy food.Chen Chunni: Otherwise, we are friends. I also like to eat spicy food. Unfortunately, our old man doesn't eat it, and neither do our children. After he finished speaking, he asked again: Do you, Lao Zhou, eat?The two of them didn't seem to eat spicy food after their marriage, and Lu Zhi didn't know.Lu Zhi answered truthfully, and then said: But I want to eat. If he doesn't eat, I can do other things.Chen Chunni: I'll have some tooLu Zhi bought some eggs and potatoes. He also wanted to buy cabbage, but it was too heavy. He could buy it when Zhou Chengan came over.When they got home, Zhou Jun ran over to help Lu Zhi carry his things, and Lu Zhi gave him a non-sinkable egg as a token gesture.Lu Zhi: Let's eat in the cafeteria for lunch today, and then eat pickled shrimps in the evening.I don't know if Zhou Jun can eat it. If he can't eat it, I can make something else for Zhou Jun.Chen Chunni's expression became more determined as she carried her things home.Not only does Lao Zhou have to work, but the cub at home also has to learn from little friend Zhou Jun.As the saying goes, those who are close to vermillion are red and those who are close to ink are black. From now on, his cub must play with Zhou Jun.

There was a faucet in the yard where you could wash vegetables. Lu Zhi took a small bench, sat down in front of the faucet, poured out the shrimps and washed them carefully.Zhou Jun very obediently took a small stool and sat next to Lu Zhi.After washing the shrimps, Lu Zhi took care of them and prepared the sauce for pickling the shrimps. Finally, he added the shrimps, not forgetting to add some coriander.The quality of the dried chili peppers was particularly good. Lu Zhi took out the dried chili peppers and pounded them into chili noodles.Lu Zhi bought a lot of dried chili peppers, so it was a bit difficult.Zhou Jun stepped on the small bench and waved his little arms to help, looking serious and proud.It's great, it's another day to help my sister-in-law with work.Hearing the commotion outside, Lu Zhi stood at the kitchen window and took a look. When he saw that it was Zhou Chengan who was back, he walked out.Lu Zhi smiled brightly, his tone rose slightly, Lao

ZhouZhou Chengan couldn't help but smile when he heard this new title.Zhou Chengan looks good when he smiles. He looks even better when he smiles in military uniform.Lu Zhi's eyes curved, like crescent moons.Zhou Chengan: Sister-in-law Chunni is here todayLu Zhi: We went to the market and bought some Pipi shrimps and made them into pickled Pipi shrimps. The spicy ones are also delicious. We will make them spicy next time. I also bought some dried chilies and just ground them into chili powder.Zhou Chengan took off his coat. Next time, you can tell me these things and I will do it.After going back and changing clothes, washing his face and hands, Zhou Chengan went out to work.While Zhou Chengan was cooking, Lu Zhi leaned against the door nearby and looked at Zhou Chengan, who was wearing a white shirt and trousers. He had a belt around his waist, which made his waist look extra thin.Zhou Chengan: Can you make egg soup and stir-fry potato slices in a dry pot?Lu Zhi nodded, okay, the potato slices must be fried a little dry.There are also pickled shrimps, which are enough for the three of them.Lu Zhi asked: Zhou Chengan, do you eat spicy food?Zhou Chengan replied: Eat.Lu Zhi: Where are the pickled shrimps?Zhou Chengan: Eat, it's delicious.Zhou Chengan turned around and looked at Lu Zhi. The two looked at each other. Zhou Chengan looked at him with a slight smile and then continued cooking.During dinner in the evening, Lu Zhi successfully ate the pickled shrimps that he had been craving for.The pickled crabs can be mixed with rice, and the pickled shrimps are also delicious with rice. They are plump and fragrant. When paired with rice, it is so delicious to eat in one bite.After Lu Zhi finished a bowl of rice, he still wanted to eat it, so he filled up another half spoonful of rice.Zhou Chengan helped Lu Zhi put the shrimps in the bowl. I have free time these days. Let's go to the kindergarten together. He has to go to kindergarten.Zhou Jun, who was cooking, looked up and was confused for a moment, then shook his head like a rattle.Don't want to go to kindergartendon't want to go to schoolI want to play with my sister-in-law and help her with her work.Lu Zhiminen: You don't want to be a primary school student. If you don't go to kindergarten, you won't be able to learn anything in kindergarten. How can you be a primary school student?Zhou Jun blinked, it seemed right.Zhou Jun immediately said: I want to go to kindergarten, go to kindergartenAfter successfully solving the problem, Lu Zhi continued to work with satisfaction.Well, the dry pot potatoes their Lao Zhou made today are still good, and they are delicious when eaten with rice.After the meal, Zhou Chengan cleared the table, and Lu Zhi took Zhou Jun to play in the yard.Lu Zhi: Lao Zhou, let's plant some fruits and vegetables in the yard these days.Fatty Zhou Jun laughed hahahahaha, Old Zhou, Old Zhou.Lu Zhi pinched Zhou Jun's cheek and said, "Kindergarten kids, stop laughing."Zhou Chengan looked at the big one and the small one for a while, then asked: What kind of vegetables are they growing?Lu Zhi also has little experience. Tomorrow, I will go to my second sister's house to see. There are also vegetables planted in the yard of my second sister's house.Zhou Chengan nodded, okay.

Li family.Chen Chunni looked at the father and son at home, while Li Changyuan and Li Weidong looked at each other in confusion.Chen Chunni: What are you looking at? Why, you can't do anything. Lao Li, you tell others to learn with an open mind, and you must also learn with an open mind. From today on, our family will eat Pipi shrimps for a week.Therefore, Li Changyuan wants to be like Zhou Chengan.Li Changyuan looked at the sky speechlessly. Zhou Chengan had mistaken him.He also didn't know that Zhou Chengan had a double standard, treating his wife and other people completely differently.From now on, I will never learn from Zhou Chengan again.Chen Chunni: I found that I really like Lu Zhi so much. I must go out with Lu Zhi more in the future. This is my favorite friend.friendThis morning, before Li Changyuan went to the military camp, he specifically told Chen Chunni not to forget to find Lu Zhi. Lu Zhi had just moved here with the army. How could they become friends so quickly?Wait, what did his wife just say?Ah ah ah ah, Zhou Chengan, your double standards should be limited and don't go too far.Li Changyuan: I, what are you talking about?Chen Chunni: What did you say?Li Changyuan: It's okay.

Lu Zhi and Zhou Jun were playing in the yard.

Although there were no vegetables growing in their yard, it was still fun. For example, enjoying the cool air was very interesting.When he returned, Lu Zhi went to take a shower.When they came out, Lu Zhi came out and Zhou Chengan went to take a shower. He was stunned by the steam that hit his face.By the time Zhou Chengan came out, the signal was almost blown out.Lu Zhi was already drowsy and almost fell asleep.Now Lu Zhi has a very good schedule and goes to bed very early. Of course, going to bed early is one thing. She is still a good sleeper and likes to sleep in.It was raining heavily outside.Lu Zhi listened to the movement outside and asked: Zhou Chengan, is it raining?Zhou Chengan: Well, it's raining. Go to sleep.It's raining. If it rains again in the morning, she can probably sleep until noon.

When I woke up in the morning, it was already past ten o'clock.Lu Zhi opened the curtains and took a look. It was wet outside, as if the rain had just stopped.When we got downstairs, Zhou Jun was playing.Zhou Jun ran over, sister-in-law, my brother asked me to tell you that he went to the military camp, and breakfast was brought back from the canteen and was on the table.Lu Zhi: Have you eaten?Zhou Jun: No, I'm waiting for my sister-in-law.Lu Zhi took a look at today's breakfast and found that it was porridge, vegetarian pancakes and cold kelp shreds. The cold kelp shreds were spicy and sour today.Because Zhou Jun hadn't eaten yet, Lu Zhi heated up the food, and the two of them sat at the table and ate breakfast.Lu Zhi:

After we finish eating, we will go to the second sister's house.Yes, Lu Zhi and Zhou Jun's second sister were stopping by to see their little nephew.Zhou Jun sat up straight seriously, looking like a little uncle, okay

After taking Zhou Jun out, Lu Zhi went to find Lu Yue.Lu Yue's family was far away from Lu Zhi, so Lu Zhi and Zhou Jun were not in a hurry and took their time.When neighbors meet Lu Zhi and know that they are family members who have recently moved in to join the army, they will say hello or say a few words to her.Are you from Vice Leader Zhou's family?it's beautiful.Is this the younger brother of Deputy Commander Zhou?I know you, your sister even mentioned you to me.When Lu Zhi arrived at Lu Yue's house, it was more than ten minutes later.Lu Zhi: Sister, I'm here.Lu Yue was coaxing her children in the house. When she heard Lu Zhi's voice, she came out holding Tuan Tuan in her arms. Zhi Zhi came over.

Chapter 15Tuantuan is only seven months old and less than a year old. The little one made babbling noises when he saw Lu Zhi dancing around.Lu Yue gave Tuan Tuan to Lu Zhi, who just reached out to hug Tuan Tuan and kissed Lu Zhi on the face, looking even more excited.Lu Yue: It's my aunt. This is my aunt.Tuantuan, who could not speak, continued babbling, seeming to want to say the name aunt.Lu Yue squeezed Tuantuan's hand. When your brother-in-law saw it, he was probably jealous. Tuantuan doesn't like being hugged by your brother-in-law. I suspect it's because your brother-in-law looks a bit rough.Got it, she's a bit of a face-controller, but she's Lu Zhi's niece. In this regard, the two of them are exactly the same.Lu Zhi looked at Lu Yue's vegetable garden. It was already the harvest season for Lu Yue's vegetable garden.Cucumbers, eggplants, cabbage, cilantro, potatoes, peppers, and an apple tree.Lu Zhi was already moved.In addition to growing vegetables, you can also grow some fruits.At noon, Lu Zhi ate at Lu Yue's place. Lu Yue went to the kitchen to be busy, and Tuan Tuan stayed at Lu Zhi's place.Zhou Jun squatted in front of Tuantuan and blinked at her. Zhou Jun had seen the child before, but this child was different. He called him uncle.Tuantuan used his hands and feet to crawl and crawl.He hugged Lu Zhi's thigh and laughed so hard that his saliva almost flowed out.Tuantuan kid, you are really cute, do you know?A little clingy spirit followed Lu Zhi, and Lu Zhi simply hugged and coaxed her for a while.The little Zaizai quickly became sleepy and wanted to play with Lu Zhi, refusing to sleep.But I was so sleepy.Tuantuan has a cradle for sleeping, and Lu Zhi and Zhou Jun watch Tuantuan sleeping next to the cradle.Zhou Junchao whispered, sister-in-law, Tuantuan likes you as much as I do.Lu Zhi touched Zhou Jun's hair, yes, Tuantuan likes me just like you.Lu Yue went to catch the sea a few days ago. There was a lot of seafood at home. At noon, she steamed a large pot, picked eggplants and peppers in the yard, made fried eggplants and peppers, and stewed cabbage vermicelli.Soon, dinner was ready.Lu Yue: For a while, you can take a nap here, just in Tuantuan's room. You can go back in the afternoon.Lu Zhi had no objection and was busy cooking.Lu Yue: Is the house tidied up?Lu Zhi: After cleaning it up, there is nothing to clean up in the first place.They were talking while eating.At noon, Lu Zhi took Zhou Jun to take a nap at Lu Yue's place. When he woke up, he and Lu Yue enjoyed the cool air again.Li Cuihua, who lived next door to Lu Yue, came over, saw Lu Zhi and smiled and asked: Lu Yue, is this your sister?Lu Yue nodded, yes.At this moment, the courtyard suddenly became lively.Li Cuihua was also a military wife who came to accompany the army. She sat on a stool and talked non-stop. You know Chen Yu, the manager of the state-owned hotel.Li Cuihua was a down-to-earth person, and she was worried that Lu Zhi wouldn't know, so she actually explained it seriously.Li Cuihua: It's the state-owned hotel on our island. This Chen Yu was new here some time ago.Lu Zhi nodded, and then what?Li Cuihua saw Lu Zhi's expression of wanting to know. She looked very kindly on Lu Zhi and talked to Lu Zhi intently.Li Cuihua: The person Chen Yu is dating is the sister of Deputy Battalion Commander Zheng. Deputy Battalion Commander Zheng despises him and has been in a cold war with his sister these days.Lu Zhi didn't even know him, but that didn't stop her from eating.Lu Zhi: Why don't you look down on it?Li Cuihua: I'm curious too, but looking at it, this Li Yu seems to be pretty good. But Deputy Battalion Commander Zheng is also very good. He has always been a good person. He has helped many people. If he looks down on him, there must be something wrong with him.Unfortunately, Li Cuihua and Lu Yue only knew Deputy Battalion Commander Zheng, but not Lu Zhi. The three of them couldn't figure it out together.Li Cuihua: My brother works in a state-owned hotel. I'll ask again later. I'll tell you when I know.good guyLi Cuihua really eats melon with everyone, and there is even follow-up service.The more she thought about it, the more uncomfortable Li Cuihua felt, so why on earth did Deputy Battalion Commander Zheng disagree?When Li Cuihua went back, she didn't forget to tell Lu Zhi that the leek and squid dumplings served by the state-owned restaurant on Monday were delicious. You can try them on Monday.Leek and Squid DumplingsLu Yue nodded, that's right. Li Cuihua's younger brother works as a cook in a state-owned hotel, and he made these leek and squid dumplings.Lu Zhi thought she could try it because she had never eaten leek and squid dumplings.Just as he was talking, Tuantuan woke up from his sleep.

Zhou Chengan and Li Changyuan stopped by and returned from the military camp together.Li Changyuan felt miserable. He felt that he had lived a comfortable life before, but now he had to imitate Zhou Chengan's gentleness and considerateness.Li Changyuan: I'm talking about Cheng'an, why didn't I realize before that you would be so obsessed with your wife once you got married?Zhou Chengan stopped and Li Changyuan straightened his back.Zhou Chengan: Zhizhi is not at home. I will go to the second sister's house to take a look.As he said that, he walked hurriedly to another location.Li Changyuan stood in a mess in the wind.No, was he listening to himself just now?

Zhou Chengan arrived at Lu Yue's house and slowed down when he saw Lu Zhi.Lu Zhi: You are back from the military camp.While he was looking at the group, he forgot that Zhou Chengan was coming back from the military camp at this moment.Lu Zhi comes over and looks at Tuantuan.Lu Zhi teased Tuantuan seriously, with a gentle expression and a much softer voice, "Tuan Tuan, who is this?"Zhou Chengan replied: Tuantuan, this is my uncle.Lu Zhi looked up and found that Zhou Chengan was not looking at Tuantuan, but at himself.AhhhhhhhLu Zhi: Yes, it's my uncle.Lu Yue stayed with them for dinner again, and they didn't go back until they finished eating.Tuantuan was still in Lu Zhi's arms, and Xiaopang was holding the corner of Lu Zhi's clothes, babbling, so happy.Lu Zhi: Tuantuan, I'm going back. Can I come see you next time?Tuantuan: Yeah yeah yeah.Lu Zhi gave Tuan Tuan to Lu Yue, and Tuan Tuan lay in his arms, still dancing to Lu Zhi.Lu Zhi: Goodbye.Zhou Jun wanted to say goodbye to Tuan Tuan, but Xiao Douding could only raise his head. Lu Zhi wanted to pick Zhou Jun up, but then found that he could not hold him.Zhou Chengan smiled softly, hugged Zhou Jun, and said goodbye to Tuantuan.Zhou Jun: Goodbye TuantuanThe family of three went back.The wind blowing from the beach at night is very comfortable.Lu Zhi told me the vegetables he wanted to grow, cabbage, potatoes, green peppers and onions. Also, I want to grow fruits, jujube trees.Zhou Chengan listened carefully and nodded, okay.Seeds can be bought, but jujube trees may not be easy to get.Lu Zhi: Also, on Monday we are going to a state-owned restaurant to eat leek and squid dumplings, which I have never eaten before.Zhou Chengan also made a note of it. At noon, you go first. Can I go to the state-owned hotel to find you?Lu Zhi nodded, no problemZhou Chengan told Lu Zhi again how to get to the state-owned hotel.Zhou Jun: Sister-in-law, I rememberHe can help his sister-in-law find the way.For a moment, looking at the large and small children, Lu Zhi doubted whether he really didn't know where the state-owned hotel was.Lu Zhi: I remember it. I remembered it after you said it last time.Zhou Jun: Sister-in-law is greatIn this way, you will also be praised.

Li Cuihua couldn't sleep at night. She tossed and turned and woke up her man.Li Cuihua: Tell me, Deputy Battalion Commander Chen, why do you disagree?Li Cuihua and her man:Go to sleep, go to sleep quickly.This apparently happened more than once.The man Li Cuihua said perfunctorily: Go to sleep quickly, I will help you inquire when I am free.After a while, Li

Cuihua felt really sleepy and fell asleep with her pillow on her head.Deputy Battalion Commander Chen is a good person, so it must be Chen Yu's problem. If this is Chen Yu's problem, she has to tell her brother to stay away from Chen Yu in the future.

Monday.Lu Zhi took Zhou Jun to a state-owned hotel, holding hands with one parent and one child while Lu Zhi sang softly.It's just that the weather is a little hot today.Lu Zhi went to find Lu Yue and wanted to go with Lu Yue.Lu Yue: I won't go. Tuantuan is sleeping. Some of my former classmates went to the countryside to work as educated youth. When they arrive, they will come over and have a look.Not forgetting to give Lu Zhi money and tickets.Lu Zhi took the ticket and said with a smile: Second sister, I'm already married.Lu Yue and Lu Zhi lived together before they got married. Every time Lu Zhi went out, Lu Zhi always gave Lu Zhi money and tickets to eat whatever he wanted. Later, when Lu Yue got married and came to the island, she always wrote to Lu Zhi alone. The letter contained Lu Zhi's pocket money and some tickets.Lu Yue: Now that you are married, I am also your second sister.Lu Zhi nodded quickly, OK, OK, thank you, second sister.Continue to the state-owned hotel.When passing by the supply and marketing cooperative, Lu Zhi took Zhou Jun to buy a bottle of soda at the supply and marketing cooperative.Standing outside the state-owned hotel, Lu Zhi just wanted to sigh that he was so right in buying soda.The island they are on is a very big island. Because of this, there are many fellow villagers on the island and many people eating in state-owned restaurants. They are still queuing up at this moment.Lu Zhi and Zhou Jun quickly went to line up.Zhou Chengan comes over, Zhizhi, you go in and find a seat and sit down, I'll just line up here.Lu Zhi wanted to take Zhou Jun back, but looked up at Zhou Chengan's thin layer of sweat. He must have been in a hurry, so he came running.After finding the handkerchief, Lu Zhi handed it to Zhou Chengan. He watched Zhou Chengan wipe his sweat and gave him his soda. Zhou Chengan took a sip, and Lu Zhi was about to go in.Looking at the two tired people, Li Changyuan twitched the corner of his mouth. He and his wife were not so tired when they just got married.Li Changyuan: You guys are so annoying.Zhou Chengan turned around and restrained the corners of his mouth from turning up. Do you think we are disgusting?Lu Zhi is tired of himLi Changyuan: Oh, Zhou Chengan, you must be promising.Hearing Li Yuanhua's voice, Lu Zhi turned around and asked, Li Yuanhua, when did he come here? Why didn't he see him just now?

There are empty seats in the state-owned hotel, and some people like Lu Zhi came in early.At this time, state-owned restaurants were divided into several types. Some had fixed supply, and you could pick up the food yourself after ordering, which is similar to the future fast food model. There was also a type of a la carte, where waiters served the food. The state-owned restaurants here are former.Lu Zhi found a seat by the window and sat down, looking at the scenery outside and then at Zhou Chengan, who was lining up in the crowd.Well, after all, the man she fell in love with was so eye-catching among the crowd.He's so good-looking.Some more people came to line up outside, and Lu Zhi heard the people at the next table talking.These are the educated youth on our island.It seems so.It's an educated youth.Lu Zhi remembered that a classmate of her second sister was also among the educated youth sent to the countryside this time.She probably didn't know him, otherwise her second sister would have told her that the former friends of second sister Lu Zhi also liked Lu Zhi, and Lu Yue always liked to take Lu Zhi to play with them.Lu Yue didn't say anything, but they were probably classmates who didn't have a very good relationship with each other, and had some ordinary relationships with them.After some informed discussion, they also went into the state-owned hotel to wait.The target of Lu Zhi and Zhou Chengan's gaze smiled at him.Li Changyuan: Cheng'an, these are the educated youth here, Cheng'an, you and I, you guys, I can't learn, I can't learn.This is really embarrassing for him, Li Changyuan.Lu Zhi held her chin with both hands. She didn't know how long it had passed before she heard someone calling her from beside her.Lu Zhi.Looking at the man in front of him, Lu Zhi was slightly stunned.Really, I didn't expect to meet him.This was Lu Zhi's blind date before Zhou Chengan.Chen Yu, the manager of the state-owned hotel, why is he here?Oh hahaThis is not what Li Cuihua said. The brother-in-law whom Deputy Battalion Commander Chen disagreed with turned out to be her previous blind date.Comrade Lu Zhi, I know you are beautiful, but you have no job.You don't really think that just because you have a good face, you can seduce the son of a factory director, and you don't want to see if the factory director's family can agree to marry you, an unemployed person.Lu Zhi was really impressed by these things. Later, Lu Zhi felt that Li Yu was better. After all, there was comparison.Later, Chen Yu was severely beaten by Brother Lu and apologized to Lu Zhi.Yesterday, Li Cuihua said that Chen Yu and Lu Zhi didn't expect this blind date. They didn't expect it to be him.Lu Zhi frowned.Chen Yu: educated youthAs he spoke, there was a proud look on his face.When Lu Zhi rejected him at first, he thought of various ways and even begged Lu Zhi. He thought that Lu Zhi could find someone, but he didn't expect that Lu Zhi would go to the countryside to become an educated youth and could not find a good marriage partner.At this moment, Chen Yu was also lucky. He was lucky not to marry Lu Zhi in the first place. Now he was going to be with Deputy Battalion Commander Chen's sister.Chen Yu: Comrade Lu Zhi, I didn't expect to meet you here. By the way, I forgot to introduce myself. I am the manager of this state-owned hotel. He smiled, stood upright, and continued, if you have any questions in the future, you can come to me. Although we did not have a successful blind date at first, I am the most generous person. If you ask me for help, I can Helpful.Lu Zhi:It really hasn't changed at all.Zhou Chengan's voice was cold, "If there is any problem with my lover, I won't bother you."

Chapter 16Lu Zhi heard the sound and looked over.Chen Yu's appearance is good, otherwise no one would have introduced him to Lu Zhi in the first place. Even if some people were too weird, the conditions for introducing him to Lu Zhi were not very good, and the Lu family would not agree to the introduction. look.Brother Lu, who has a bad temper when it comes to his sister, can rush up and start a fight.But when Chen Yu and Zhou Chengan stood together, they immediately became much inferior.Chen Yu turned around, his eyes blank.Lu Zhi introduced, by the way, let me introduce, this is Zhou Chengan, my lover.Chen Yu had just arrived to work in a state-owned hotel on the island, but Zhou Chengan still knew about it.I don't know how many girls on the island like this guy. He looks so capable. If he didn't have a cold face and a cold personality all day long, many people would pounce on him.I heard that when I went to see the leader and entered the sorority, the girl's face turned red.Zhou Chengan: This isLu Zhi thought for a while, passerby AChen Yu's face turned ugly again.He admitted that he missed Lu Zhi. Ever since he met Lu

Zhi for the first time, he had been thinking about Lu Zhi, and he was even more reluctant to do so later.Now, Lu Zhi actually said lightly, Passerby AZhou Chengan looked over casually, but his expression was very cold. Passerby A, look, it turns out to be Comrade Lu.Comrade LuLu Zhi couldn't help laughing, and Chen Yu ran away.When Lu Zhi met Zhou Chengan's eyes, he felt a little guilty.Then he felt confident again, he had nothing to feel guilty about, this was not his ex-boyfriend, he was just a blind date, a rejected blind date.She didn't believe that Zhou Chengan only had her blind date.Lu Zhi smiled and said: Comrade my dear, Comrade Li Changyuan is still watching the show.Zhou Chengan's expression softened, and I went to line up.Li Changyuan doesn't like eating melons and is not interested in them, but if it's Zhou Chengan's melon, he has to eat it.What happened just now?Who is he?Talk about it.Zhou Chengan looked calm. Just now, she called my lover comrade.That look seemed to be asking, has your wife ever called you that?Li Changyuan:Hahaha, his wife has never called his lover "comrade", but he knows that Zhou Chengan is getting better and better at spreading his tail.Li Changyuan looked in front of him and shouted, "Cheng'an, your sister-in-law and I have been married longer than you. How long have we been married? Are you right?"Show off hardLi Changyuan: When your sister-in-law and I met, it was the same thing. On the first blind date, we decided to get married.Zhou Chengan: Dumplings.Li

Changyuan: What?Zhou Chengan handed over the ticket and money first. I want the leek and squid dumplings.Li Changyuan:Quickly taking the money and tickets, Li Changyuan also made dumplings.Li Changyuan wanted to go home, so he took two portions of dumplings before going back.After telling Chen Chunni, he went back to make leek and squid dumplings.

Lu Zhi looked at the leek and squid dumplings in front of him, picked one up with chopsticks and ate it into his mouth.It's indeed an islandWhat about leek and squid dumplings? Let's just call them squid dumplings.There is a lot of squid in the dumplings, but not too many leeks. It can even be said to be a side dish, just for the taste of the leeks. When you bite into it, the squid meat is firm and elastic, and it is also juicy.Zhou Chengan: This is vinegar.Lu Zhi dipped the dumplings in vinegar and ate them, because the sour taste of vinegar gave them a different taste.Woo woo woo woo.It's so delicious.Lu Zhi succeeded in stuffing himself.Next time, she can try making this dumpling by herself.Fatty Zhou Jun was holding the dumplings. He could eat one in two mouthfuls and concentrated on cooking.Lu Zhi found that fat little Zhou Jun seemed to eat dumplings and didn't like to be dipped in vinegar.Look at Zhou Chengan again.The two brothers seem to have different tastes. Zhou Chengan likes to eat them with vinegar.What Lu Zhi and Zhou Jun couldn't eat gave to Zhou Chengan, and the whole family watched Zhou

Chengan eat the remaining dumplings.Zhou Jun: My sister-in-law likes to eat dumplings. I will learn to make dumplings in the future.WowWhat an ambitious bastard, hahahaha.After Zhou Chengan finished eating, he said: I can.

When Li Changyuan came home, he always seemed hesitant to speak.After finishing the meal, Chen Chunni had a cold face, Li Changan, why don't I tell you to come back and bring dumplings? If Lu Zhi told Chengan to bring dumplings, Chengan would definitely not be like you when he comes back.In order for Li Changyuan to explain himself, they went to eat together today.Chen Chunni: What do you mean? I'll go with you.Li Changyuan felt aggrieved, and then said seriously: Then Lu Zhi still calls Comrade Cheng'an Lover, why don't you call me Comrade Lover.Chen Chunni: Love, comrade, this title starts from the time you learn to wash dishes.It's great that his man has made another step towards becoming a gentle and considerate husband.But my lover, comrade, I'm so sorry. How can I shout this out to Li Changyuan?

After returning home, Lu Zhi took a shower.It's really too hot. If you go out in the heat, you'll be sweating when you come back.When he came out, Zhou Jun had already finished taking a shower and was sitting on the bed wearing a tank top and shorts.After pinching Zhou Jun's face, Lu Zhi said: Okay, you can take a nap.Holding the fat little Zhou Jun in his arms, Lu Zhi fell asleep quickly after smelling his fragrant scent.Feeling a little hot, I rolled to the side and continued to sleep.When Lu Yue came over, Lu Zhi hadn't woken up yet. She called Lu Zhi a few words downstairs, and Lu Zhi rubbed his eyes and got up from the bed.Opening the window, Lu Zhi said: Second sister, I'm upstairs.When I went downstairs, I glanced at Zhou Jun next to me. I was really envious of this Zaizai's sleep quality. He was not woken up, but his eyelashes trembled slightly.Lu Yue downstairs said: Today a classmate of mine came to the island to become an educated youth.Lu Zhi nodded, I know.Lu Yue: I accompanied her to the resettlement site for educated youth, and then came back. Guess who I met?What could make Lu Yue so excited was Chen Yu, whom Lu Yue had complained about for several months.At this time, it would be better to let Lu Yue say it herself, after all, she was excited.Lu Zhi: Who is it?Lu Yue: Chen Yu, I finally know why Deputy Battalion Commander Chen didn't agree to your blind date, Chen Yu.Lu Zhi listened to Lu Yue complaining about Chen Yu for more than an hour.You look down on him, but he actually thinks you want to rely on your beauty to climb highThis kind of man, this kind of thinking, can marryAt first, your elder brother and I were so angry that we couldn't even eat.Now that I have said it, we are pretty, we are smart and kind, but people like him only know how to look.Very good, my confidence level is through the roof, okay?Lu Yue thought of Tuantuan. I asked Li Cuihua to help watch Tuantuan, so I went back first.

Lu Zhi felt bored and Zhou Jun didn't wake up. She sat on the edge of the bed and poked Zhou Jun's cheek, then squeezed his fleshy little hand.Kids, this is really fun.That is, if he sleeps like this, will he really not be able to sleep at night?When Zhou Jun finally woke up, he still looked a little dazed.Zhou Jun was swaying, as if he was about to fall asleep again, sister-in-law.Lu Zhi: Get up. My sister-in-law will make spicy strips for you.spicy stripsThe sleepy Zhou Jun's eyes seemed to have been opened by Kazilan's big eye special effect.Lu Zhi: Wow, you also like spicy stripsZhou Jun: Sister-in-law, what are spicy strips?You don't know, you're still driving Kazilan's special effects?Lu Zhi: Spicy strips are very spicy and delicious.When they arrived in the kitchen, Lu Zhi started to get busy.She likes spicy strips very much.Lu Zhi used to use beef tendon noodles to make spicy strips, but now she can't buy beef tendon noodles, so she makes spicy strips made of rice and flour.Lu Zhi rolled the prepared vegetables into dough cakes with a rolling pin, and then began to cut them into long strips, not forgetting to press the noodles on the spicy strips to make long strips.Put it into the pot and start steaming.Zhou Jun stepped on the small bench, is this spicy strips?Lu Zhi: Wait a moment, it will be steamed, then we will pour the seasonings on and mix it.Since there are not a lot of seasonings now, Lu Zhi can only make a simple version, but the chili powder is enough.Finally, the spicy strips are steamed.In order to take care of the children, Lu Zhi made two types:

very spicy and slightly spicy.Pour the prepared seasoning powder on the steamed spicy strips, then pour hot oil on it, and the spicy flavor will be stimulated immediately.Zhou Jun, who has always been a manly man, couldn't help but drooled.Not like a little man at all.He is also a Zaizai who is crazy about snacks.Lu Zhi tasted one. It was very good and very tough.Hiss~The point is, it's really spicy.This dried chili is really good.When Zhou Chengan came back, he saw Lu Zhi and Zhou Jun playing a plate in front of him. He didn't know what it was.Lu Zhilan's lips were red and she was still eating.Zhou Chengan couldn't help his Adam's apple twitching.Zhou Jun jumped up and was very proud. Brother, do you know what this is? These are spicy strips. My sister-in-law made them for me.That's right, my sister-in-law cooked it for him.Zhou Jun: How about you give it a try?Zhou Chengan took off his coat and walked over. He sat down and looked at the two spicy strips, which he could tell had different spiciness, and took the one from the plate in front of Lu Zhi noodles.Lu Zhi was looking forward to it, and Zhou Chengan ate one.Hiss~It's really spicy.Zhou Chengan: Delicious.Zhou Jun: Brother, it's very delicious.Zhou Chengan: It's very, very delicious.Zhou Jun puts his hands on his hips, it's very, very, very, very delicious.Lu Zhi was in a daze. Unknown to him, he thought that if the hot strips made for her were in the future, he would be able to start a business and reach the pinnacle of his life.Continue to eat the spicy strips.

It is really spicy, but it is also really delicious.After eating too much spicy strips, Lu Zhi found that he became picky about food at night and ate very little.The kid Zhou Jun even used spicy strips to make a bowl of rice.Lu Zhi was a little ready to make a move.Spicy strips and rice might be delicious.

Chapter 17Spicy strips and rice, really deliciousZhou Chengan gave Lu Zhi some green vegetables, and Lu Zhi ate them seriously, leaving nothing behind.Zhou Jun had a look of admiration on his face.Ah ah ah ah ahHis sister-in-law is really awesome. She eats spicy strips and is willing to eat green vegetables.Zhou Jun is no longer picky about food, and is busy eating.Lu Zhi was obsessed with Zhou Chengan's hands. They were so beautiful. Even if they were very bland vegetables, Lu Zhi was willing to eat them.

Li Changyuan and Chen Chunni were walking and passed by Zhou Chengan's home, so they stopped by to take a look.Everyone lives very close to each other.Chen Chunni: Why don't we go to the beach together later? Let's go to the beach and enjoy some fresh air. It will be cool and comfortable.Li Yuanyuan's footsteps pausedI really forgot that Zhou Chengan is no longer the Zhou Chengan before. If Zhou Chengan does something, he will have to follow suit when he returns.Li Changyuan: I thought about it for a moment. These two people are newlyweds. If not, we might as well not bother them.

Novel reading public account: Jiuju tweetsWhen Li Changyuan wanted to go back, Lu Zhi and Zhou Chengan came out.Chen Chunni was silent.Looking at the red lips of the two people, she felt that what their old man Li said was not unreasonable.Lu Zhi: My sister-in-law is here. Come in and sit for a while.Chen Chunni was also embarrassed and couldn't help it.Li Changyuan smiled awkwardly, we were just passing by, so we went back first and will have dinner together next time when we are free.Lu Zhi looked at their backs, they were so strange.Turning around, he met Zhou Chengan's eyes.Zhou Chengan pointed to his lips, and Lu Zhi came closer.WowIt looks like jelly.Zhou Chengan couldn't hold it back anymore. When he leaned down and kissed Lu Zhi, his heartbeat accelerated a little.They have been married for some time.The difference is that they seemed to have gotten married because of a quick blind date. On the wedding night, Lu Zhi mentioned that he did not want children for the time being. They spent an ordinary wedding night. After that, the two people's state was more like In love.Lu Zhi bit it lightly.Well, it does look like jelly.When they separated, Lu Zhi discovered that Zhou Chengan was already red from his neck to his ears.At this moment, it is not easy for Lu Zhi to know whether Li Changyuan and Chen Chunni are embarrassed.It's quite a bit embarrassing.

At night, the lights-out horn sounded.Lu Zhi: Lao ZhouZhou Chengan turned off the light and got into bed. The electric fan didn't work and it was extremely hot today. Zhou Chengan still fanned Lu Zhi with a cattail leaf fan.Lu Zhi: Let's not sleep for now. Let's go see Zhou Jun who is not asleep. He slept for a long time today.After waiting for a while, Lu Zhi and Zhou Chengan went out very lightly. They went to Zhou Jun's room to have a look.The little fat man was lying on the bed, hugging a pillow, and his legs seemed to be split.good guyThis sleeping position is worthy of posting on Moments.Unfortunately, I can't post it to Moments.Lu Zhichao whispered and fell asleep againZhou Chengan: He was able to sleep better when he was a child.I saw Zhou Jun turned over again on the bed, and then fell into another sleeping position.This time I didn't do the splits, this time it looked more like I was about to dance, hahahaha.The two of them went back, and Lu Zhi was lying on the bed. Only then did he realize that Zhou Chengan seemed to have a particularly good sleeping position. Lu Zhi occupied a large space when sleeping, but Zhou Chengan was different.Lu Zhi: Did I hit you when I was asleep?Zhou Chengan: No.Very good, Lu Zhi was relieved.Lu Zhi turned over again without falling asleep. I think it is necessary for my sister-in-law and the others to try the spicy strips. You can invite them over for dinner tomorrow. I will steam some shrimps, swimming crabs and conches.Soak some dried beans and roast the potatoes to eat. I saw them at the market last time. They were very small potatoes. I peeled them and added them directly.Lu Zhi was fearless and saved them from embarrassment.Zhou Chengan: Okay, I'll tell them tomorrow.Now that she thought about eating spicy strips wrapped in rice, she still felt a little aftertaste. She didn't expect that there was such a way to eat spicy strips. Children are indeed very creative.The first time I ate spicy strips, I actually knew how to eat them with rice.

A new day begins.Lu Zhi planned to go to the market. She got up early today and saw Zhou Chengan wearing a hat. She reached out and straightened the hat again.She didn't know how to say it because she couldn't hold it back.Lu Zhi: That's fineZhou Chengan looked at Lu Zhi's back in the mirror, Lu Zhi was facing him.Lu Zhi: Is that true? It's almost as if it has been measured with a ruler.When she was talking, a few strands of hair on her casually tied low bun in the mirror were swaying.This seems to be the feather duster method that Lu Zhi mentioned.He didn't know, but he knew that Lu Zhi's hair was really beautiful.Lu Zhi felt a little confident. After all, they had a marriage certificate.Lu Zhi: Don't forget to tell your sister-in-law and the others.Zhou Chengan looked at Lu Zhi and promised to complete the task.Suddenly, Lu Zhi was amused.

Li Changyuan looked at Zhou Chengan. His CPU was almost burned out and he didn't know what spicy strips were.I've never heard of this stuff.But it sounded very spicy. He, Li Changyuan, is not picky about food, but he just can't eat spicy food.Li Changyuan: I can't eat spicy food, but your sister-in-law and your nephew like it. I'll go back and talk to them later, and we'll have a drink then.Zhou Chengan frowned, forget about drinking, let's just chat.When they were both single in the past, they sometimes had some sad things, but they would occasionally drink together and not drink much. Later, Li Changyuan got married, and the two of them drank less frequently. Some.But Li Changyuan didn't expect that Zhou Cheng'an would stop drinking when he got married. He stopped drinking.Forget it if he doesn't drink it. He doesn't want to take out the wine he treasured yet.Li Changyuan shook his head and sighed, tut tut.After walking a long way, Li Changyuan's expression changed, and the speed he ran back almost exceeded his limit.Li Changyuan: Zhou ChenganZhou Chengan looked at him.Li Changyuan: Zhou Chengan, be a human being and never tell your sister-in-law about this matter, otherwise I will only be able to keep my treasured wine in the future.Li Changyuan spent a lot of effort to buy those wines, and then brought them all the way from his hometown.

Lu Zhi and Zhou Jun had breakfast, and after asking Zhou Jun's opinion, they went to the market with Zhou Jun.Although Zhou Jun is a child, children sometimes have their own ideas.Children Zhou Jun can be exercised in such small matters.Zhou Jun: Sister-in-law, shall we go cycling?Lu Zhi looked at the cars in the yard. I might not be good at riding a bike.Not to mention taking Zhou Jun with him.This is why Lu Zhi initially suggested that Zhou Chengan buy a men's bicycle. Zhou Chengan thought it was for Lu Zhi and he could ride the women's model, so he bought the women's model.Lu Zhi is worried that Zhou Jun will be disappointed. Next time, how about you ask your elder brother to take you to the market on a bicycle?Zhou Jun likes his sister-in-law so muchHe is better than the adults he has met. Although his eldest brother is also very good, he is not as gentle as his sister-in-law.Zhou Jun patted his chest, "You don't have to wait until I grow up, I can take you on a bicycle. My sister-in-law is sitting on the back seat of the bicycle, and I am riding in front. I must be better than my elder brother."Wuwuwuwuwu, what kind of repayment is this?Lu Zhi pinched his cheek and said, "Okay, sister-in-law, I will wait for you to ride with me when you grow up. Maybe you can also drive with me."Zhou Jun raised his chubby hand, okayTake Zhou Jun for a walk and go to the market.Finally arrived at the market.There were a lot of seafood in the market today. Lu Zhi bought the shrimps, swimming crabs and conches he wanted to buy.Ah, I just can't get enough of the Pipi shrimps.I ate pickled Pipi shrimp last time. Let's make some soy crab bibimbap this time, but I'm afraid I have to wait a while before I can eat the soy crab.When buying seafood, Lu Zhi bought some swimming crabs.Lu Zhi also bought the small potatoes he wanted to buy.What else?Lu Zhi looked around, wanting to buy some more meat, which could be added to beans and potatoes, but he found that the queue outside was very long.It's also very hot.When Lu Zhi was hesitating, Li Cuihua waved her arm to Lu Zhi, Lu Zhi, Lu Zhi, come here.Lu Zhi went over, but Li Cuihua didn't buy the meat either. He gave his place to Lu Zhi. You queue up here to buy it. If you buy it in a while, can we share half of it?Lu Zhi nodded, okayLi Cuihua seemed very anxious. I just saw Deputy Battalion Commander Chen and her sister. They looked like they were angry. I want to go take a look. After you finish shopping, just wait for me here. Don＇t wait for me. You You can also send the things directly to your second sister's house.Don't forget to give the meat coupons and money to Lu Zhi.It's okay. If you get more refunds and less subsidies, and advance money for advance checks, everyone is not well-off.Besides, looking at Lu Zhi's appearance, you can tell that she is a good girl, so there is no need to worry about anything else.Lu Zhi:Oh my gosh, Li Cuihua's dark circles couldn't be because of Deputy Battalion Commander Chen's sister.Deputy Battalion Commander Chen had to squeeze out a few tears after hearing this. He didn't expect that there was someone who cared more about his sister than him.Lu Zhi looked at Li Cuihua squeezing in and just wanted to say, what a talent.After queuing up and approaching Lu Zhi, she took a look and saw that there were still pork belly and tenderloin left.Lu Zhi found his ticket and bought pork belly. At this time, this kind of pork belly was also more popular than tenderloin because of its fat content.If it were Li Cuihua, she would definitely buy pork belly instead of tenderloin.After buying the pork belly, Lu Zhi and Zhou Jun held hands, and then, under Zhou Jun's expectant eyes, they handed the meat to Zhou Jun.Lu Zhi: Okay, we can go back

Chapter 18Lu Zhi went to find Lu Yue first.After hearing the whole story, Lu Yue was very calm. After all, this was something Li Cuihua could do.Lu Yue: She is a nice person, but she really thought about these things for a long time and said, she was so enthusiastic.Taking the pork belly to the kitchen, the two pieces of pork belly were about the same size. Lu Zhi took one piece for Li Cuilan, then calculated the money and tickets, and gave the extra to Lu Yue.Lu Zhi gave some of the remaining meat to Lu Yue.Lu Zhi: Second sister, not much, but I have enough. I plan to make beans, potatoes and pork belly tonight. Political Commissar Li and Sister-in-law Chen will come to our house for dinner.She continued, I also made spicy strips and I will bring you some next time.Looking back, Lu Yue was so moved that she almost cried.Lu Zhi:It seems like she just did a very small thing.Lu Yue: We are childish, and we are so kind to our second sister. I will write a letter to your elder brother soon.He said, looking proud.Lu Yue started looking for something and told Lu Zhi to wait for him. Lu Zhi took Zhou Jun to see Tuantuan.Tuantuan is sleeping. At his age, Tuantuan sleeps a lot.Lu Zhi touched the chubby hands and couldn't help but smile.This niece of hers is really cute.Zhou Junchao whispered, sister-in-law, she fell asleep.Lu Zhi: Yes, she is asleep. When Tuantuan can walk, you can play with her.Zhou Jun: When will Tuantuan be able to walk?Lu Zhi really didn't know this.Before learning to walk, Tuantuan still needs to learn one thing, and that is to speak.Lu Zhi: Before walking, Tuantuan can talk. You can call me aunt and you uncle.Zhou Jun stood up straighter when he thought about Tuantuan calling him uncle.This is my nieceLu Zhi: Our Xiaojun is so awesome that he is now our uncle.Zhou Jun: I will be a very good uncleWhen Lu Yue came back, he found brown sugar and honey for Lu Zhi. There was not a lot of brown sugar, but a lot of honey.Lu Yue: Take these back and drink them with water. It's sweet.

In the evening, it gets cooler.Lu Zhi got up and stood in front of the window looking at the scenery outside. Unfortunately, he couldn't see the seaside at a glance from the second floor. He had to go to the terrace upstairs.Lu Zhi casually tied his thick long hair into a low bun and went to the kitchen to cook.Zhou Jun followed behind Lu Zhi, sister-in-law, are you going to cook?Lu Zhi: Yes, your Uncle Li and Aunt Chen will come over for dinner later.After a pause, Lu Zhi remembered one thing. Do they have children? How could she forget about it? Just tell them to come with their children.In the kitchen, Lu Zhi looked at the dried beans that she had soaked when she came back. The dried beans were already soaked. She took out the dried beans, washed them for a while, and processed them again.After that came the pork belly and baby potatoes.When the oil was hot, Lu Zhi fried the pork belly in the pot. It quickly became fragrant, and then added dried beans and potatoes.After adding the seasonings, Lu Zhi stir-fried the vegetables together.Zhou Jun stepped on the small bench and swallowed his saliva intently.Zhou Jun: Sister-in-law, are you okay?Lu Zhixiao, "It needs to be stewed before it's ready. Get me some water."Zhou Jun immediately went to get water for Lu Zhi. Lu Zhi poured the water into the pot and closed the lid.The fragrance is getting stronger and stronger.During this time, Lu Zhi cleaned the seafood again and steamed it.Lu Zhi deliberately kept swimming crabs, and planned to start making soy crabs.Zhou Chengan came back and entered the kitchen. If there is anything left to do, let me do it.Lu Zhi: I want to stick corn tortillas in the pot. You can do this.Zhou Chengan smelled the aroma in the kitchen, and the seafood had been steamed. The swimming crabs in Lu Zhi's place were probably not meant to be steamed.Zhou Chengan: I want to make soy crabsLu Zhi: Yeah.The two of them were busy in the kitchen together.Zhou Junzuo looked around again, got off his little bench, took his own little bench, sat aside, and looked at them with his chin in his hands.Lu Zhi couldn't help but ask: Sister-in-law, do they have children?Zhou Chengan: I have a son named Li Weidong, who is the same age as Zhou Jun and is now in kindergarten.Lu Zhi: I forgot about this.Zhou Chengan: It's okay, they will bring Wei Dong with them.There is no need to say these things. Zhou Chengan and Li Changyuan have a really good relationship.Dried beans, pork belly and potatoes are stewed. The potatoes inside look very soft and waxy, the pork belly is ruddy in color, and the dried beans are very appetizing.Zhou Chengan took the corn dough and pasted it on the edge of the pot. He pasted a dozen or so in total before he stopped.The tortilla began to be soaked in the soup little by little, and it must be a little crispy but soft when eating.Lu Zhi's pickled crabs were also wrapped in sauce and put away by Lu Zhi.Little kid Zhou Jun was almost drooling, but he was not stubborn enough to eat a piece first.Lu Zhi picked up a piece of pork belly and asked Xiaojun to take a bite.Zhou Jun akimbo, sister-in-law eats firstWhile Zhou Jun was talking, Zhou Chengan had already put a piece of pork belly to Lu Zhi's mouth.Lu Zhi and Zhou Chengan looked at each other.Zhou Chengan: YeahLu Zhi: Do you know? It's beautiful and delicious.Hearing this, Zhou Chengan's eyes and eyebrows were filled with smiles, knowing it, just like I am looking at you now.Lu Zhi:Ah ah ah ah ah.It was her who flirted with Zhou Chengan.Forget it, let's eat firstWell, soft and waxy, delicious, very delicious.

Li Changyuan, Chen Chunni and their son Li Weidong smelled the fragrance before they arrived at Lu Zhi's home.There were also many people talking around.Who is cooking here?It smells so good.It seems to be beans.I'll eat beans too today.Li Changyuan: This tastes really good.Xiaodou Ding Li Weidong nodded in agreement.Finally arriving at Lu Zhi's house, the three members of the Li family were stunned when they smelled the smell.Wait, this smell comes from Lu Zhi's family.When Lu Zhi came out, she smiled and said: Sister-in-law, you are here, sit down quickly, Cheng'an will put out the dishes, and we will start dinner.Chen Chunni: It's the food you cooked at home. It tastes so delicious. I didn't expect Cheng An to do it.You can also make such good meals.Zhou Chengan came out, not me. You came here today because of your childishness.Chen Chunni: Oh my God, Cheng'an, you are really lucky to get married.Zhou Chengan smiled and said: Yes, you have married a treasure.There is obviously a difference between marrying a treasure and marrying a treasure, but only Lu Zhi seems to have noticed.Lu Zhi put his hands behind his back and gently touched Zhou Chengan's hand, only to be held by Zhou Chengan.Soon, the four adults and two Zaizai officially started eating.Li Changyuan was so delicious that he almost criedThe corn tortilla soaked in soup was so delicious when he took a bite. With the unique texture and the aroma of corn, he had never tasted such delicious corn tortillas.He hated, hated why he had eaten in the canteen at noon, why when he met Deputy Battalion Commander Li in the afternoon, Deputy Battalion Commander Li gave him fruit, and he ate a lot of it.It's delicious, it's really delicious, but he can't eat it anymoreChen Chunni: Wei Dong, from now on Xiaojun will go to a kindergarten with you, and maybe he will go to elementary school together, so you can play together.Chen Chuni was still cooking. After waiting for a while, Li Weidong still didn't answer.Wait, her son is very obedient, why doesn't he speak?good guySon, your head is almost buried in the bowl.It's a bit embarrassing.The two cubs finished eating first, we talked, and the cubs went to play in the yard.Li Weidong stood in the yard and looked around.The yard of Lu Zhi's house is empty now and has not been tidied up yet. After all, he just moved here.Li Weidong: Wow, your yard is so fun, you can run aroundLu Zhi came out and fell into deep thought.It turns out that her yard can still be praised even though she has not grown vegetables or has tables and chairs to enjoy the shade.Li Weidong's eyes are sparkling. Auntie, do you want to do a backflip?Oh my god.You versatile Zai Zai, look at itLu Zhi: You can do backflipsLi Weidong is proud and knows how toThe three people in the room who were talking happily all paused when they heard some back flips.Chen Chunni held her forehead, but she didn't have the eyes to see. She simply didn't have the eyes to see. Maybe she should just send Li Weidong back.In the yard, Li Weidong rushed out quite far and reached a wall of the yard.Lu Zhi was in awe, but also worried that Li Weidong would be injured, so he planned to stop Li Weidong first. After all, he was still a kid. Weidong, youLi Weidong moved with difficulty, and then rolled around.No, who taught you to do a backflip like this?

The Li family of three was about to go back, and Lu Zhi remembered the spicy strips and brought them some spicy strips.Chen Chunni: This looks delicious.Lu Zhi: You can usually make snacks. This one is slightly spicy but not very spicy, and this one is very spicy.I think it was made from the chili I bought last time.Yes, it is made from the chili I bought last time.Li Changyuan lowered his head and looked, but it was a pity that he couldn't eat spicy food.When she went back, Chen Chunni felt that the people enjoying the cool air and talking outside looked a little envious of them.Come to think of it, how could you not be envious? Who wouldn't be confused by the smell of Lu Zhi's cooking?

Lu Zhi put on the cream, and the more he thought about it, the more interesting it became. He was very curious about who taught Li Weidong such a backflip.Zhou Chengan: Me.Lu Zhi:Zhou Chengan recalled that before he came to the island, he often went to Li Changyuan's house for dinner, so he was very familiar with Li Weidong, a kid.Li Weidong heard something about Zhou Chengan and insisted on learning a backflip from Zhou Chengan. Li Changyuan told Zhou Chengan that he could just fool around.Who knows, Li Weidong is a little stupider than they thought.From then on, the Li family had one more conspicuous bag.Li Changyuan couldn't hear the words "backflip", couldn't hear them.If this could be photographed and recorded, and Li Weidong could see it when he grew up, he would definitely be embarrassed and just solve the problem of three bedrooms and one living room.Wait, take photos and record themYou can't post it to Moments, but you can take photos and record them yourself.Lu Zhi: Lao Zhou.Zhou Chengan: YeahLu Zhi: I want to buy a cameraZhou Chengan: I'll buy it on the weekend.Wow, wow, wow, this kind of love words is really beautiful.Lu Zhi's eyes moved, and she smiled and said: So, you really have married a treasure, so you have to take care of it, right?Zhou Chengan looked at Lu Zhi under the light.The trumpet sounded.The room became dark.Lu Zhi heard Zhou Chengan say in her ear: Yes, baby.The sound is nice, deep and magnetic.

Chapter 19This is what Grandpa Zhou said on the phone before the blind date. His personality is a bit cold and he doesn't like to talk very much, but he is responsible and responsible.AhhhhhhhHe calls himself baby.Zhou Chengan's voice is really confusing.He gently kissed Lu Zhi's earlobe.No matter what Lu Zhi said, someone who has experienced the 21st century, how could he be so indifferent.Lu Zhi kissed Zhou Chengan's lips, and the two lingered for a long time before they separated.

In the morning, after Lu Zhi woke up, he opened

the curtains and took a look at the weather outside. The weather was very good, with clear skies.Downstairs, Zhou Chengan had breakfast in the cafeteria, and Zhou Jun was playing, waiting for Lu Zhi to have breakfast with him.Zhou Jun: Sister-in-law, there are steamed buns todayThe cafeteria made steamed buns today, stuffed with shrimp and cabbage. Of course, the cabbage inside is more like a side dish, and the shrimp is the main ingredient.One bite, full of springy shrimps, so delicious.Today is another day of seafood freedom.Lu Zhi bit the bun, let's go to the beach to watch the sea today.Zhou Jun's cheeks were bulging while he was eating, and he nodded vigorously.He likes the sea, especially the seaThere were still some steamed buns left, so Lu Zhi put them in the pot and heated them up at noon. Then he could continue to eat them without having to cook or go to the canteen.After the meal, Lu Zhi tidied up, put on his floral skirt, locked the door and took Zhou Jun out.Zhou Jun: I know, sister-in-law, let's move forwardLu Zhi: Okay.Zhou Jun: Sister-in-law, we are going to turn left.Lu Zhi: Turn left, turn left, la la la la.After turning left. Lu Zhi saw the endless sea.The sea breeze blows and I just feel comfortable.There are already many people playing here at the beach. Many of them are not yet in kindergarten, because those who are in kindergarten are now in school.There are also family members like Lu Zhi who went to the island with the army, or fellow villagers and educated youth who went to the countryside.Lu Zhi found a seat and sat down, looking at the sparkling sea.Zhou Jun stood next to Lu Zhi with his hands on his hips. Sister-in-law, look, it's a seagull.Lu Zhi looked over and saw several seagulls flying over the sea in the distance.When Zhou Chengan passed by the beach, he looked at the two figures on the beach, stopped and looked over.Lu Zhi has a slender figure, her skirt is flying, and her skin is as bright as glowing in the sun.Several people following Zhou Chengan couldn't help but look over.Look, who is that?This is too pretty.Zhou Chengan turned around with a cold face, does it look good?No one spoke.Zhou Chengan withdrew his gaze, you sister-in-law.Everyone:Oh my god, theysister-in-lawAhhhhh, why are they still single, but their cold-faced, rigid and serious deputy leader Zhou can marry such a wife.

Lu Zhi didn't eat the buns she left in the morning, but she didn't eat them at noon. After enjoying the wind at the beach, she stopped by her second sister's house and stayed there all afternoon.Holding Tuantuan in his arms, Lu Zhi had a great time playing with her.Lu Zhi: Isn't it Tuantuan? You are Tuantuan. Who am I? I am Tuantuan's aunt, right?Tuantuan: Yeah yeah yeah~Smiling so happily.Lu Yue looked at them. At this moment, if his brother-in-law is okay, he will probably be here soon.As he said that, he also asked: I really don't want to eat here tonight.Lu Zhi: I made soy crab. I'm going back today to eat soy crab bibimbap.Lu Yue: I see, let alone Tuantuan drooling, you are almost drooling.Hahahaha.But the pickled crab is really delicious.Zhou Chengan came over and called after entering: "Second sister."Lu Yue was satisfied. This brother-in-law looked good no matter what. Look, he is so sensible. When he came in, he called his second sister.Wait, her brother-in-law Zhou Chengan is sensibleBecause of this realization, Lu Yue couldn't help but twitch her lips, and when she looked at her sister, she calmed down again.Normally, if another man married her sister, he would probably be sweeter and more sensible than Zhou Cheng.The family of three went back.Lu Zhi: I went to the beach with Xiaojun today, and then came to my second sister's house. I haven't finished the buns you brought back this morning. I'll go back later. You can stew some rice and eat the soy crab. We'll have the soy crab bibimbap and then heat up the steamed buns.Listening to what Lu Zhi said, Zhou Chengan nodded, and then held Lu Zhi's hand.Zhou Chengan: I listen to you.Lu Zhi couldn't help but smile. Who knows if you will always listen to me.Zhou Chengan thought carefully for a moment, then nodded, yes.

When he got home, Zhou Chengan was going to cook.Lu Zhi leaned over, took his arm and looked up at him, "Thank you for your hard work, Lao Zhou."Zhou Chengan: It's not hard, it's not hard at all. Why should I work hard to marry you?I just like to see Zhou Chengan being serious and saying things like this.Lu Zhi took a shower upstairs and went downstairs. Zhou

Chengan also prepared dinner.Lu Zhi looked at the pickled crabs on the table with special anticipation.Zhou Chengan brought all the dishes to the table. Now, we can start eating.Zhou Chengan helped Lu Zhi handle the sauce crab, and the crab meat was all in Lu Zhi's bowl.Lu Zhi took a bite of the soy crab bibimbap and his expression lit up.The crab meat is soft and delicious, and it goes into your mouth with the rice. There is also the fragrance of crab roe in it.Zhou Jun's first time eating it, wow, it's deliciousLu Zhi: Next time I go back, I must bring soy crabs to my eldest brother and the others.Zhou Chengan: You do it, and I'll help you find someone to send it over.Lu Zhi took another bite of rice, okayAfter one meal, Lu Zhi was a little full.Lu Zhi took Zhou Jun to play on the terrace. Each of them took a small bench and sat on it.The wind is blowing, it's really cool.When Zhou Chengan came out, Lu Zhi and Zhou Jun waved their arms to him. They both sat on the small bench. Zhou Jun was still leaning on Lu Zhi's shoulder and followed Lu Zhi.Lu Zhi: Lao Zhou, come up.Zhou Jun: Brother, come up.Soon, Zhou Chengan also took a small bench and sat with them.The starry sky today is exceptionally bright.It's so beautiful.

At Li Changyuan's house, his family of three were enjoying the shade in the yard.Li Weidong took the spicy strips and ate them. Li Weidong was the most spicy in their family. The spicy strips he ate were the spiciest. Chen Chunni ate slightly spicy ones, but Li Changyuan didn't eat them.Li Weidong took a sip of water. It was a good time, a good time.Chen Chunni couldn't help but eat the spiciest one and nodded in agreement, "Yeah, it's delicious, it's delicious."Looking at them, Li Changyuan thought about Lu Zhi's cooking, but he was still not interested in spicy strips.Chen Chuni and Li Weidong almost finished the spicy strips. Chen Chuni gave one to Li Changyuan. You can try one.Li Changyuan looked at Chen Chunni and handed him the spicy strips, and he took a bite.Li Changyuan:This taste, this texture, this is spicy stripsLi Changyuan ate faster and faster. After eating, he looked at Chen Chuni and Li Weidong again.Finished eating, they finished eatingChen Chuni and Li Weidong stood up contentedly and stretched together.Okay, after eating, you can brush your teeth, wash your face, and go to bed.Li Changyuan:Spicy strips, he wants to eat spicy strips.

It's a new day.Lu Zhi prepared the pickled crabs for his elder brother and the others, and went to call them.The phone call had just been connected, and on the other side of the phone was the voice of the Lu family talking.ChildishWhy did you call me?How are you doing?I know you like to eat bacon, so I finally found some for you here. Your Grandma Zhou also pickled pickled beans and dried cucumbers for you. She said she was worried that you would have difficulty eating vegetables.Lu Zhi smiled, everything is good here. The swimming crabs here are particularly delicious. I made some pickled crabs. When the time comes, Chengan will find someone to help you and deliver them to you.The person holding the phone was Li Lan. She listened to what Lu Zhi said and nodded quickly, okay, okay.Lu Xiangde also quickly took the phone, "Zhizhi, when we are free, we will go see you."Lu Zhi: Okay.Lu Zhi: How are you all?Lu Xiangde: Everything is fine. I have prepared very well for the exam. I am confident that I can become a level seven fitter. Your eldest brother and sister-in-law, your mother is watching them study, and they are also very serious, as well as your niece. , your niece was praised by the kindergarten teacher.Lu Zhi: Really.Hearing the mention of himself, Xiaodou Ding Lu Anan waved his arms vigorously, "Sister-in-law, sister-in-law"Lu Zhi: Well, I heard it. Please help me tell An An to study hard and I will give her a small schoolbag.The phone bill was very expensive, and there were people waiting in line to make calls. Lu Zhi talked to them for a while before going back.Unexpectedly, I met Li Cuihua.Lu Zhi: Come and make a call too.Li Cuihua: I'll fight later. I'll fight later. Come over here and let me tell you something.She looked very excited.Outside the phone room, Li Cuihua lowered her voice. Do you know why Deputy Battalion Commander Li disagreed?too strongIt's really too strongReally, in the future, if she doesn't become a reporter, she will be delayed in her ability to shine.Lu Zhi: Why?Li Cuihua recalled how she met Deputy Battalion Commander Li and his sister in the market that day.Deputy Battalion Commander Li: Let me tell you, Li Yu can't do it. He doesn't like you and your character isn't very good. Now you're looking for your husband. He doesn't like you and your character isn't very good either. , and a bit narcissistic, what are you trying to do?Then there was a quarrel between the two people.I do not care.you are crazyI'm going to marry himBelieve it or not, I will break your legs.After Li Cuihua finished speaking, she was still talking with gusto. Tell me, Battalion Commander Li wouldn't really hit his sister.This Deputy Battalion Commander Li is quite powerful.Li Yu is narcissistic, he knows it.Lu Zhi: Deputy Battalion Commander Li can watch his sister.Li Cuilan: As you can see, the two of them are still together now, and they don't know what they will do in the end.As he spoke, he shook his head.Li Cuilan looked at the person who came to call. After she finished speaking, she hurried in and continued to line up to make calls.Lu Zhi took a look and could only say that he was so talented that he was still standing in the queue at the back, not where he was just now.

canteen.Zhou Chengan looked at Li Changyuan who smiled sincerely at him.Zhou Chengan: It's been all morning.Li Yuanyuan has been like this this morning. His attitude towards Zhou Chengan is simply too good. You can tell at a glance what Li Yuanyuan wants to say to Zhou Chengan.Li Changyuan: Cheng'an.Zhou Chengan: Yeah.Li Changyuan: You are such a good wife.Hearing this, Zhou Chengan couldn't help but pursed his lips and smiled, and then.Li Changyuan: You have good taste, and so does your wife. From now on, the two of you will enjoy a golden marriage and grow old together.Zhou Chengan didn't speak, and Li Changyuan was still thinking about how to praise the two of them, but he really couldn't think of anything.It cannot be said that Zhou Chengan really has double standards.Li Changyuan: Anyway, you guys are so sweet. After saying that, he smiled and said, "Look, when are you going to make this spicy strip?"Zhou Chengan: You are not, you can't eat spicy foodLi Changyuan: People will change.Zhou Chengan would not agree to Li Changyuan. This was Lu Zhi's business, even if it was for making spicy strips.While Zhou Chengan was eating, I went back to ask her if she was free recently and if she could do it. She was very busy recently.Li Changyuan: It's okay. Next time she does it, just help me do it a little bit.No, that's not what he thinks.

Chapter 20On the weekend, Lu Zhi and Zhou Chengan are going to the city.Although supplies are scarce now, Lu Zhi is still very happy about going shopping. In addition to cameras, she can always buy some things she needs.Before the wake-up call sounded, Lu Zhi got up and washed up, while Zhou Chengan got up and went to the canteen to get food.The cafeteria was particularly awesome today. They even made seafood porridge.The boiled and blooming rice contains scallops, shrimps and crab meat.It's still a day that has a lot of seafood ingredients.The staple food includes Erhe noodles steamed buns and cold kelp shreds.Lu Zhi took a spoon and took a sip. The main thing was delicious. It was so delicious.Lu Zhi: This Yao Zhu is delicious.Taste firm and toughLu Zhi planned to buy some scallops when he went to the market next time, which he would use to make porridge or cook dishes.Before the older one and the younger one even started eating, they found all the scallops in their seafood porridge and gave them to Lu Zhi.Zhou Jun is serious, sister-in-law, you need to eat more to grow taller.Lu Zhi:Lu Zhi looked at Zhou Chengan, who was 1.85 meters tall, with an expression on his face, "I can't grow any taller."Fatty Zhou Jun was confused as to why he couldn't grow taller.It seems that the food in front of me no longer tastes good.Lu Zhi's expression didn't change, because your eldest brother is 1.85 meters tall and I am standing next to your eldest brother, right at his shoulders. What if I grow taller and am taller than him?There is no psychological burden at all to fool children.Zhou Chengan is very serious, I am 1.85.5 meters tall.Lu Zhi:After the family of three finished their meal, they set off to the pier.Lu Zhi held Zhou Jun's hand, and Zhou Jun was still immersed in things about whether eating would make him taller.Although Lu Zhi had already explained to him that adults should eat well, but it would not be possible to grow taller.Zhou Jun: Sister-in-law, sister-in-law, I understand.Lu Zhi: Well, what do you know?Zhou Jun: I want to eat more than my elder brother, so that I can be 1.86 meters tall in the futureHaving said that, I'm still a little shy, but 1.86.6 is fine.Good guy.You are really promising.

There are a lot of people at the pier today.The sea surface was different from when Lu Zhi first came to the island to take a boat. It was a little rough and rough.Lu Zhi looked up and looked at the weather, Lao Zhou, will it rain today?Zhou Chengan replied: No, I listened to the weather forecast on the radio and it was just a little stormy today.Lu Zhi got on the boat and went to the deck again.Many people couldn't help but look at it.Lu Zhi shuttled through the crowd like a beautiful landscape.Wearing a navy-style dress and small leather shoes, she had long, thick black hair tied into a half bun at the back, and she also wore a particularly beautiful hairpin.The boat swayed with the waves on the sea, and Lu Zhi held on to the railing to stand firm.There was another wave. Before Lu Zhi could step back, he was held down by Zhou Chengan and stood firmly on the spot.His arms were strong and strong, and his body smelled of clean soap.It feels so safe.Lu Zhi turned around and met Zhou Chengan's eyes.Zhou Chengan: Do you want a coat?Lu Zhi shook his head, no.Just, my heart is beating a little fast.

On weekends, there are also many people in state-owned shopping malls.In many places, there are almost long queues.Fortunately, there is no need to queue up to buy a camera. This thing is expensive, and not many people buy it.The salesperson cheered up when she saw them. What do you want to see?Lu Zhi:

Camera.Hearing this, the salesperson looked at this handsome family, her eyes fell on Lu Zhi, and she became even more envious.After buying a camera, I still have to continue shopping in state-owned shopping malls.Zhou Jun was going to school, so Lu Zhi bought Zhou Jun a new schoolbag and stationery, as well as pencils, erasers and notebooks.Six feet of navy blue fabric.A packet of jujube cake.Two clam oils, two bottles of shampoo, two bars of soap.Bought another can of biscuits.There are also many types of vegetable seeds.Lu Zhi saw a store selling hairpins and carefully selected a few.Although their hair is sparse, they are also fair, tender and cute little girls. They will definitely like it if they receive hairpins.Lu Zhi: Let's buy another pair of small leather shoes for my second sister.With that said, Lu Zhi went to choose small leather shoes again and chose a black classic model.When he turned around, he found that Zhou Chengan had taken a pair.Lu Zhi asked doubtfully: This pair looks better than the one I got.Zhou Chengan handed it over. This pair will look good on you.Their old Zhou is promising.Lu Zhi: Do they look better than the little leather shoes I'm wearing now?Zhou Chengan lowered his head and looked over. He thought carefully about it. You are good-looking and you will look good no matter what you wear.It seems extremely sincere.He had many experiences of being praised for his good looks, but when he was praised for his good looks with an expression like Zhou Chengan's, Lu Zhi couldn't help but feel a little shy.

I caught the last boat back to the island. When I returned to the island, it was already getting dark.When passing by Lu Yue's house, Lu Zhi gave him the small leather shoes he bought for Lu Yue and the hairpins he bought for Tuan Tuan.The bright smile on Lu Yue's face couldn't be concealed. Why are you still thinking about me? Our feet are the same size. Why don't you wear them? I have shoes here.Lu Zhi: I also bought a pair.Lu Yue accepted it now. Don't go back. You have to cook when you go back. Eat some with me.Very good, you can start cooking nowLu Yue went to catch the sea today and came back with a lot of seafood. He steamed a pot of seafood, stewed a cabbage and tofu, and fried a spicy crab.Lu Zhi thinks the spicy crab is delicious, spicy and spicy.She likes to eat spicy food. She ate spicy crab and a bowl of rice.Lu Zhi: Second sister, I haven't crossed the sea since I came here. Next time you go to catch the sea, ask me to come with you.Lu Yue: OK, next time I go to sea, I'll call you.This does not mean they can catch the sea whenever they want. It depends on the weather and the tide.After Lu Zhi finished eating, he was babbling in Lu Yue's arms. He saw Lu Zhi looking over and giggling.Lu Yue: Hey, you are quite sensible. You know to wait until the aunt has finished eating before letting her hold you. Auntie bought you a lot of hairpins today.Lu Zhi hugged Tuan Tuan into his arms, a soft ball.At first, Lu Zhi was nervous holding Tuantuan. After all, it was such a small one, but now he just felt so soft and comfortable to hold.Lu Zhi squeezed Tuantuan's little hand and waved to Zhou Cheng'an on the side. Look, it's us Tuantuan.Zhou Chengan and Tuantuan stared at each other with big eyes and small eyes, one looked serious and the other looked confused.Zhou Chengan: I am my uncle.Tuan Tuan: Kick Kick~

I am really tired today.After returning home, Lu Zhi took a shower and lay down, hugging her quilt and unwilling to move. She even felt that her fingers were a little weak.Thinking about the camera, Lu Zhi got up from the bed and found the camera.Lu Zhi felt that he could still learn how to operate it by tinkering, but this thing required film. Lu Zhi didn't want to waste it, so he played with the camera and waited for Zhou Chengan to come out.The camera focused on Zhou Chengan coming out of the bathroom.Lu Zhi:Zhou Chengan washed his hair. It was a little damp, probably because he had just taken a shower, and his eyes seemed to have been washed with water.Zhou Chengan: Press the button on the right hand.There was a scratching sound.The first photo taken by the camera was of Zhou Chengan wiping his hair with a towel and looking back.Also greatIf this photo were posted to Moments, it would probably get a lot of likes, and you can imagine the comments below.Drool, saliva~Zhou Chengan spent a while and explained the operation of the camera to Lu Zhi.In the future, she can start to use a camera to record these aspects of her life, otherwise it would be a pity to not even be able to find a few photos in retrospect.Fortunately, I bought a lot of film.After learning, Lu Zhi lay flat on the bed.I yawned and moved my shoulders again.Zhou Chengan: Let me press your shoulders for you.Lu Zhi would definitely not miss such a good thing, so he quickly sat up.Zhou Chengan's pressing force was a little light at first, but after asking Lu Zhi several times, the force became just right.Lu Zhi was drowsy.Lu Zhi: Zhizhi.Lu Zhi: YeahZhou Cheng settled down for a moment before saying: I'm 1.85.5 meters tall.Lu Zhi:

After Lu Zhi married on the island, people in the courtyard envied her for a long time.The man Lu Zhi married was really great.Chu Tong felt uncomfortable and panicked, feeling that everyone looked at her differently. He Li and Li Yu spent a lot of effort to coax her.Chu Tong felt a little more comfortable after being held by others.In the evening, every household is busy cooking, and when they have free time, they chat in the yard.Chu Tong took things from her husband's house and returned to her parents' house. She was flattered by her parents' family and looked proud when she came back.He Li: I' m back. Have you eaten yet?Chu Tong: After eating, my parents asked me to bring you some dumplings. They said, they are embarrassed that you always ask me to bring things back, but they are also happy that we married into your family.Hearing the dumplings, He Li felt that her back straightened up again.Although she really felt sorry for the things she gave to the Chu family.Tell me, what dumplings are you bringing? Just eat them.It's not easy for you to marry a daughter. You should go back often and bring them something.Let me see what the fillings of these dumplings are.Chu Tong: Stuffed with pork and cabbage.Of course, it's mainly cabbage, with only a little bit of pork, but it's also stuffed with pork and cabbage.Sister-in-law Lu and Li Lan listened to the commotion outside. They were not too angry, but they missed Lu Zhi a little, and even worked slower.Sister-in-law Lu: They perform every day at home, and they make noises at night with the door closed, so they don't think others don't hear them.Li Lan also remembered the quarrel behind closed doors at their house. They lived close to each other, so they heard it very clearly.Jiang Dong came over and stood outside the courtyard and shouted: Uncle Lu is there, is Aunt Li here? It's deputy captain Zhou and my sister-in-law who asked me to come over and deliver things to you.

Chapter 21Sister-in-law Lu rushed out and saw Jiang Dong standing at the door of the courtyard.The Lu family also came out quickly one after another.They all remember Jiang DongWhen Lu Zhi and Zhou Chengan went to the island, it was Jiang Dong who drove here. They remembered it clearly. Even if they met Jiang Dong by chance on the road, they would still remember it if it wasn't Jiang Dong who came to look for them.Lu

Zhi made a total of more than 30 kilograms of pickled crabs. In addition to the Lu family, some were given to Grandpa Zhou and Grandma Zhou.Jiang Dong gave them the pickled crab, which was made by our sister-in-law.woo woo woo woo.Because he helped deliver the pickled crabs, Jiang Dong also ate the pickled crabs made by Lu Zhi. It was really delicious. He had been to the island for a long time, and this was the first time he had eaten such delicious pickled crabs.Lu Xiangde reached out to carry something. How is Lu Zhi doing on the island?Jiang Dong: Uncle Lu, don't worry, my sister-in-law will be fine on the island.Lu Xiangde nodded. Although Lu Zhi and Lu Yue both called and said it was fine, they still wanted to ask, so that they felt at ease.Lu Xiangde: Are you ready to eat? Come in and sit down. Let's have a meal together and then go back.Jiang Dong: Uncle Lu, you're welcome. You're really welcome.Jiang Dong wanted to refuse, but the Lu family was so polite that they almost gathered him at home.Sauce crab.The two sisters of the Lu family really miss their family.They found the man well.When Lu Yue came back before, he brought a lot of dried kelp, dried shrimp scallops and the like. There seemed to be dried oysters and fresh seafood.He Li's face was extremely ugly. During these days, she had been uncomfortable because of trying to please Chu Tong, and now she was even more uncomfortable.Some people looked at He Li and Chu Tong's mother-in-law and daughter-in-law, and felt that these two people were simply asking for humiliation.How is someone's life going? They live in a large courtyard. Can't you tell?No matter how good the acting is on the surface, it is still acting.Look, there will definitely be a quarrel in their house these days.Chu Tong often went to her parents' house to get things.Now when I see Lu Zhi delivering pickled crabs to his house, can I not be jealous?Inside the house, Mrs. Lu opened the package of pickled crabs and couldn't help but make a sound. These pickled crabs are so good.Jiang Dong, who was sitting aside, couldn't help it anymore and swallowed again.Yes, this sauce crab is goodThe soft meat, fragrant crab roe, and rich flavor made him never taste such delicious pickled crab.

Zhou Jun has been playing on the island for a while and is familiar with the environment here.Going to school must be put on the agenda.When Zhou Chengan proposed to take Zhou Jun to the kindergarten to report, Zhou Jun was lying on the coffee table with his shoulders slumped.I don't want to go to school, I really don't want to go to school.Why, can't you become an adult now?Lu Zhi was making spicy strips in the kitchen, and this time she made more. She added various seasonings to the spicy strips, and finally poured hot oil on them.After mixing the spicy strips, it's done.Lu Zhi took some spicy sticks and put them on the coffee table. Zhou Jun, who seemed to be very excited about eating spicy sticks just now, suddenly felt as if he had beaten eggplant with frost.Lu Zhi: What's wrong with you?Because of his concern, Lu Zhi looked very gentle.Zhou Jun stood up, put his hands on his hips, sister-in-law, I'm going to kindergarten. I have to study hard and make progress every day. In the future, I will become a man and take care of my sister-in-law.Zhou Chengan:The two brothers looked at each other, and Zhou Jun pushed out his chest.It's not that I don't want to go to kindergarten.Lu Zhi applauded, wow, Xiaojun is great.Zhou Chengan took a sip of water and looked at Lu Zhi. Lu Zhi discovered that he could see a trace of grievance in his eyes.No, this is impossible, this is not Zhou Chengan's character

Zhou Chengan had already arranged for Zhou Jun to go to kindergarten.There is only one kindergarten on the island, and there is nothing to choose from. Just send Zhou Jun there.Lu Zhi got up early.After washing up, he went to Zhou Jun's room. Zhou Jun was wearing clean blue and white striped short-sleeves and shorts, and was carrying the cross-body schoolbag Lu Zhixin bought for him.Zhou Jun: I brought pencils, erasers and notebooks.Lu Zhi: Wow, our Xiaojun is so awesome.He actually packed his schoolbag himself.In addition to these, Lu Zhi found a kettle for Zhou Jun and filled it with cold water. He also took a lunch box and chopsticks and put them in Zhou Jun's schoolbag.A family of three set off to kindergarten.When I arrived at the kindergarten, there were many people outside the kindergarten.The children were chattering.Lu Zhi was a little worried about child Zhou Jun. Although he had gone to kindergarten before, this was his first time in a kindergarten on the island.Child Zhou Jun: Sister-in-law.Lu Zhi was nervous and began to think quickly about how to comfort him.Go to school well and she will pick him up after school.Make him something delicious for dinner.What to eat? Why not make spicy squid bibimbap and drink a bottle of soda to enjoy it.Zhou Jun: Sister-in-law, I have to go to school. You have to have a good meal at noon. If there is any work, you can wait until my elder brother or I go back to do it together.Lu Zhi nodded.Wait, Zhou Xiaojun, something is wrong with you.Zhou Jun looked a little worried, sister-in-law, I have weekends every week, as well as winter and summer vacationsFor a moment, Lu Zhi felt as if many people around her were looking at her, and she actually felt envious.Okay, you can be proud.Teacher Xiao Feng stood at the entrance of the kindergarten waiting for the children, and was shocked by the scene in front of her.She actually saw this kind of cub.I almost cried with envy.When Zhou Jun arrived at the entrance of the kindergarten, he turned around and waved his arms to Lu Zhi and Zhou Chengan, "Brother and sister-in-law, I'm going to school."Lu Zhi felt a little sad in his heart.Zhou Chengan: Zhizhi, what are you having for dinner?Lu Zhi looked at him and talked happily, "Spicy squid with rice, I have to go to the supply and marketing cooperative to buy soda."Seeing Lu Zhi become happy, Zhou Chengan didn't consider his brother going to kindergarten at all. Zhou Jun still understood.When going back, Lu Zhi met Chen Chunni and Li Weidong.Li Weidong: Aunt, Xiaojun has gone to kindergarten.Lu Zhi was stunned when he looked at Li Weidong's sausage mouth.Good guy, how many spicy strips have you eaten? Why are you so spicy?Looking at Li Weidong's little hand, he was still holding the spicy strips tightly.Lu Zhi replied: Yes, Xiaojun goes to kindergarten, you are in the same class.Li Weidong's steps were much faster, and he rushed towards the kindergarten.Li Weidong: Xiaojun, XiaojunThen I stuffed a bite of spicy strips.Chen Chunni: Hahahaha.It's okay, not embarrassing, not embarrassing at all.

Lu Zhi and Chen Chunni went to the market together.The market is also very lively today, with a lot of seafood.Lu Zhi bought squid, and Chen Chunni also bought some.Chen Chunni: What are you going to do?Lu Zhi told Chen Chunni how to cook spicy squid, and you can go back and cook it too.Chen Chunni nodded, obviously hearing it, and then bought some more squid.Thinking of the spicy squid that Lu Zhi taught her to make today, Chen Chunni could hardly hold back her laughter.Lao Li, just wait to show shock and applaud for her.There are also a lot of Yao Zhu here, and Lu Zhi bought another Yao Zhu, after all, she really likes to eat them.After returning home, Lu Zhi put his things in the kitchen and took some time off.The sun was particularly good today. Lu Zhi took out the quilt and dried it in the yard.After returning to the house, he found a book and brewed a cup of honey water. Lu Zhi was half-lying on the sofa downstairs, looking very relaxed.At noon, Zhou Chengan came back.Looking at the man standing in front of him, Lu Zhi was surprised, Lao Zhou, why are you back?Zhou Chengan: Get the lunch box, let's go to the cafeteria to eat.Ahhhhhh.Therefore, Lao Zhou was worried that she would be boring, so he came back to have dinner with her.The corners of Lu Zhi's eyes and lips curved, Zhou Chengan, come here.When Zhou Chengan stopped in front of Lu Zhi, Lu Zhi put her arms around his neck and kissed him on the cheek.After a few minutes.Lu Zhi regretted a little.What's wrong with her lips? Maybe she ate too many spicy strips today.

There are many people in the cafeteria.Lu Zhi found a seat and sat down, while Zhou Chengan went to line up for food.Lu Zhi saw a few familiar people, who seemed to be Zhou Chengan's soldiers. They were enthusiastic and cheerful.Hello sister-in-law.sister in lawHello sister-in-lawLu Zhi: Hello.Soon, Zhou Chengan came back from cooking.The canteen has a lot of seafood.Most of the dishes in the canteen are seafood, but there are not many vegetables. Most of the time they are potatoes and cabbage.Zhou Chengan knew that Lu Zhi liked to eat Pipi shrimps, so he gave Lu Zhi some Pipi shrimps, which were fried Pipi shrimps.People at the table next to me were talking.Make a bet, make a bet.Yes, yes, I am not convinced.I'm not convinced either.Thinking about what happened last time, Feng Jianshe, who became the biggest winner, smiled honestly.Han Zhi said: Today, we will make a bet whether our deputy leader Zhou will be able to help my sister-in-law wash the lunch box. Whoever wins this time will not have to do any work in the dormitory.Feng Jianshe was a little slow, and because no one else chose Zhou Chengan to help Lu Zhi wash the lunch box, he chose this.Feng Jianshe scratched his head and then busied himself with cooking.Everyone laughed.Everyone quietly looked at Lu Zhi and Zhou Cheng'an.Zhou Chengan helped his sister-in-law peel the shrimps.Zhou Chengan helped his sister-in-law pick up the food.Zhou Chengan cleared the table and started washing the lunch boxes.

No, it was not like this when Zhou Chengan trained them.The cook, Feng Jianshe, finally finished his meal, and then he realized that everyone was very envious of him.Ah, what's going on?Lu Zhi thought of the wedding candies at home, she went over and said with a smile: Hello everyone.Everyone stood up one after another.The voice is very loud, hello sister-in-lawLu Zhi felt that everyone in the cafeteria was looking at him. When Zhou Chengan heard the sound and looked over, Lu Zhi became calmer.Lu Zhi found wedding candies for them, wedding candies.Thank you sister-in-lawSister-in-law, I wish you and our deputy leader Zhou a happy son soon.

AhhhhhhhTheir voices seemed to be getting louder, and more and more people seemed to be watching her in the cafeteria, and some even followed them to bless her and Zhou Chengan.Lu Zhi felt himself blushing, but Zhou Chengan seemed very happy

Chapter 22Lu Zhi was at Lu Yue's house in the afternoon.Lu Yue had to work and tidy up the house, so Lu Zhi was left with the task.They took a nap together with Tuantuan in his arms. When Lu Zhi woke up, Tuantuan was already awake and was chewing his little fist obediently.Really so sensibleZhou Xiaojun is very easy to lead, and Tuan Tuan is also super easy to lead.Lu Zhi pushed Tuantuan gently, and Tuantuan rolled to the side on the bed.Tuantuan: Giggle, giggle~At seven months old, he can already roll over.Tuantuan clenched her fists hard on the bed, turned over, waved her fists with Lu Zhi, and continued to play.Lu Zhi pushed Tuantuan over again, and this time Tuantuan even kicked his little fat legs.Tuantuan: Yeah yeah yeah~Oh hahaIt's pretty awesome, and it turned over again.The two played tirelessly several times, and Lu Zhi teased her for a while with the rattle.Lu Yue heard the sound and came in. He woke up and came down to eat some watermelon.Lu Zhi: Watermelon, second sister, where did you get the watermelon?Lu Yue: It was given by Li Cuihua next door. I sent her some seafood last time I went to sea.Of course, not a whole watermelon, but a quarter of a watermelon.The watermelon cut into pieces looked very refreshing. Lu Zhi took a bite and felt it was refreshing and relieving the heat. It tasted quite sweet.Lu Zhi's hair was gently blown by the hot breeze in the afternoon, and he took another bite of watermelon.Tuantuan was whining and slurping at the side, eating watermelon in small mouthfuls.Lu Yue sighed, these days passed so quickly, it has been almost eight months since then.As he said that, he felt very relieved to see Lu Zhi and Tuantuan sitting together.Well, they are all on their way to becoming adults.Lu Yue took the handkerchief and handed it to Lu Zhi to wipe his mouth.Lu Zhi looked at Lu Yue with some suspicion. She suspected that in Lu Yue's heart, there was no difference between herself and Tuantuan.Lu Yue took Tuantuan's handkerchief again and wanted to wipe it with Tuantuan, but looking at her little hand holding the watermelon, she thought it would be okay to wash it together later.Lu Zhi: Second sister.Lu Yue: YeahLu Zhi: There are differences between Tuantuan and I.After finishing speaking, Lu Yue performed a spitting watermelon seed show on the spot.Lu Yue:Oh, there is a difference when you grow up. There is no difference. To her, they are all children.Look at what this person is doing, what is the nature of a child if he is not a child?

Kindergarten was over, and Lu Zhi went to wait for Zhou Jun to finish school.The kindergarten is very close to Lu Zhi's home. Zhou Chengan can drop Zhou Jun off when he goes to school, and he can go back by himself after school, or he can solve all the problems of going to and from school by himself.Today is special, it is Zhou

Jun's first day out of kindergarten.Li Qiaozhen, the daughter-in-law of Deputy Battalion Commander Chen, was waiting for her son. After seeing Lu Zhi for a few more glances, she said hello: You are from Deputy Commander Zhou's family, right? I live next door to your home. My name is Li Qiaozhen.Oh hahaIt's her.As neighbors, the two of them exchanged a few words and were considered acquainted.Zhou Jun was the first Zaizai to rush out from the kindergarten. Sister-in-lawThere was a follower, Li Weidong, behind him. When Li Weidong looked at Lu Zhi, his eyes were full of longing.Then, one cub, two cubs, three cubsWait, what is going on?Li Qiaozhen looked at Lu Zhi's figure and couldn't help but sigh: This deputy battalion commander Zhou's wife is really nice, and the children also like her.Ah.It's just the charm of spicy strips.Li Weidong stretched out five fingers.Lu Zhi didn't understand what Li Weidong meant, so he extended his hand with Li Weidong.Yeah, I successfully high-fived Li Weidong.Not to be outdone, Zhou Jun, the little fat man, jumped up and wanted to high-five Lu Zhi. Lu Zhi was also very cooperative.Li Weidong: Today I gave the spicy strips to five children to eat together.He said, feeling a little uncomfortable.Although each of them was given only a small piece, no matter how small the mosquito was, it was still meat.Li Weidong looked at Zhou Jun enviously and asked a question, why are you not my sister-in-law?Ah, this

Lu Zhi arrived home and went to the kitchen to get

busy.Wash the squid and blanch it. When the oil is hot, stir-fry it with minced garlic, green onions, and dried red pepper. The aroma of the seasoning will be instantly stir-fried, with a hint of garlic flavor in the spiciness. .Then add Lu Zhi's homemade hot sauce.Finally, stir-fry the squid and green chili pepper in the pot again, so that the squid is all covered with the soup that is stir-fried in the pot.On top of the fragrant rice on the plate, there is a layer of spicy squid. There is enough squid, and it seems to be more than the rice.Lu Zhi was cooking, and many people around him smelled the aroma.Zhou Chengan returned home under the envious eyes of everyone.Deputy Battalion Commander Chen shook his head while holding the kettle. It smelled spicy. It must be the smell of chili peppers. What else could it be? It smelled like squid.Not only did Deputy Battalion Commander Chen smell it, but everyone else also smelled it.So, the next door guy just made a spicy squid dishDeputy Battalion Commander Chen: When will we have dinner?Li Qiaozhen was pleasantly surprised and wanted to eat it now.Because of his sister's incident, Deputy Battalion Commander Chen has no intention of eating these days.I really want to thank Lu Zhi.

Lu Zhi watched Zhou Chengan open the soda easily, and they started eating.Lu Zhi mixed the rice with a spoon. The squid and rice were wrapped in the soup. When he took a bite, it had a rich texture. The slight spiciness stimulated his taste buds and made him sweat a thin layer.At this time, it is really delicious to take a sip of soda.It seems to be an orange flavored soda.Zhou Chengan asked Zhou Jun: How was it in kindergarten todayZhou Jun answered truthfully, and everything was fine. But he looked at Lu Zhi, and then said hesitantly: I don't like Li Weidong anymore.Zhou Chengan: Why don't you like Li Weidong?Zhou Jun: He likes my sister-in-law and hopes to be my sister-in-law's younger brother. It's impossible. If you marry your sister-in-law, she will be my sister-in-law.He said in a low voice, Brother, Mom said, she liked our dad at first because she fell in love with his face. She also said, who doesn't like good-looking men? You can put on the cream from now on, and I'll do the same.Zhou Chengan made a move.Lu Zhi couldn't help but laugh.After Zhou Jun finished eating and went out to play, Zhou Chengan asked: Are you satisfied with my current face?Lu Zhi: Satisfied, very satisfied.If Zhou Chengan wasn't good-looking back then, Lu Zhi really might not have agreed.

Li family.Today, Chen Chunni was determined to impress Lao Li and Xiao Li, locking them out of the kitchen while she was tinkering in the kitchen.Finally, Chen Chunni came out.Li Changyuan and Li Weidong's stomachs had begun to growl.Chen Chunni's guilty conscience suddenly stopped.Chen Chunni: Are you hungry and want to eat?Li Changyuan:Ever since Lu Zhi came to the island, his wife has become more and more different from before, always doing strange things.Li

Changyuan's stomach growled again. Yes, he was hungry.Chen Chunni took out the spicy squid bibimbap she made with satisfaction.Li Changyuan and Li Weidong feel that there is no difference between the spicy fried squid cooked by Chen Chunni. The only difference is that this time it is served with rice.Looking at the two people eating with big mouthfuls, Chen Chunni said: Sure enough, the food I made today is delicious, but you should eat slowly, don't be in a hurry, don't be in a hurry.Father and son: two:Forget it, let's get to work first.

It's a new day.Zhou Chengan took the time to go home and plowed the ground in the yard so that he could grow vegetables.The vegetable patch in the yard is not big to begin with, but it was quickly filled up.Zhou Chengan held the seeds again and watched the vegetable seeds being sown skillfully.Cabbage, green onions, coriander, spinach, radishLu Zhi looked at the sweaty man and felt that he couldn't get enough.Li Qiaozhen, come here. She's at home.Lu Zhi got up, sister-in-law Qiaozhen.Li Qiaozhen held the basket. When she saw Lu Zhi, Lu Zhi, who smiled sincerely, was a little stunned.Although I had a few words with Li Qiaozhen yesterday, Li Qiaozhen is not like this now.Li Qiaozhen: That's not true. There are a lot of cucumbers in the yard at home. I'll bring some for you.As he said that, he looked at Zhou Chengan and asked, are you growing vegetables?Lu Zhi: Yeah.Li Qiaozhen took out all the cucumbers. Okay, I can grow vegetables in this yard, and I can usually be self-sufficient. If I have nothing to do in the future, I can come to my sister-in-law's house to play.Lu Zhi asked: Lao Zhou, you and Deputy Battalion Commander Chen have gotten closer recently.Zhou Chengan shook his head.Lu Zhi: This is strange.Although, Lu Zhi took the cucumber and thought it would be good to eat cucumber at night, it was refreshing.It's okay to wash one and eat it nowLu Zhi went to wash a cucumber under the faucet. After breaking it open, he gave half to Zhou Chengan and ate the other half himself.Lu Zhi: Lao Zhou, come onZhou Chengan wiped his sweat, Lu Zhi.Lu Zhi: YeahZhou Chengan: Do you think I look good like this?Lu Zhi was so calm that he even looked at it up and down. It looked good.Unable to hold back, Zhou Chengan pinched Lu Zhi's cheek.Lu Zhi: Ah, ah, don't pinch it. I won't pinch it next time.When Zhou Jun came back from kindergarten, Lu Zhi told Zhou Jun that from now on, he could no longer play in the vegetable garden. There would be a lot of food here soon.Zhou Jun salutes and promises to obey orders

In the next few days, Lu Zhi lived leisurely.Everything is fine, the only thing I'm not happy about is probably that she might be a little fat.Looking at himself in the mirror, Lu Zhi felt that he had to lose weight anyway.While he was thinking about it, he heard Lu Yue calling him outside.Lu Zhi ran downstairs, second sister.Lu Yuexi smiled brightly. Your brother-in-law is back. He will be home soon around dinner time.

He also asked someone to help deliver some things. There are gifts for you. We will go there to have dinner together in the evening.Brother-in-law is backLu Zhi really hadn't seen his brother-in-law for a long time, and he was also very happy. Okay, I'll take Cheng'an and Xiaojun there in the evening.

Chapter 23When Lu Zhi arrived at Lu Yue's house, Jiang Hao was cleaning up the yard.Lu Zhi: brother-in-lawJiang Hao is tall and good-looking, although he is a bit rough, but his strength makes him feel very safe.Jiang Hao is also a man who really dotes on his wife.Jiang Hao: My little sister is here. I brought you a gift. It's in the house. Go and have a look.Lu Zhi: Thank you, brother-in-lawWhen he arrived in the living room, Lu Zhi started looking for his own gifts. Jiang Hao always liked to bring gifts to Lu Zhi in the past, and even mailed gifts to Lu Zhi several times.This time Jiang Hao went to the capital, and among the things he brought back were roast duck, snacks, and fabrics, all of which were for Lu Zhi.Lu Yue: This hairpin is yours too, one for you and Tuan Tuan.It's a hairpin with a bow, and the butterfly's wings can move.Lu Zhi shook his head at Lu Yue with the hairpin in his hand, and the butterfly wings on it swayed rapidly.Tuantuan held the bow hairpin and began to shake it vigorously. The wings of the butterfly hairpin swayed together.In addition to these, there are gifts.Lu Zhi was pleasantly surprised. She didn't expect her brother-in-law to come back with rice noodles.Lu Zhi was holding rice noodles. This brother-in-law also bought them in the capital.Lu Yue: No, it was given by a comrade. He said it was made by himself. He gave a lot of them. Do you know what this is?Lu Zhi: This is rice noodles. She paused. It was very delicious.Lu Yue: Okay, you can take it all back.Lu Zhi: If you can't eat it, I'll just take these. I'll come over next time and teach you how to make them. It's delicious.Lu Yue: OK.Finally, Lu Yue remembered the two men still in the yard.One is a flower of the high mountains and the other is taciturn. How do they communicate when they are together?Thinking about it, Lu Yue felt very embarrassed.Lu Yue hurried out.In the yard, the two people seemed to be communicating very happily.Jiang Hao: If your wife is angry, just admit your mistake directly, and your attitude must be sincere. Your face is not as important as your wife.Zhou Chengan nodded, his brother-in-law was right.Jiang Hao: Have you ever had any quarrels since you got marriedZhou Chengan shook his head, with a faint smile on his lips. Their relationship was very good and stable, and they had never had any quarrels until now.Hearing this, Jiang Hao continued to tell Zhou Chengan his experience. If there is a quarrel, just remember three words.Zhou Chengan listened carefully, brother-in-law, tell me.Jiang Hao: Thick-skinned.

Lu Yue was busy cooking in the kitchen, and Jiang Hao came over to help.During this time, Jiang Hao seemed to look stronger.Lu Yue: What did you and Chengan talk about just now?Really curious.Jiang Hao recalled it for a while, and then started talking about when Zhou Chengan and Lu Zhi entered their yard.Ah ah ah ah ahThere is no need to explain it in such detail.In detail, I am going to talk about the punctuation marks.Jiang Hao: After that, I asked him how he and Lu Zhi got together.Okay, I know the answer.Lu Yue: Go out and wash the seafood.Jiang Hao easily picked up the seafood that Lu Yue brought back, said "good", and went out to work neatly.

In the evening, the two families had dinner together.Lu Zhi was not without a wink. He had to go back after the meal without delaying the couple's conversation.A family of three is walking on the road.Lu Zhi was jumping up and down, followed by Zhou Jun.Lu Zhi: Zhou Chengan, let's take a detour to see the sea and then go back.Zhou Chengan: OK.They deliberately took a long way to the beach.There are a lot of people at the beach, enjoying the cool weather and playing with their children.Lu Zhi found a seat and sat down, while Zhou Jun ran to the beach to find Li Weidong.Zhou Chengan sat down next to Lu Zhi.What a nice viewLu Zhi was sighing, but his eyes couldn't help but fall on a man and a woman on the beach.The man is Chen Yu, Lu Zhi's narcissistic blind date. In this case, it goes without saying that the woman is the sister of Deputy Battalion Commander Chen.Deputy Battalion Commander Chen's sister looks innocent and cute. If we just talk about her appearance, Lu Zhi is very fond of her.Lu Zhi: Lao Zhou, Lao Zhou.After waiting for a while, Zhou Chengan didn't say anything. Lu Zhi looked over and found that Zhou Chengan was looking at her with his lips pursed.No way, Lao Zhou, you are so jealous.Otherwise, give me some coaxingZhou Chengan: It's all my fault. I wish I had gone on a blind date with you earlier.Lu Zhi:good guyIt's actually possible to do this.Chen Yu felt nervous when he saw Zhou Chengan and Lu Zhi, worried that these two people would mess up their affairs.Chen Ting found that Chen Yu was absent-minded, what's wrong with you?Chen Yu: I want to confess something to you. Before I came to the island, my family pressed me to get married, so they forced me to go on several blind dates, but I didn't fall in love with them.These words made Chen Ting laugh. Are you confessing to me that you only like me, or should you confess to me.Chen Yu: One of my blind dates went to the island with the army. She was reluctant to talk to me before, but I rejected her. If she says anything to you, don't believe it. This person is a little bit obsessed with love. Crazy.Chen Ting feels sorry for him, who is it?Chen Yu: Let's not talk about it for now. She is married. It would be best if she can think things through. If she can't think things through, don't believe her.Chen Ting: Yeah, yeah, I believe youThe two people looked at each other, as if their eyes were full of affection.Lu Zhi was still looking at the beach, and Zhou Chengan said: Let's go home. We'll clean up soon and turn out the lights.Lu Zhi stood up, XiaojunZhou Jun, who was playing, looked back, spoke to Li Weidong, and quickly ran towards Lu Zhi.

In the evening, it was extremely quiet.Deputy Battalion Commander Chen, Chen He couldn't sleep, so he turned over. When she came back today, her smiling eyes were almost narrowed into slits. She must have met Chen Yu again today.Li Qiaozhen: You can't look at her.Chen He: Otherwise, don't take this class. Anyway, I don't agree. You didn't see how she was controlled by that Chen Yu. Besides, that Chen Yu's character doesn't look right to me. What's real?As she said this, she sighed, I was really worried because of her, but she still thought that I was planning to arrange a marriage for her and that I was the one who arranged the marriage.Li Qiaozhen: That's true.Chen He: I, I have made progress. I am not planning an arranged marriage. I just want her to find someone with good character.As a man, he also felt that Chen Yu didn't like his sister Chen Ting at all.

Today is the weekend.When Lu Zhi got up, Zhou Chengan and Zhou Jun were playing with Li Weidong in the yard, and the other was reading the newspaper in the living room.Lu Zhi went out, but before he could say anything, Li Weidong ran over and hugged Lu Zhi's thigh.Lu Zhi: I have a task for you. Can you help me go to my second sister's house? Tell them that I will make rice noodles for lunch today and ask them to come with me.Li Weidong can take Zhou Jun with him.The two Zaizai said in unison, ensuring that the task would be completed.Seeing them running out of the yard, Lu Zhi went to see Zhou Chengan again.Lu Zhi: Lao Zhou, go to the market and buy some shrimps and swimming crabs. I will make shrimp balls and crab balls for rice noodles.Zhou Chengan put down the newspaper a long time ago and helped Lu Zhi open the lunch box. I'll go right away. You come over first and have breakfast. Today is your favorite seafood porridge.Lu Zhi was indeed interested.Sitting on the chair, Lu Zhi took a spoon and drank in small sips. By the way, soak the rice noodles in warm water first.Zhou Chengan soaked the rice noodles and came out of the kitchen. He wiped his hands again. I went to the market and will be back in a while.Clay pot rice noodles.Lu Zhi was really greedy.But now it can only be called rice noodles, because Lu Zhi doesn't have a casserole to use for the time being.After Zhou Chengan came back, Lu Zhi taught him how to make crab balls and shrimp balls, and the two of them were busy in the kitchen together.Lu Zhi: I really like eating shrimp balls.The shrimp balls on the market that Lu Zhi ate before did not contain much shrimp, but the shrimp balls he made were different.Zhou Chengan: I will do more.Lu Zhi: Okay.Lu Zhi stir-fried the rice noodle base for the casserole and added water to it. When the water began to boil, she added the rice noodles, and then started adding meatballs and vegetables.The rice noodles look delicious, delicious, and make you salivate just by looking at them.You don't need to think about it to know how delicious this rice noodle can be.The group of people outside were laughing. Before they arrived at Lu Zhi's place, Lu Zhi heard the noise outside.Lu Zhi goes out, second sister, second brother-in-lawLu Yue: You made the rice noodles, right?Lu Zhi: I did it with our old Zhou.Zhou Chengan was kind to Lu Zhi, which made Lu Yue happy and smiled gently at Jiang Hao.The taciturn Jiang Hao is really a good brother-in-law.Next door, Chen He is also off today.Chen He was quarreling with Chen Ting.Chen Ting: You don't know, you don't know Chen Yu's character, you don't understand him, why do you disagree with us being together? He loves me very much, and I love him very much too.Smelling the fragrance next door, Chen He was intoxicated, and he was very irritable because he couldn't eat rice noodles.When he heard what they said outside and what Chen Ting said, Chen He felt that he understood.Chen He: What kind of person do you think Zhou Chengan is?What kind of person is Zhou Chengan?Chen Ting followed Chen He here. At first, she came to help take care of the children. Later, she found a temporary job and worked here. She knew about Zhou Chengan.Before, Chen Ting had participated in a social gathering and met Zhou Chengan at the social gathering. Afterwards, she heard about how many girls were pursuing Zhou Chengan, but in the end, Zhou Chengan ignored them at all. Some girls even stuttered when they saw him because of his cold personality.Chen Ting: He, he is good at everything, but he has a cold personality. He is a flower of the high mountains.Chen He: This kind of man can now cook for his wife. This is love, this is love. If you think Chen Yu treats you better than Zhou Chengan treats his wife, I agree with you. marry.

Chapter 24The steaming rice noodles also come with separate chili oil and vinegar. If you want to eat it, you can add it yourself.Lu Zhi added some chili oil to himself before starting to eat.When the delicious and smooth rice noodles are eaten, your taste buds seem to be activated instantly. They are soft but chewy and have a bit of spiciness, which is simply delicious.Not to mention the shrimp balls, which contain almost 99% of shrimp. The main thing is that they are tender and elastic.The crab balls are different, they have a rich flavor and a soft texture.It's so deliciousThis bowl of rice noodles is extremely delicious because of the shrimp balls and crab balls, and even the soup.Jiang Hao kept a straight face and refrained from touching the rice noodles in front of him. "Little sister, it's not like you didn't know how to cook before."Did Zhou Chengan bully Lu Zhi? Otherwise, what happened to Lu Zhi's cooking skills?Yesterday, I was discussing with myself how to be a husband. Is it all a lie?Lu Zhi: Brother-in-law, I am interested in cooking and learned from reading books.Jiang Hao was relieved.In one meal, there was no rice noodles or even soup left.Jiang Hao was enjoying the meal and was waiting for me to ask my comrades to order this rice noodle.This is not difficult.Jiang Hao and Lu Yue often mail seafood from the island to some people, and the relationship between that comrade and Jiang Hao is also very good.

Chen Ting was looking around outside and came in carrying a watermelon. Is Sister Lu Zhi there?Zhou Chengan came out and pointed upstairs. My wife is taking a nap. Is there something wrong?Because Zhou Chengan spoke very quietly, Chen Ting did not dare to speak loudly, especially when she saw Zhou Chengan, she was even more nervous.Maybe Zhou Chengan didn't feel it, but when Chen Ting saw Zhou Chengan, she felt her feet were a little weak and scared.Chen Ting: My sister-in-law told me to give this to Sister Lu Zhi.After delivering the things, Chen Ting ran out quickly and patted her chest.When Chen Ting returned home, Deputy Battalion Commander Chen was reading the newspaper in the yard.Deputy Battalion Commander Chen: I'm backChen Ting: Brother, you haven't seen how Chen Yu treats me. That deputy captain, besides having a nice face, being able to cook and work, what else is good about him? Big deal, I told Chen Yu to learn how to cook, that would be great.Deputy Battalion Commander Chen: You have never seen Deputy Commander Zhou treat his wife well.Chen Ting doesn't believe it, she definitely doesn't believe itChen Yu was kind to her.Fortunately, both brothers and sisters thought they had won and were the victors. Today, the Chen family's yard was actually a little clean and there was no quarrel.

When Lu Zhi woke up, he found Zhou Chengan gently fanning himself with a cattail leaf fan.There is a fan at home, but Lu Zhi feels uncomfortable when the fan blows for a long time, especially when he takes a nap. The fan blows for several hours and he wakes up, which makes him feel a little uncomfortable.Lu Zhi rubbed his face.She must be in a mess now, and she wants to wash her face when she gets up.Zhou Chengan looked at her and smiled.Lu Zhi: Why are you laughing?Zhou Chengan: Cute.When he got to the bathroom, Lu Zhi looked at himself in the mirror and fell silent.Lu Zhi:So, that is, do their aesthetics really differ, or does Zhou Chengan have a filter for himself? This is a question worth thinking about.Lu Zhi came out: Is Xiaojun back?Zhou Chengan: I haven't come back yet. I'm probably still at my second sister's house.The kindergarten was also on holiday, and Zhou Jun went back with Lu Yue and Jiang Hao.Just as he was talking, Zhou Jun came back.Zhou Jun: Sister-in-lawZhou Jun ran up quickly. He was sweating from running, and he felt hot just looking at him.Lu Zhi: Take a rest, drink some water, and wash your hands.Only then did Zhou Chengan think of watermelons. The man next door had just come over and brought some watermelons.Lu Zhi: Who sent it here?Zhou Chengan: Deputy Battalion

Commander Chen's sister.Lu Zhi:Forget it, you still have to eat watermelon.Downstairs, a family of three was eating sweet and refreshing watermelon in the yard.After Zhou Chengan finished eating, he went to water the vegetable garden again.

Deputy Battalion Commander Chen's family had already given gifts to Lu Zhi and the others twice, and Lu Zhi had to return the gift no matter what.There aren't many things that can be given in return at this time.Therefore, Lu Zhi and Zhou Chengan's topic at night turned to giving something to Deputy Battalion Commander Chen's home.Lu Zhi: Is it good to dry vegetables?Before Zhou Chengan could answer, Lu Zhi denied it again.Lu Zhi: Pastry bar, there are still some unopened pastries that my brother-in-law brought back.Zhou Chengan: OK.Lu Zhi: Okay, that's it, we've decided to send cakes.Now sleeping in the same bed as Zhou Chengan, Lu Zhi doesn't feel any psychological pressure at all, and sometimes even falls asleep in his arms.Zhou Chengan sighed slightly, then got up and went to the bathroom.It's best if everything works out as it should.

Lu Zhi was a little busy on Monday.Lu Zhi received a letter from Chen Jiaojiao in the capital, and also received a letter from her parents, eldest brother and sister-in-law. Together, there were twenty or thirty letters.Lu Zhi probably took a day to write a reply.In addition, there are also Chen Jiaojiao's remittance orders and tickets, which are for Zhou Jun's living expenses.Grandpa and Grandma Zhou also presented pickled sour beans and some dried vegetables they had dried. Lu Xiangde and Li Lan also presented some tickets.Beside the window, Lu Zhi sat on a chair and read the letter seriously.Sister Lu's work has been going very well recently, and Brother Lu seems to be becoming a regular employee. Lu Xiangde is preparing for the exam, and Li Lan is also working hard, preparing to take the factory officer exam.Li Lan supervised Brother Lu and Sister Lu's studies, and also followed suit. This learning was remarkable.If anyone in the family is not motivated, Li Lan will have a heart-to-heart talk with them about such things as ideological enlightenment.Li Lan also told Lu Zhi a secret, that is, she was going to take the officer exam, which made her feel a little uneasy.Lu Zhi wrote the most replies to Li Lan and kept encouraging Li Lan.Lu An'an, the youngest of the Lu family, couldn't write letters. Sister-in-law Lu helped convey the message. Lu An'an told Lu Zhi to eat well. Lu Zhi even laughed out loud and asked her friends, Zhou Jun.Therefore, the child Lu Anan also received a reply alone.Lu Zhi's mother-in-law, Chen Jiaojiao's letters are particularly interesting. They are all about things that usually happen to her in the factory.Lu Zhi was amused several times.One of the funniest things was that Chen Jiaojiao said that when young people in their factory fall in love, it seems that some kind of confession is popular, but Lu Zhi's father-in-law never confessed to him at first.Chen

Jiaojiao was too embarrassed to tell Lu Zhi's father-in-law about this matter. Although Chen Jiaojiao was now doted on by Lu Kai, she always felt that she was the mother-in-law, so she was embarrassed.Lu Zhi suggested that Chen Jiaojiao could try saying "I like you" to Lu Kai, and maybe there would be a surprise.Lu Zhi's replies were all very serious. Just like these letters he received, you can see their seriousness between the lines.Lu Zhi's hands were a little sore.When Zhou Chengan came back, Lu Zhi called him and told him everything.Lu Zhi cooks delicious food, but rarely cooks. Most of the time, Zhou Chengan cooks or cooks in the canteen.Zhou Chengan, who was planning to go to the cafeteria, saw Lu Zhi putting letters in envelopes and reached out to help.Zhou Chengan: What did my mother say?Lu Zhi: I don't want to tell you.Zhou Chengan raised his eyebrows and stopped asking. Looking at Lu Zhi's look, he knew that she and Chen Jiaojiao were writing letters and seemed very happy.Lu Zhi waited for a minute, and the envelopes were all packed.Lu Zhi was shocked. You really stopped asking.Zhou Chengan nodded.Oh my God, when Li Cuihua saw Zhou Chengan, she probably didn't know what to say.Lu Zhi: You really don't want to knowZhou Cheng settled down for a while and sat down aside. What did my mother say?Lu Zhi took the envelope back, I won't tell you.Zhou Cheng Ansi took the exam for a while and couldn't help but chase him out. Zhizhi, just tell me, okay?Ah ah ahTheir old Zhou really knows how to fall in love.Lu Zhi kept a straight face and said nothing.Zhou Chengan called him "Zhizhi" in a low voice.Comrade Zhou, you committed a foul, do you know it?Lu Zhi won't let himself show other expressions. You go back and see for yourself.Zhou Chengan: I want to hear what you say.Lu Zhi finally reached out and pinched Zhou Chengan's cheek, "Old Zhou, are you self-taught?"Zhou Chengan: This is considered self-taught.Lu Zhi: Why can't he be considered self-taught?You tell meDon't tell me, don't tell me, you can see for yourself, I'm going to go next door to deliver snacks.Today, he was busy reading and replying to letters. Lu Zhi ate lunch and made do with leftovers from the morning, and then continued writing replies after waking up from his nap, forgetting about the pastries.When Lu Zhi arrived next door, Li Qiaozhen was washing vegetables in the yard.Lu Zhi: Hello, sister-in-law. My brother-in-law brought some pastries back for you. They are quite delicious. The ones with jujube paste are especially delicious.Li Qiaozhen enthusiastically helped Lu Zhi sit down in their yard.Li Qiaozhen: Look, you are still thinking of me. You are sitting, and the vegetables in the garden are ripe. I am picking some cucumbers for you, and there are radishes for you to eat.Lu Zhi:Li Qiaozhen picked a full basket for Lu Zhi.Lu Zhi: Sister-in-law, that's not necessary.Li Qiaozhen: I live next door to my neighbor, so please don't be polite to me.Deputy Battalion Commander Chen Chen He came back, and Lu Zhi stood up. Deputy Battalion Commander Chen, I am Lu Zhi, Zhou Chengan's lover next door.Chen He: Oh, Qiaozhen, why don't you pour her a glass of water? Sit down quickly and I'll pour you some water.This is really passionate, so passionate.Chen He poured water for Lu Zhi, which was still brown sugar water.Brown sugar water is a good thing at this time.Lu Zhi felt a little embarrassed.When they returned, Lu Zhi was still carrying a basket of vegetables. Li Qiaozhen said it was for Lu Zhi, cucumbers and radishes, but in fact it also contained green onions and coriander for Lu Zhi.Li He: If you have free time these days, let's come over for dinner.Lu Zhi:

The evening breeze blew the curtains gently.Zhou Chengan looked at the letter written by Chen Jiaojiao and paused slightly when he saw that Chen Jiaojiao said that two young people in their factory confessed their love.Hearing the noise outside, Zhou Chengan put the letter away and went downstairs.Zhou Chengan: The cakes were delivered.Lu Zhi: I sent it to their house. They were so enthusiastic.The enthusiastic Lu Zhi even doubted whether they were his relatives.Zhou Chengan: Passionate.Lu Zhi nodded, yes.Zhou Chengan: Fortunately, I acted quickly.Lu Zhi raised his eyes and looked at him, so you are praising me.Zhou Chengan: Yes.Ah ah ah ah ahIt feels like my mouth is grinning.

Chapter 25, Zhou Jun came back from school.As a

repaying favor, Zhou Jun came back from kindergarten with clean clothes and schoolbag. He squatted under the faucet in the yard and washed his chubby hands.Lu Zhi brought Zhou Jun soap, and Zhou Jun washed it seriously.Lu Zhi: Who did you play with in kindergarten?Zhou Jun frowned and then said: There are many children playing together.They all want to play with him.The one who had the best time was Li Weidong, because Zhou Jun knew Li Weidong before he went to kindergarten.When Zhou Jun was trying to rinse his hands with water, Lu Zhi foamed up some soap and spread it on Zhou Jun's face.Lu Zhi: Okay, let's wash our faces too.Dinner is served tonight.What Zhou Chengan brought back today was spicy fried clams made in the cafeteria, as well as a dish of fried potatoes and winter melon clam soup.Lu Zhi was more interested in the winter melon and clam soup because the soup was light and fresh. She drank a small bowl of winter melon and clam soup and only ate a little rice.Lu Zhi: Today, I received a letter from my sister-in-law. An An doesn't know how to write letters, so my sister-in-law conveyed it to you and asked you.Speaking of which, it's still a bit weird.But there is no way, Zhou Jun is senior, and together with Lu Zhi, they call Brother Lu and Sister Lu "big brother and sister-in-law".Zhou Jun: I also want to play with An An. I like playing with An An the most.Lu Zhi: Where is Tuantuan?Zhou Jun is a little confused, An AnGood guy, I'm still An An.Lu Zhi: Wait a minute, I am writing a letter to tell my sister-in-law that

I will call you and An An on the next weekend, okay?Zhou Jun said happily: OK

After Lu Zhi finished taking a bath, he went to check on Zhou Jun. Zhou Jun was already asleep.very goodChildren go to kindergarten, so they will be tired when they come back, and then they will fall asleep quickly.Lu Zhi went back and got his camera and called Zhou Chengan, "Old Zhou, I want to take pictures."Zhou Chengan wanted to get a flashlight, but Lu Zhi said: The lights haven't been turned off yet.When they arrived at Zhou Jun's room, Lu Zhi looked at Zhou Jun who had kicked the quilt away again. It was a small one but occupied a large space. He took a camera and took a quick photo.When going out, Lu Zhi did not forget to pull up the quilt for Zhou Jun.Lu Zhi remembered something. Tomorrow, let's take some more photos. After they are developed, I will mail a few to my parents, and my second sister will also take a few together.After Lu Yue got married on the island, she also sent photos to her family, but not many, just a few. This time Lu Zhi also took more photos for them.Zhou Chengan: OK.It was almost lights out, and Zhou Chengan went to take a shower.Finally, they also stopped.Zhou Chengan: Childish.Lu Zhi: YeahZhou Chengan: I like you.Lu Zhi, who originally planned to go to bed and was waiting for him to help fan him in Zhou Chengan's arms, subconsciously raised his head and met Zhou Chengan's lips.His lips were soft.At first it was just kissing, but later it turned into rubbing hands.Zhou

Chengan: Zhizhi, I like you.Later, when Lu Zhi was extremely sleepy, he glanced outside and saw that it was almost dawn.

It was already noon when Lu Zhi woke up. She hadn't slept in like this for a long time.There was a note left by Zhou Chengan on the table. He went to the military camp and gave Lu Zhi breakfast, which was downstairs.After reading the note for a while, Lu Zhi got up and went to wash up.She felt that if she were the female protagonist, Zhou Chengan would be a standard male protagonist.Zhou Chengan made a special trip back at noon.When Lu Zhi saw him, he had just come down from upstairs and his face was slightly red.Hold it backShe is not embarrassed.Then I discovered that Zhou Chengan's ears seemed to be red.Zhou Chengan: I came back from lunch.Lu Zhi: I haven't had breakfast yet.At noon, Zhou Chengan had breakfast with Lu Zhi.They seemed to be getting closer.

In the afternoon, Lu Zhi took his camera to Lu Yue's house.Lu Yue: My camera. It's a good camera. I just took a few photos and mailed them back together.Lu Zhi: That's what I mean, let's take pictures of Tuantuan.Tuantuan sat in the cradle, yawning, and when he saw Lu Zhi looking at him, he immediately waved his chubby arms to Lu Zhi.Wow, so cuteLu Zhi quickly took a picture of Tuantuan.Li Lan and Lu Xiangde have always liked the vegetable garden. They couldn't grow vegetables in the courtyard, so Lu Zhi took Tuantuan to the vegetable garden again to take pictures of Tuantuan.After that, he took another photo of Li Lan.On an island, you always have to go to the beach to take pictures.Lu Zhi: When our old Zhou, brother-in-law and Xiaojun come back, let's go to the beach to take pictures together.Lu Yue: Okay, let's eat in the cafeteria tonight, and I'll go find some clothes and put on makeup.Lu Zhi didn't need to clean up, she was wearing her own navy-style skirt.Tuantuan was handed over to Lu Zhi, who put the camera away and picked up Tuantuan. We were so cute together. After a while, we went to the beach to play and take pictures.I don't know if Tuantuan can understand it, but Lu Zhi plays with her and talks to her, which makes her very happy.Lu Zhi was a little panicked and wanted to go back with Tuantuan in his arms.Li Cuihua who was passing by saw Lu Zhi coming. Lu Zhi was coming.Lu Zhi: Sister-in-law Cuihua.Li Cuihua: Is it hot? Wait, I'll get you some fruit.Lu Zhi: No need, Sister-in-law Cuihua.Li Cuihua: Don't be polite to me. Wait a minute.Soon, Li Cuihua came back and brought Lu Zhi a pineapple.Lu Zhi was surprised, it was a pineappleLi Cuihua: My relatives brought this to me. They brought a lot of it. Eat it quickly. This fruit is quite delicious. It's a little bit chewy when you eat it.After thinking about it for a long time, Li Cuihua remembered how to say, "It's so scary to prick it." It's strange. You said this fruit, how can it be so prickly?Lu Zhi: Soak in some water, salt water.Li Cuihua was surprised that fruits can still be soaked in water.If Lu Zhi wanted to explain to Li Cuihua, it would probably take a long time, and Li Cuihua might not be able to understand it. The key was that it was a bit troublesome, so she simply said directly: "I read it in a book, just soak in it for ten minutes."Lu Zhi gave the pineapple to Li Cuihua to help look after it. She went to the kitchen to process the pineapple, then soaked it in salt water before coming out.While Lu Zhi was waiting for the pineapple, he was talking to Li Cuihua.Li Cuihua: Let me tell you, do you know the house next door to your sister?Lu Zhi looked over, then shook his head, I don't know.This is another melonLi Cuihua: The man in their family had his first love on the island. Before, his first love went to work in the city. Recently he was transferred back, but there was some quarrel.As he spoke, he looked excited.Lu Yue came out of the shower, Sister-in-law Cuihua.Lu Zhi: Second sister, come here quickly, this pineapple is ready to eat.Pineapple is sweet and so deliciousLu Zhi was still thinking that it would be nice if there were more pineapples to make fried rice.Li Cuihua took a bite and patted her thigh. Really, there was no prick at all. This was also the first time I had eaten this thing.Saying that, wait a minute, I will bring you two more pineapples. My relatives gave me a lot this time.Very good, pineapple fried rice is ready to eat.Lu Zhi: Thank you, sister-in-law Cuihua.Soon, Lu Zhi and Lu Yue each got another pineapple.

Lu Zhi went to pick up Zhou Jun from school, and then brought Zhou Jun over, but Tuantuan in his arms always wanted to be with Lu Zhi.Lu Zhi: No, it's a bit far. I can't hold you. You're too tired.Tuantuan: Yeah yeah yeah.Lu Zhi: I'll be back in a while.Tuantuan: Yeah, yeah, yeah.Lu Zhi: Okay, it's settled, you wait for me.Tuantuan: Yeah yeah, yeah yeah~After giving Lu Yue a hug, Lu Zhi went to kindergarten.When I went out, I met Zhou Chengan.Lu Zhi: Lao ZhouJust in time, you can go with Zhou Chengan, or Zhou Chengan can go to the kindergarten to pick up Zhou Jun.Lu Zhi was a little confused.Zhou Chengan was not in a hurry and looked at Lu Zhi.Lu Zhi: Okay, you go to the kindergarten to pick up Zhou Jun.Zhou Chengan smiled, okay, can I bring you ice cream when I come back?Lu Zhi nodded, okayAfter returning, Lu Zhi hugged Tuan Tuan in his arms again.Lots of surprises: babble ah ah ~Looking at the young and old, Lu Yue couldn't help but smile and shook his head, "Zhizhi, do you prefer a son or a daughter?"Lu Zhi: I like both my daughter and my son.Of course, it doesn't matter if you have a daughter or a son, it's best if you can be like Tuantuan, Zhou Jun, and An An.Ah ah ah ah ahHow could she forget that she did not plan to have children for the time being, and her family, Lao Zhou, was still using birth control.

When the four adults and two Zai Zai arrived at the beach, it was very lively.Lu Zhi took the camera and took individual photos of each of them, and then group photos.When taking a group photo, Zhou Chengan asked Jiang Dong, who happened to be at the beach, to help them take a group photo together.Lu Zhi held the camera. Let me take a picture for you. I will give it to you after it is developed.Jiang Dong: Thank you, sister-in-lawLu Zhi: Lao Zhou, why don' t you buy some more film and ask your people who want to take pictures to help take a group photo together and then mail it back.Zhou Chengan looked down at Lu Zhi and smiled softly, "Okay, I will listen to you."Jiang Dong: Sister-in-law, you are so kind

Chapter 26The two families went to the cafeteria to eat together.What we ate in the cafeteria tonight were noodles or noodles with soybean paste, which was a very surprising thing.The rich-colored sauce is mixed into the white noodles, and is garnished with refreshing cucumber shreds. It tastes really refreshing.Lu Zhi didn't have any leftovers today. He ate very cleanly. He was probably a little tired from playing today.Tuantuan likes to cling to Lu Zhi, but he is very sensible and waits until Lu Zhi has finished eating before asking Lu Zhi to hug him.When he went back, Tuantuan was always in Lu Zhi's arms.Lu Zhi: Even if you are young now, I won' t be able to hold you when you are older.How could Tuantuan know this? She just thought Lu Zhi liked her.Soon we arrived at Lu Yue's house.Lu Yue took over the tuan tuan, okay, here we are. After finishing speaking, he looked at Lu Zhi again, Zhizhi, don't forget to bring the pineapple. By coincidence, I have some shrimps here, you can take them back together.Lu Zhi smiled, "Okay, second sister."Lu Yue stood outside the yard with Tuan Tuan and Jiang Hao in her arms. Seeing Lu Zhi and his family of three, she couldn't help but smile with joy.

Finally arriving home, Lu Zhi lay on the bed and was too lazy to move. He was really tired.Fortunately, he had already taken a shower before, otherwise it would be impossible, absolutely impossible for Lu Zhi to get up from the bed.Zhou Chengan took out the film. Tomorrow, I will ask someone to take it to the city to develop the photos. Should you mail it back with the letter, or wait until the photos are developed?Lu Zhi: How long will it take to get the photos back after developing them?Zhou Chengan: It will take a few days.Lu Zhi: Let's mail the letter together and develop the photos a little more. In addition to the ones for them, we'll also keep a copy.Zhou Chengan nodded, okay.When he was about to turn off the lights and go to sleep, Lu Zhi met his eyes and quickly turned over.Impossible, absolutely impossibleThe fact that she is so tired today has something to do with Zhou Chengan.When the room became dark, Lu Zhi felt himself being held in Zhou Chengan's arms.Zhou Chengan: Zhizhi, good night.Fortunately, he is still very considerate.

Chen He and Li Qiaozhen are not asleep yet.The couple talked.Chen He: It would be best to create opportunities for Lu Zhi and Li Ting to get along. She snorted softly as she spoke. Seeing how proud she was, the state-owned hotel was serving steamed buns today, so Chen Yu brought some for her.Li Qiaozhen: I have an idea.Chen He: What method?Li Qiaozhen: I heard that the food factory is looking for temporary workers, but it hasn't been decided yet. How about I reveal the news to Lu Zhi first and then think of a solution? Lu Zhi and Chen Ting are in the same workshop.Chen He: Is the situation about temporary workers true or false?It's hard to find jobs on the island.Li Qiaozhen: It's basically settled.Chen He: Yes, yes, Chen Ting should have more contact with people like Lu Zhi. Look around her. I can't look down on any of those who are good at playing.Now, Chen He was in a relaxed mood.

Early in the morning, Lu Zhi really wanted to take back his idea that Zhou Chengan was very considerate.When he got downstairs, Lu Zhi stood in the yard and basked in the sun. He was very comfortable, but a little hot.Li Qiaozhen, come here and bask in the sunLu Zhi: Sister-in-law Qiaozhen, come in quickly.When they arrived in the living room, Lu Zhi poured water for Li Qiaozhen.Li Qiaozhen is holding the water. Do you know my sister Chen Ting?Seeing Lu Zhi nod, Li Qiaozhen continued. She works in a food factory. I heard that the food factory may be hiring temporary workers. If you have ideas, take this time to learn more. Take the exam. If you don't understand something, you can ask my sister.Lu Zhi:Lu Zhi still knows that finding a job is not easy.Sometimes the main focus is an information gap.Lu Zhi: Sister-in-law Qiaozhen, you also need to prepare for the exam.Li Qiaozhen was a real person. She sighed slightly and told the whole story.Good guy.Finally I understand why the people in their family are so enthusiastic.Lu Zhi: I'm afraid that's not possible. I don't really want to go to work in a food factory.How boring.Li Qiaozhen: We, Mr. Chen, are really worried about this sister, but the bet has been won. Otherwise, you can do this favor for your sister-in-law.Lu Zhi: Sister-in-law, I won't hide it from you either. I've been on a blind date with Chen Yu before.Li Qiaozhen squirted out a mouthful of water, and then trembled with anger. He was so good at deceiving people.Chen Ting, Li Qiaozhen and Chen He told Chen Yu that his blind date came to the island to join the army. What did he say? He said that this blind date liked him and was a little crazy after being rejected by him.Lu Zhi:Li Qiaozhen, get up. I'll be back soon. I want to see if Chen Ting is also blind.

The episode at Deputy Battalion Commander Chen's house did not affect Lu Zhi. She slowly and simply made lunch for herself and spread the quilt.When Chen Ting came over, her eyes were a little red.As soon as she entered Lu Zhi's courtyard, she saw a picture of a beautiful woman.Is there anything else you can ask?How could this man be so dishonest?Chen Ting stamped her feet and ran away crying.Li Qiaozhen looked at Lu Zhi sheepishly, and after saying a few words, she quickly chased after him.After Zhou Chengan came back, Lu Zhi told him about it.Zhou

Chengan asked: Do you want to work?Lu Zhi: It's not that it's hard to find a job on an island. After that, he added: I don't want to go to a food factory, it's boring.Zhou Chengan: Where is the teacher?Teachers with winter and summer vacationsLu Zhi: Is the school looking for a teacher?Zhou Chengan helped her tuck her hair. There were more and more children on the island, and there were also a lot of new students entering school next time. Therefore, the island needed to recruit teachers, but they also had to take exams. In a few days, the news would be announced.Lu Zhi: Okay, I'll prepare for the exam.This is much more interesting than temporary work in a food factory.

Today Lu Zhi is going to make pineapple fried rice. Lu Zhi specially kept the pineapple from yesterday.Lu Zhi plans to use half of the pineapple for fried rice, and half of the pineapple will be soaked in salt water and eaten directly.Pineapple fried rice is simple. Cut the pineapple pulp into pieces. When the oil in the pot is hot, add the eggs and shrimps and stir-fry. Then add the rice. When it is fried, stir-fry it with the pineapple for a while. .Lu Zhi directly served the fried rice with pineapple skin cut into two pieces, and placed another portion on a plate.Zhou Jun looked at it eagerly, sister-in-law, why can fruits also be fried rice?Lu Zhi: Yes, it's delicious.Children who have never eaten fruit fried rice will probably like the taste after eating it, not to mention that Zhou Jun seems to like eating pineapple.But what if you don't like it?Do you want to do something else?Zhou Jun: Wow, sister-in-law, you are so awesome.Looking at the pineapple fried rice, Zhou Jun's eyes were shining.Okay, no need, just have pineapple fried rice.Zhou Jun particularly likes the pineapple fried rice, which is sweet and not greasy at all. It is also very novel.Lu Zhi and Zhou Jun ate fried rice served with pineapple skins, while Zhou Chengan served it on a plate.When Li Cuihua passed by Lu Zhi, she didn't forget to shout, "Lu Zhi, Lu Zhi, the state-owned hotel is busy, hurry up, hurry up, hurry up"Without thinking, I knew it must be Chen Yu and Chen Ting.As one of the protagonists, Lu Zhi felt that he had better go and see it, otherwise he would be framed by Chen Yu, and it would not be easy to explain when the time comes.When Lu Zhi got up, Zhou Chengan knew what Lu Zhi meant and said, "I'll go with you."Zhou Jun hadn't finished his meal yet, so he wanted to go out with them.Lu Zhi: Children, please cook well at home.Zhou Jun ran over again and continued to cook.

When we arrived at the state-owned hotel, it was very lively outside.Everyone who was eating inside had come out, and there was an outrageous number of people squatting outside with their bowls in their hands to watch.Chen Ting burst into tears, liar, you liar, you said that your blind date was rejected by you, but in fact, it was you who rejected the blind date, are you crazy?Chen Yu didn't expect that Chen Ting would cause trouble like this.Lu Zhi knew why. Chen Ting was a bit of a love-minded person. It was true that she was willing to go on a blind date with Chen Yu, and it was also true that she collapsed because of Chen Yu.Chen Yu is anxious. You must have been deceived by her. Let's talk about it when we go back. Don't talk about it here.Li Qiaozhen: Don't say it here, don't say it here, you continue to lie to my sisterChen Yu: I really don't.Chen Ting shouted loudly: Chen Yu, do you think I am blind or do you think my eyesight is not good enough? You don't even look at who your blind date is, who actually said such things.Everyone wants to know who it is.Who is Chen Yu's former blind date?I don't know, but it must look good.Is it possible that Chen Ting misunderstood?What's going on?Li Cuihua was next to Lu Zhi. She never stopped talking and looked extremely excited.Chen Yu saw Lu Zhi and Zhou Chengan, but he was betting that these two people would not come forward, and Chen Ting's family would not tell them either.Chen Yu: Chen Ting, you have to believe me, feelings are not about looks or knowledge.Lu Zhi thinks Chen Yu's acting skills are also great.As expected, some people around him began to believe what Chen Yu said.Lu Zhi felt Zhou Chengan hold her hand. She looked over and saw Zhou Chengan nodded to her.If Lu Zhi wants to help, Zhou Chengan agrees.Lu Zhi said nothing. She was waiting for the reaction of the Li family. If they said it, Lu Zhi would not come forward. If they did not say it, Lu Zhi would come forward.After waiting for a while, Chen Yu had already started to say: Everyone, please stop standing here, the restaurant is still open. After saying that, she looked at Chen Ting, "Okay, let's go back and say, you have to believe me, I really only like you," she said. She didn't say anything about my blind date.Lu Zhi smiled and said: What happened to me?Everyone looked towards Lu Zhi.Li Cuihua: Oh my god, it's youAt this moment, someone actually laughed.Ha ha ha ha ha ha ha.Chen Yu, where is your face?Lu Zhi went crazy because of youChen Yu's face was extremely ugly, and there was a lot of ridicule around him.If it was Lu Zhi, no one would believe what Chen Yu said.

Chapter 27Chen Yu wanted to explain, but he stood in front of Lu Zhi and couldn't utter a single word of sophistry.After organizing the words, because Zhou Chengan stood beside Lu Zhi, looking at him coldly, he felt as if his throat was blocked again.Listening to the ridicule of the people around him, Chen Yu blushed and ran back.I have to say, it's good to see that Lu Zhi has this kind of ability at his level.Deputy Battalion Commander Chen and his family looked grateful, and Chen He even stepped forward to thank Lu Zhi.Chen Ting and Chen Yu are in a free relationship, and they are still a bit shaky at this time. Lu Zhi is hesitant to speak.Lu Zhi would definitely not do such a thing as comforting a lovelorn person.Lu Zhi: Let's go to the beach first.Lu Zhi specially went to the beach with Zhou Chengan. This time he didn't take Zhou Jun with him, just the two of them.Seems a bit romanticZhou Chengan did not go back directly with Lu Zhi. The two of them walked on the beach together for a while. Lu Zhi stepped on the beach and looked at Zhou Chengan's feet. Only then did he realize that Zhou Chengan's feet were They all seem beautiful.Lu Zhi couldn't hold back and lightly stepped on Zhou Chengan with his sandy feet.Zhou Chengan looked at Lu Zhi with a smile.Lu Zhi is confident and good-looking.Zhou Chengan looked down at his feet and then at Lu Zhi's feet. He felt that his feet were not good-looking, but Lu Zhi's feet were good-looking.

Zhou Jun was very obedient. He ate at home and then played in the yard.Now I am squatting here in the vegetable field, looking at the sprouting seeds in the vegetable field.Lu Zhi also went over and squatted down together. Wow, it has sprouted. We will be able to eat the vegetables we grew ourselves soon.She didn't forget at all that she didn't seem to be working in this vegetable field. The one who did the work was basically Zhou Chengan.Zhou Jun: Sister-in-law is really greatLu Zhi: I also think our Xiaojun is great too.All the children, one big and one small, were very happy.After returning home, Lu Zhi was even more surprised to find that Zhou Jun had cleared all the tables.Back upstairs, a family of three was listening to the radio in the house.The most laid-back person was Zhou Jun, lying on the bed shaking his legs, while Lu Zhi and Zhou Chengan were having fun.

Early in the morning, Li Qiaozhen came to Lu Zhi and gave Lu Zhi many things.Yesterday, Li Qiaozhen and Chen He had been persuading Chen Ting. It was almost dawn when the two of them went to bed. Chen He went to the military camp early in the morning, but Chen Ting couldn't sleep and woke up too.There is a bag of food, most of which are dried seafood and a portion of ribs.Lu Zhi: You really don't need it, it's just a little effort. I'm embarrassed if you do this.Li Qiaozhen pushed the thing into Lu Zhi's hand. Just take it. You don't know what we, Lao Chenchou, were like some time ago. After saying that, he hurried back, not forgetting to wave his arm to Lu Zhi, "Go back quickly."Lu Zhi had no choice but to take the things back, planning to tell Zhou Chengan when he came back, and then give something to Li Qiaozhen and the others. This would make things even.After eating the breakfast that Zhou Chengan brought back, Lu Zhi went upstairs to read.By the time it was noon, Lu Zhi felt so tired that his waist was a little sore, so he got up and stretched out for a walk.Today on the island, everyone is discussing the island's recruitment of teachers. Many people are ready to make a move. If it weren't for the lack of education of some people, there would probably be a quarrel by now.Lu Zhi knew about this and was not surprised.After wandering around, we arrived at Lu

Yue's house.Lu Yue saw Lu Zhi and said angrily: "You do know how to be a hero."Lu Zhi: Second sister.Lu Yue: I don't care about others, I only care about you, and you can just rely on your appearance. After finishing speaking, he let Lu Zhi come in and poured brown sugar water for Lu Zhi.Lu Zhi: Do you know that the school is looking for a teacher?Lu Yue: I know, but I still have to lead the group.I'm so successful today, I'm actually crawling around and trying to stand up.There is really no way to take care of the child, otherwise Lu Yue would like to give it a try. It would be easy if Tuantuan goes to kindergarten, but that's how taking care of children is.In the afternoon, Lu Zhi played with Tuantuan. Tuantuan, a little Zaizai, played with Lu Zhi for a while and then fell asleep in the cradle.Lu Zhi stood next to the cradle and poked her fair and tender face.Well, that's fun.Lu Yue: You and Cheng Anye have been married for a month or two, right?Lu Zhi understood the implication of Lu Yue's words, pursed his lips and smiled without saying much.

In the evening, Lu Zhi cooked pork ribs.Blanch the pork ribs and take them out. Heat the oil in the pot and stir-fry the sugar with white sugar. After the pork ribs start to stir-fry, they will soon be coated with sugar and look very appetizing.If there is rock sugar, it is best to use rock sugar, but unfortunately Lu Zhi only has white sugar now.The pork ribs in the pot continued to simmer. Lu Zhi also added two kinds of seasonings and vinegar, white vinegar and mature vinegar, and also added some white sugar.Zhou Chengan smelled the fragrance when he came back, and it tasted very similar to sweet and sour.When he got to the kitchen, Zhou Chengan asked: What are you doing?Lu Zhi: Sweet and sour pork ribs.After telling Zhou Chengan what happened today, Lu Zhi said: I originally planned to think about how to return the gift, and it was considered even. When I was doing it, I found that there were quite a lot of ribs. I would send some to them later. Then I'll give you something else next time.Zhou Chengan nodded, okay.After the ribs were done, Lu Zhisheng came out and asked Zhou Chengan to deliver them while she and Zhou Jun cleared the table for dinner.Zhou Jun's mouth almost watered.Zhou Jun: Sister-in-law, sister-in-law, why is there no fruit in this, but it is sweet and sour? The ones I have eaten before did not taste like this, and were not as fragrant as this one.A child, a young child, has a hundred thousand reasons.Lu Zhi thought about how to answer.Zaizai, who repays his kindness, has already thought of the answer by himself. I know it is because my sister-in-law is the most powerful, right?Lu Zhi:Very good, very good, let's continue according to this logic from now on, little fat man.Zhou Chengan took the ribs to the next door.Chen He was intoxicated by the smell next door and munching on steamed buns. When he saw Zhou Chengan, he came over and asked, Deputy Commander Zhou, why are you here.In fact, looking at the sweet and sour pork ribs held by Zhou Chengan, I felt like I was almost running over there.This,

this, this, this is giving them better sweet and sour pork ribsZhou Chengan: My lover told me to send it here.Chen He: How embarrassing. After finishing speaking, the conversation changed. I am not a pretentious person, and I will not be polite to you anymore.Seeing Zhou Chengan go back, Chen He quickly went back with the sweet and sour pork ribs. The next door brought sweet and sour pork ribs.Chen He helped with the work, and soon the Chen family had dinner.Chen Ting is still immersed in the emotion of breaking up with Chen Yu. No, they haven't broken up yet, and she hasn't officially said they broke up yet.Smelling the smell of sweet and sour pork ribs, Chen Ting, who didn't want to eat, swallowed.Chen Ting was very reserved at first. When she ate the sweet and sour pork ribs, she just wanted to cook.Chen Yu will talk to you later.The sweet and sour pork ribs are juicy and delicious. When paired with a mouthful of rice, Chen Ting felt that she had never eaten such delicious pork ribs.After the meal was finished, the three people looked at each other in confusion.Chen He: Vice leader Zhou, this is a lucky marriage.Just smelling the smell next door, he felt that he was satisfied after eating it. Now that he had eaten it, Chen He felt that it would be even more difficult to smell the fragrance next door in the future.Chen Ting looked at the plate of sweet and sour pork ribs and felt even more uncomfortable.Ahhhhhhh, I want to eat sweet and sour pork ribs.That night, Chen Ting couldn't sleep, not because of Chen Yu, but because of the sweet and sour pork ribs

When Chen Ting found Lu Zhi, Lu Zhi was also a little surprised. She thought that Chen Ting wouldn't want to meet her because of Chen Yu, but she didn't expect that she would take the initiative to find her.Chen Ting looked hesitant, sister-in-law, can you accompany me to find Chen Yu? I want to formally break up with him.Lu Zhi: I won't accompany you, but I want to go to a state-owned restaurant for dinner, is that okay?Chen Ting: Thank you sister-in-lawThe two of them set off together.When we arrived at the state-owned restaurant, one went to order food and the other went to find Chen Yu.Chen Ting calmed down. She looked at Chen Yu who was standing opposite her, thinking that Chen Yu would defend herself. However, Chen Yu didn't say a word, and Chen Ting was even more disheartened by him.Chen Ting: Let's break up.Chen Yu: Just this matterChen Ting slapped him in the face, and this matterLu Zhi:Good guy, call me Li Cuihua, Li Cuihua will probably join you.Chen Yu touched his burning cheek. He was already embarrassed. When he saw Lu Zhi eating in a state-owned restaurant, he felt even more uncomfortable.Chen Yu: Is there anything else?Chen Ting was so angry that she slapped him again.Chen Yu:Chen Yu swallowed what he wanted to say and turned back to the state-owned hotel. The two of them officially broke up.Chen Ting and Lu Zhi ate together in a state-owned hotel. She ate faster and faster, but Lu Zhi said nothing.When the two of them were approaching home, Chen Ting looked at Lu Zhi and said in a serious tone, "Sister-in-law, thank you."Lu Zhi: Go back quickly.

When Zhou Chengan came back, Lu Zhi talked to him about becoming a teacher.Zhou Chengan had no objection and had told Lu Zhi about this matter before.Zhou Jun, the little fat man, looked at Lu Zhi with bright eyes, "Sister-in-law, I have become a primary school student. You will be my teacher, right?"Lu Zhi smiled, but shook his head, no.Zhou Jun looked at Lu Zhi eagerly, "My sister-in-law must have her reasons if she doesn't want to be my teacher."Lu Zhi couldn't help but pinch Zhou Jun's cheek.She didn't want to be Zhou Jun's teacher, not because she didn't want to teach Zhou Jun, but because Zhou Jun was learning from her every day, and now that she was back, maybe she would continue to teach Zhou Jun, which was boring.Lu Zhi: But, I like you.Zhou Jun suddenly smiled, sister-in-law, I like you too

Chapter 28It's another new day.Lu Zhi and the others got back the photos they took. Lu Zhi opened the envelope containing the photos and looked at them carefully one by one.The little fat Zhou Jun stood next to Lu Zhi. This is me, this is the sister-in-law, this is the eldest brother, this is the second sister, this is the second brother-in-law, and this is TuantuanZhou Jun raised his hand, my sister-in-law is the prettiestZhou Jun's eyes were sparkling, and he didn't look like he was lying at all. He was so sincere.Although Lu Zhi knew that he was good-looking, he felt a little embarrassed after being praised.Zhou Jun pushed his eldest brother who was sitting on the other side of Lu Zhi, eldest brother, you said what I said, right?Zhou Chengan looked serious. Well, you are right.For a moment, Lu Zhi seemed to see the mutual recognition between the two brothers.Ahhhhhh, you two are enough. If you are like this, she will drift off.

Lu Zhi took Zhou Jun to send photos to Lu Yue. Lu Yue looked happy while holding the photos and looked at them over and over again.Lu Yue: This one looks good, this one also looks good, and this one looks good to me.Lu Zhi was playing with Tuan Tuan. His white and tender little fingers did not grab Lu Zhi's hair, but only held Lu Zhi's clothes.Before crossing over, Lu Zhi had met some naughty children and some children who were only a few months old. However, he did not expect that after crossing over, all he would see were cubs who were repaying their kindness. ah.Tuantuan pulled Lu Yue's hair a few days ago. Lu Yue was in great pain. She talked to Tuantuan for a long time and acted like she was about to cry. As a result, Tuantuan cried, but she didn't like it very much afterward. Pulled hair.Lu Yue: At home, I will probably receive it tomorrow.Lu Zhi: You should receive it tomorrow.Lu Yue got up, I will put it away first. When I buy a photo album, I will buy a photo frame to store it properly.While the two were talking, Lu Zhi saw Tuantuan turning over in her cradle. She stood up excitedly, Second Sister, Second SisterLu Yue: What's wrong?Lu Zhi: Tuantuan just turned overEveryone gathered around, holding the rattle and shaking it hard with their little hands, but unfortunately they refused to turn over again.

As soon as Lu Zhi got home, Chen Ting came over. She must have been listening to the noise next door.Chen Ting looked good, and Lu Zhi was a little surprised. He thought that based on Chen Ting and Chen Yu's previous relationship, even if they knew Chen Yu's true face, they ended their relationship as boyfriend and girlfriend. Chen Ting, she It will also feel uncomfortable for a few days, or even for a long time.Maybe it's because he doesn't want to show it in front of outsiders like himself.Chen Ting brought the abalone over. Sister-in-law, this is the abalone. Take it as a token of my appreciation.Lu Zhi looked at the abalone in the net and smiled, doing it with just a few clicks.Chen Ting pushed it over, "Sister-in-law, just keep it. These things are not valuable on the island." I just put in some effort and went to sea with my brother in the morning.Lu Zhi: OK.Chen Ting: Sister-in-law, please come and sit at our house when you have time.Lu Zhi sat down in front of the faucet in the yard with a bag of abalone and began to handle the abalone. Zhou Jun sat aside and watched for a while, learned the lesson, and began to help seriously.Zhou Jun: Do we want to eat abalone tonight?Lu Zhi: Well, let's eat braised abalone.After processing the abalone, Zhou Chengan hasn't come back yet. He must be a little busy today.Blanch the abalone meat in the pot, don't throw away the abalone shells, blanch the abalone in water, it will still be useful after a while.After the oil in the pot was hot, Lu Zhi added chopped green onion and minced garlic, and the sound of sizzling was heard.After the braised sauce was made, Lu Zhi put the abalone in. After a while, the taste suddenly became delicious.One abalone shell and one abalone meat. Finally, pour the braised broth and sprinkle with a little fresh green onion.Zhou Jun swallowed hard, and Lu Zhi handed one to Zhou Jun first. It was a bit hot, so slow down.Crispy and tender abalone meat, rich sauce, and a little bit of green onion flavor, it is so deliciousZhou Jun: My sister-in-law is the best sister-in-law.Lu Zhi touched his hair. I went to the next door and will be back soon.

Li Qiaozhen cooked a meal and asked Chen Ting to eat. Although she had always felt that Chen Ting was confused, she felt distressed now.Li Qiaozhen: You said, you have to eat. Eat some. Today you and your elder brother went to sea. Instead of bringing abalone back, I made abalone.Hearing this, Chen Ting shook her head, I don't want to eat, sister-in-law, I really can't eat, you don't have to worry about me, I will just rest for a few days.Li Qiaozhen: Look what you said, if you don't eat, how can I not worry about you? Even if I go back, your elder brother will come to persuade you soon.Chen He was listening to their movements. When Li Qiaozhen mentioned himself, he strode over, "Chen Ting, let's eat."Chen Ting: Brother, I really can't eat, just let me take a rest.Chen Yu was Chen Ting's first date. At this moment, Chen Ting was still a little sad. She had sweet memories with Chen Yu. Now that she thought about it, she still felt like a fool.Chen Ting: Brother, sister-in-law, I went to see Chen Yu today to formally break up with him, and even slapped him, but I feel that I am still a little bit upset. When we first met, I blushed when I saw him for the first time.She was still recalling what happened between herself and Chen Yu.Lu Zhi came over: Sister-in-law Qiaozhen, I just made abalone and sent you some.What fish, abalone?Who did it? Lu Zhi did it.Chen Ting looked up and saw that Chen He, who was still frowning, had run out.Li Qiaozhen: Little sister, let me go out and take a look first.Chen Ting ran past Li Qiaozhen.Li Qiaozhen:When Chen Ting saw Lu Zhi, she seemed to be in a better mood than when she had just given the abalone to Lu Zhi. She even smiled, "Sister-in-law, I gave it to you, and you have already prepared it and delivered it to us." How embarrassing. Besides, I'm at home. Just call me and I'll come over.Lu Zhi was about to pass the plate to Chen Ting, but Chen He caught Lu Zhi's plate before Chen Ting.Lu Zhi: It's a bit troublesome to arrange the dishes, so I'll go back first. When you are free, just send me the plates.If it wasn't abalone that was brought over, they would probably have to scoop out the contents of the plate and give Lu Zhi the plate that Lu Zhi brought over, which would be more convenient.Chen He: Okay, I understand, wait until I clean it for you and send it over.When Lu Zhi was about to go home, they found that the Chen family next door were too enthusiastic and sent her to the door. If Lu Zhi hadn't stopped them, they would have sent Lu Zhi back.Chen He put the abalone on the stone table in the yard, and Chen Ting had already come over.Chen He: Didn't you say you don't want to eat?Chen Ting's face turned slightly red. Who said she wouldn't eat? This is the wish of the sister-in-law next door. I don't want to eat. I'm so embarrassed.After taking one bite, Chen He's expression lit up.Delicious, really delicious

After Zhou Chengan came back, he explained to Lu Zhi that he had to temporarily handle some things today.The family of three was preparing to have dinner. Zhou Cheng Ansai gave Lu Zhi some fruits and then went to work.Sitting on the armrest of the sofa, Lu Zhi watched Zhou Chengan busy.The fruit was very clean, and it looked like it had been washed. She was worried that it was a little sour, so she took a small bite and found that it tasted very sweet.Lu Zhi: You went to the mountains todayZhou Chengan: Well, I just came back from the mountains. Someone on the island said that they saw wild boars on the mountains. We looked around and couldn't find them. They were probably hidden. We have to go there again in the next few days, so you and Zhou Jun should not run to the mountains for the time being.Lu Zhi: Got it.Dinner includes braised abalone, spicy and sour cabbage, and a cabbage and tofu soup.Zhou Jun likes to eat rice with soup. One bowl of rice is not enough. After eating, he takes his rice bowl and goes to the kitchen to fill it up.Lu Zhi ate a bowl and wanted to serve some more. Before he could get up, Zhou Chengan reached out and took Lu Zhi's bowl. Half a bowl was still a full bowl.Lu Zhi: A little less than half a bowl.Zhou Chengan: OK.He held his chin with his hands and looked at Zhou Chengan. Who wouldn't like this kind of man?Zhou Jun came out, sister-in-law, do you want to serve rice? I can help you.Zhou Chengan: This is my wife. You can give her to your own wife from now on.Zhou Jun looked at Zhou Chengan with his hands on his hips, looking angry.Very good, as expected of you Zhou ChenganZhou Jun: Sister-in-law, when you are old, I will help you carry it. When the time comes, my eldest brother will be old too.Very good, as expected of you Zhou Jun, you understand your youth, no, you understand your youth.Zhou Chengan carried Zhou Jun to his seat. Thank you for reminding me. I will continue to exercise well in the future. My wife does not need you to serve food.

In the evening, Lu Zhi was a little full after all, so she was enjoying the cool air in the yard.Zhou Chengan was washing dishes in the yard, while Zhou Jun was playing in the yard. Looking at the two of them, Lu Zhi couldn't help but smile.This feeling is really good.

Chapter 29Lu Zhi was busy reviewing elementary school textbooks. Thanks to her experience as a tutor when she was in college, this did not trouble her.Knowing that it is not easy to find a job now, Lu Zhi is extra serious.The floral curtains were blown gently by the breeze. Looking at the scenery outside the window, Lu Zhi took a rest.After all, work and rest are combined.Think about it, the Lu family has probably received the letter.

Lu Xiangde received the letter and took it home without opening it. He waited until his family members came back from get off work and told them about it.Li Lan: You said you, but you didn't even look at what Zhizhi wrote when he came back, if something happened.Opening the envelope, there were more than a dozen photos inside. The first one was a photo of Lu Zhi's family and Lu Yue's family.Li Lan: Zhizhi is on the beach, and she has a conch in her hand. Xiaoyue looked a little rosier than the last time we went to see her, and her face was a little rosier. This one is Tuantuan, so cute.They huddled together at a table.Li Lan held the photo, this one, this one is beautiful, and she is still holding her arms tightly.Lu Anan, aunt, is auntSister-in-law Lu rubbed her daughter's soft hair, yes, it's aunt, these two are aunt, second aunt and younger aunt.Lu Anan nodded seriously, I will remember it.In addition to the photos, there is also a letter, also written by Lu

Zhi.The person who read the letter was Lu Da's sister-in-law: Mom, dad, brother, sister-in-law, and An'an, how are you doing lately? Everything is fine on the island. The house I live in is not by the sea, but I am here. You can see the sea from the terrace, which is similar to the second sister's house. A few days ago, I bought a camera and took some photos. I thought you were thinking of me. After I took the photos, I developed some more and mailed them to you.Sister-in-law Lu read very slowly and her voice was very soft. As she read, Hai couldn't help but laugh along with her.Li Lan: You bought a camera. It's good to buy a camera. Once you buy a camera, you can take more photos, and then mail them back to us after you take them.Everyone nodded in agreement.Sister-in-law Lu continued to read the letter. Now the swimming crabs are plump and plump. I have been pickling some for you in the past few days, as well as Pipi shrimps.After reading this, Mrs. Lu became a little greedy.The rest of the Lu family also remembered how delicious the pickled crab Lu Zhi sent back last time was.Already starting to look forward to it.

There will be a great harvest at sea today.Lu Zhi went to find Lu Yue, and the two of them went to the market to buy swimming crabs, and Lu Zhi made sauce crabs.Lu Yue wanted to give a larger portion. Lu Yue liked to eat it, and so did her brother-in-law. The Chen family next door gave some. They thanked Lu Yue. Lu Yue felt that it was not necessary, but was embarrassed to only accept their things. And She also wants to give some to Li Changyuan.These are not enough, I still have to give back to my family, from Zhou Chengan's grandparents.If we calculate ten jins per household, it would still cost 60 jins. There are also Pipi shrimps. Nowadays, Pipi shrimps are plump and pickled. If we calculate five jins per household, this would cost thirty jins.Lu Zhi also planned to send them some asparagus, kelp, dried abalone and the like.It was a bit irritating to buy too much at once. Lu Zhi said: Second sister, you and I buy it separately, and each of us buys half.Lu Yue: OK.The market is busy now, and the seafood is all fresh. When Lu Zhi finished shopping and was about to go back, his expression moved when he looked at the fresh shrimps.Drying some dried shrimpsIt's just right to eat as a snack.As she said, Lu Zhi bought another ten kilograms of shrimps. She would dry some of these to taste for herself. If they tasted good, she would dry some more.Fortunately, Lu Zhi pushed the bicycle over, so the two of them were not too tired when they went back.Lu Zhi pushed the bicycle for a while, Lu Yue asked her to rest, and she started pushing.Lu Yue: How was your review?Lu Zhi: Not bad.Although he felt stable, before Lu Zhi won this job, it was better to keep a low profile.Lu Yue: You are smiling, your mouth is almost grinning.Lu Zhi:

Thinking about the delicious pickled crabs, Lu Zhi was a little busy, but he wasn't tired either.She found that the most difficult thing to deal with was the swimming crabs and Pipi shrimps, which had to be cleaned. It was faster with Lu Yue's help.When Li Cuihua came over and saw these things, she was not too surprised. It was nothing. She once drove out to sea and brought back dozens of kilograms of things.Li Cuihua: How do you eat this?Lu Zhi: Make pickled crabs and send them to home.Thinking that the Lu family was far away from their island, she felt a little envious that these things were just the right thing to send there to eat. Her family was not as close to the island as the Lu family was, but it was not too far away.When the washing was almost finished, Lu Zhi went to the kitchen to make the marinating soup. Fortunately, Lu Yue had all the seasonings.After finally putting all the things on, Lu Zhi stood in the yard, washed his hands and stretched, "Second sister, please find me some clothes. I'll go upstairs to take a shower and change into clean clothes."Lu Yue: The clothes are all in the cabinet. You can find them yourself. I'm tidying up the place.Lu Zhi: Okay.When passing by Tuantuan, Tuantuan reached out her hand and made babbling noises. She asked Lu Zhi to hug her, but Lu Zhi refused. She had better go upstairs and take a shower.

For today's dinner, Zhou Cheng'an steamed steamed buns and made porridge, and Lu Zhi made spicy and sour potato shreds and cold asparagus. Zhou Cheng'an took care of all the dishes, making them easy to make.Today Zhou Jun broke open the steamed buns and ate them with potato shreds sandwiched between the steamed buns. The steamed buns were full of flavor, and when you bite into them, you will find crispy, sour and spicy potato shreds. The two textures are mixed together, and it is extremely delicious.Zhou Chengan: After dinner, let's go upstairs to enjoy the cool air.Lu Zhi nodded, okay.The family of three went to the terrace after dinner. Lu Zhi was the first to go up. She looked at the rocking chairs and table on the terrace with a pleasant expression.Zhou Chengan didn't say anything when he got it back, and quietly brought it up himself.Zhou Chengan smiled: Go up and give it a try.The rocking chair was covered with something, and it was a little soft when you sat on it. Lying on it, the rocking chair swayed slightly, and you could see the stars in the night sky without raising your head.It's so beautiful.Zhou Chengan looked at Lu Zhi and smiled softly.

On the day of the exam, Lu Zhi got up early.Zhou Chengan took Lu Zhi to the island's primary school on his bicycle.The number of people who came to take the exam was quite impressive. Lu Zhi looked around and saw that these were all qualified, but he felt a little unsure for a moment.So many people.Zhou Chengan: I'll wait for you outside.Listening to Zhou Chengan's voice, his emotions calmed down. If you pass the exam, you will pass. If you fail, you will fail. You can't force this.Lu Zhi: It's time to test the results of my study these days.

Li Changyuan passed by and saw Zhou Chengan,

and found that there was a kettle in his bicycle, and he suddenly looked complicated.You've changed, you've really changedLi Changyuan: My brothers and sisters will be out soon.Thinking of Lu Zhi, Li Changyuan was thinking a lot, thinking about Lu Zhi's cooking skills. It has been hot recently and he has lost weight. He used to eat so much, but now he eats less.Li Changyuan stood and talked to Zhou Chengan for a while.Lu Zhi: Zhou Chengan.Li Changyuan looked up when he heard the sound.When did Zhou Chengan run over?Lu Zhi: After the summer vacation, I can come over to work and teach Chinese.After getting the water bottle handed over by Zhou Chengan, Lu Zhi took a big sip and felt a little refreshed.Lu Zhi: I still need to make a phone call and talk to my parents. I will also go to my second sister's house soon.Zhou Chengan nodded and wrote them down one by one.Zhou Chengan: I will take you there now.When Li Changyuan saw Lu Zhi and Lu Zhi, he said congratulations.Lu Zhi: You look a little thinner.Li Changyuan: Yes, it's hot. I've been having trouble eating recently and haven't eaten much.Lu Zhi: Why don't you come over and eat fried noodles together in the evening? By the way, you can take the pickled crabs I made for you back with you. The pickled crabs are ready to eat.Li Changyuan started to drool a little. He couldn't eat. He couldn't eat anything, but he could eat it. He could show off three bowls of rice.

This time the school recruited a total of four teachers, and Lu Zhi was honored to become one of them.In addition to Lu Zhi's three remaining teachers, one is an educated youth, one is a fellow villager here, and the other is a military wife like Lu Zhi.They were not familiar with each other, and they might not even be able to remember their names, but since they were both working in the island's primary school, they greeted each other when they came out.Lu Zhi sat on the back seat of the bicycle, shaking his feet slightly and sharing with Zhou Chengan.When they arrived at the operator's room, Lu Zhi got off his bicycle and went in one after another with Zhou Chengan.The person who received the call was Li Lan.Li Lan: Received, received, this morning someone delivered the pickled crabs and pickled shrimps. Your dad went to the countryside to deliver things to your grandparents again, and he also brought some meat along the way. Every time your grandparents go there, they must bring something for us to bring back.After listening to Li Lan's words, Lu Zhicai smiled and said: Twenty-six dollars a month's salary.Li Lan: What＇s a monthly salary of 26?Lu Zhi: Teacher.Li Lan was cold for a while, then understood what Lu Zhi meant and became excited.

Chapter 30Lu Zhi found a job as a teacher, earning twenty-seven dollars a month. Of course, this may be a temporary salary, and there will be salary increases and various benefits in the future.Li Lan: Your sister-in-law and the others will definitely be happy when they find out. When I go back today, I will buy some wine for your dad and your eldest brother no matter what.Lu Zhi: It's better not to buy anything, eat fresh food, and try not to drink alcohol.Li Lan: OK, OK, I'll listen to you. When will you go to work? Have you told your second sister what grade you are teaching for the first time as a teacher? Do you need us to send you something?Lu Zhi: No, don't worry. I'm teaching first-grade Chinese. I'll be with my second sister in a minute.Li Lan: OK, OK.After the phone call, Lu Zhi smiled, it was really hard to be unhappy.Zhou Chengan: Teacher Lu, let's go to your second sister's houseLu Zhi: Teacher LuNot to mention before time travel, after time travel, Zhou Chengan was the first to call her Teacher Lu.

Lu Yue was a little absent-minded. Hearing the movement, he quickly walked over with Tuantuan in his arms. How about it?Lu Zhi shook his head.Lu Yue: It's okay. We'll talk about it later when we have the chance. Otherwise, if you hold Tuantuan and play with Tuantuan, Tuantuan will miss you, right?Lu Zhi shook his head again, "Second sister, you have to call me Teacher Lu from now on."Lu Yue, who was still worried, breathed a sigh of relief and reached out to pinch Lu Zhi's cheek. "You are so childish, and you still do this."Tuantuan giggled at being amused, and Lu Zhi took her over and coaxed her for a while.Lu Zhi held his little hand and greeted Zhou Chengan, "Uncle, it's uncle."

Li Changyuan looked particularly excited when he came home today.Li Chuni joked: What's wrong with you? You got promoted.Li Changyuan: Don't cook today. Lu Zhi passed the exam and is going to be a teacher in an elementary school. He even asked us to eat fried noodles together.fried noodlesLi Chunni likes to eat this.Li Chunni and Li Changyuan simply packed up and went out. First they went to the supply and marketing cooperative and bought two bottles of cans for Lu Zhi and the others, and then went to Lu Zhi's house.Li Chunni: I heard that the cans from the supply and marketing cooperative this time are different from the previous ones. They are particularly delicious.Li Changyuan: What's the difference? They're not all canned food.Li Chunni: They are all canned. Let's go back and you eat the noodles I made for you.Li Changyuan looked at the cans in the net bag and nodded after a while. Yes, what you said makes sense.As they neared Lu Zhi's house, the two men discovered that they had forgotten to call their son, Li Weidong.The two people looked at each other, then looked at the sky, and turned around in unison to go home to find their son.

For fried noodles, the sauce should be fragrant, the noodles should be chewy, and the refreshing cucumber shreds must be indispensable.Lu Zhi took a few cucumbers and washed them outside the yard before going to the kitchen.After Zhou Chengan took care of the side dishes, Lu Zhi started cooking.When the oil was hot, Lu Zhi stir-fried the sliced pork belly in the pot.A handful of chopped green onions were sprinkled in, and Lu Zhi stir-fried for a while until he felt it was almost done, so he added the sauce prepared in advance.Add seasonings, add water and slowly simmer the sauce.Zhou Chengan is very strong, so he made the noodles.As soon as Li Chuni and the others came in, they smelled the aroma of fried sauce. The aroma was so strong that it was fragrant but not greasy.When Lu Zhi came out, Li Weidong ran over and hugged him. She smiled, sister-in-law, come here. When Lao Zhou finishes cooking the noodles, we will start dinner.Li Chuni looked at this place, not to mention, it was really good. When she just came here, the vegetable garden here was still bare, but now it has sprouted.Finally dinner was served.Each noodle is coated with fried sauce. The noodles are smooth and chewy. When you take one bite, you will feel the aroma in your mouth. And because the shredded cucumber is very refreshing, it is even more amazing to eat the pork belly inside. The meat is soft and full of sauce. juice.Lu Zhi ate two bowls of noodles by himself.The two Zaizai couldn't eat any more and wanted to eat more. Fortunately, Lu Zhi stopped them.Lu Zhi: You are not allowed to play any games today. You have eaten too much. Exercise right after eating to avoid stomachache.Zhou Jun: Good sister-in-lawLi Weidong: OK

Zhou Jun is on summer vacation.This is really great for Yu Zhou Jun. He can play with his sister-in-law every day and go to see Tuan Tuan.Lu Zhi was lying on Lu Yue's bed, with two cubs playing together next to her.

She looked at the older one and the younger one, and was a little curious about how a kindergarten cub and a cub who couldn't speak yet played. So harmonious.Lu Yue and Li Cuihua went to catch the sea. Hearing them talking outside, Lu Zhi got up and went downstairs.Lu Zhi: Second sister, you are back.Lu Yue looked unhappy, and Lu Zhi asked quietly: Did you and Li Cuihua quarrel, or did Li Cuihua say something that you didn't like to hear?Lu Yue: It's not me, it's you. Aren't you going to be a teacher in an elementary school? Li Cuihua told me today that there was a teacher in the elementary school on our island who liked Lu Chengan before.Before Lu Zhi started working, Lu Yue began to worry about Lu Zhi getting along with his colleague. After all, this colleague was quite special. I heard that he was not married yet.Lu Yue looked at her calm look. You are not jealous or worried.Lu Zhi: I'm definitely not worried if I'm worried, and I'm definitely not jealous if I'm jealous.Lu Yue looked unbelieving, oh, I'm not jealous.Zhou Chengan, who came to find Lu Zhi and Zhou Jun, stood outside and heard what these two people said.

In the evening, Lu Zhi and the others had dinner at Lu Yue's house before going back.The steamed seafood is authentic and very simple.Lu Zhi came out of the shower and was slapped on the wall by Zhou Chengan. She still had a towel in her hand and her hair was wet. She looked up at Zhou Chengan. She really didn't know why the plot of such an idol drama was suddenly staged.The two have been married for a while. Even so, looking at Zhou Chengan's face, Lu Zhi's heart was still beating a little fast.Lu Zhi hugged his neck, and the two were inseparable. The difference was that Lu Zhi found that Zhou Chengan was particularly domineering today.Lu Zhi: What's wrong with you?Zhou Chengan: I've never seen you jealous.Lu Zhi:I didn't expect you to be like Zhou Chengan.

　　Large courtyard.Chu Tong and the Li family have been quarreling for a long time. Lu Zhi obviously lived a good life after marrying to the island. The more this happened, the more uncomfortable Chu Tong became, because he had no thoughts about Li Yu anymore, and the two of them were now behind closed doors. Quarrel often.He Li regretted it now, but there was nothing she could do about it now. Chu Tong was married to Li Yu, and life had to go on. She gritted her teeth and bought a temporary job for Chu Tong.After getting the job, Chu Tong and Li Yu seemed to have returned to their previous appearance.The two of them came back from the food station together, chatting and laughing, and also mentioned a lot of things.Someone in the courtyard couldn't help but ask: What kind of day is this for you? I even bought ribs.Chu Tong: It's nothing, I just have to go to work and want to celebrate.He Li came out, how could she not let everyone know about such a good thing, especially since this good thing was her credit.He Li: Yes, she is going to work. This is not to find a temporary worker for her. Although she is a temporary worker, she can become a regular worker if she works hard in the future. It is in that flour mill.How well she does as a mother-in-law?Betrothal gift, and also find a job, no mother-in-law in this large courtyard can do what she does.He Li: This job is not cheap, but I thought, for the sake of my daughter-in-law, it would be better to buy it, so that she can have a formal job and be able to stand upright when she returns to her parents' home. Do you think so?It's true that because of this job, Chu Tong is now the envy of his family.Chu Tong nodded and said, I am envious of having a mother-in-law like you.Li Lan came back from get off work and saw them talking, but didn't say much. He was anxious to go back to cook. They went to deliver pickled crabs and pickled shrimps to Zhou Chengan's grandparents. They unexpectedly And gave sausages.This Li Lan wanted to wait for Lu Zhi to come back and cook it for Lu Zhi to eat, but An An wanted to eat it, so she just made it first.He Li: What are you, Lu Zhi, doing on the island? Have you found a job?Li Lan said calmly: I found the job.Everyone became interested when they heard this and looked towards Li Lan.Aunt Li: What kind of job? Why haven't you heard of this? Have you mentioned it?Li Lan: I haven't gone to work yet. Besides, once you find a job, just work hard and do it honestly.He Li and her family looked a little ugly, but they didn't expect Lu Zhi to find a job on the island.He Li: What kind of job?Li Lan smiled, "Teacher, this is not the winter and summer vacation. If it were not the winter and summer vacation, she would be at work now." Okay, you go on, I still have to cook here.teacherLu Zhi not only married an officer who looked very fond of his wife, but he was also able to become a teacher.

Chapter 31When Lu Zhi got up on his first day at work, Zhou Chengan had already returned from the cafeteria.There are steamed buns in the cafeteria today.Lu Zhi was eating steamed buns, thinking about going to class later, and still felt a little nervous.Lu Zhi looked up and found that Zhou Chengan also seemed a little nervous and very confused.Lu Zhi: It's me who's in class, not you.Zhou Chengan hesitated to speak, lowered his head and continued to eat. After finishing the meal, he realized that what he ate today was not a bun filled with cabbage, but a bun filled with sauerkraut.Zhou Chengan sent Lu Zhi and Zhou Jun to school together.When he arrived outside the school, Lu Zhi looked at the energetic faces and the flowers of the future of the motherland. For some reason, he suddenly felt less nervous.Zhou Chengan was no longer nervous, but he looked a little angry.Lu Zhi:No, what's wrong with this man?Zhou Cheng'an: I'll pick you up after you get off work tonight.Lu Zhi: Okay.The happiest person is Zhou Jun. Lu Zhi is now in school. Although he doesn't teach Zhou Jun, they can all come to school together in the future and then go back together.Zhou

Jun was chattering, and Lu Zhi forgot about Zhou Chengan's strangeness.Lu Zhikan and Zhou Jun entered his class, and then he went to the office.When he arrived at the office, Lu Zhi introduced himself to the teacher in the same office, and then began to clean up his desk.Several people asked Lu Zhi some basic information at the same time. Lu Zhi picked a few answers that he could answer, and gave perfunctory answers to those he couldn't.There are a total of six teachers in Lu Zhi's office, including her, there are seven in total. There are quite a lot of people, so it is quite lively.Among these teachers, two were military wives, so as soon as Lu Zhi came over, they were particularly enthusiastic towards Lu Zhi.There were some questions that Lu Zhi didn't need to ask, they helped answer them.

On her first day at work, Lu Zhi felt pretty good because she was really not tired. She was teaching Chinese, and since she was a new teacher, she didn't have too many classes. The lesson plans had been prepared before, so she had free time. It's really a very leisurely time.The lunch in the school cafeteria is also quite delicious. Lu Zhi can also talk and listen to gossip with his two new military wives.When it was time to get off work, Lu Zhi waited in the office until Zhou Jun came over, then slowly went back with Zhou Jun.Zhou Jun: Sister-in-law, did your work go well today?Lu Zhi couldn't help but laugh. He is really a little grown-up, and he still knows how to ask me if my work is going well. Don't worry, it will go well.Zhou Jun is serious. Are they taking the lecture seriously?Lu Zhi rubbed Zhou Jun's hair, are you serious in class?Zhou Jun nodded, seriously, I want to study hard.The two people arrived at the school gate and saw Zhou Chengan waiting for them.Lu Zhi went over and asked: What should we have for dinner?Zhou Chengan: The eldest sister said that in order to celebrate your first day at work, she asked us to come over and have dinner together.Lu Zhi: Okay.The family of three set off to Lu Yue's house together.When Zhou Chengan asked Lu Zhi if his work was going well, Lu Zhi also replied that it was going well. There were some gossips that he wanted to talk to Zhou Chengan, but because Zhou Jun was nearby, he didn't say anything.Lu Zhi: Are you in a bad mood today?Zhou Chengan:Then Zhou Chengan seemed to be a little emotional because Lu Zhi asked him.Lu Zhi:I should have known better than to ask, but what is Zhou Chengan doing?

Chapter 32Lu Yue cooked a table of dishes to celebrate Lu Zhi's first day at work.After Lu Zhi and his family finished eating, Zhou Chengan went to help with the remaining work, and Lu Yue simply went over to talk to Lu Zhi.Lu Yue was still thinking about the fact that the person who liked Zhou Chengan before was now a colleague with Lu Zhi, so he asked carefully.Lu Zhi couldn't laugh or cry. I didn't even know who it was. Maybe I met him at school today, so I didn't even know.Lu Yue: You, be careful anyway and don't get tripped up by others.Lu Zhi: Not reallyLu Yue: Anyway, it's better to be careful. I heard that girl's personality is a bit paranoid.

After taking a shower and packing up to go to bed, Lu Zhi thought of Zhou Chengan's mood changes throughout the day and stared at him.Lu Zhi: Let me explain.Zhou Chengan: What should I tell you?Lu Zhi: What do you think?Zhou Chengan suddenly smiled and seemed to be happy. He quickly explained the matter again, down to the smallest detail.The girl who chased Zhou Chengan was the sister of Zhou Chengan's colleague. The two met once in total. Later, Zhou Chengan's colleague wanted to help as a matchmaker but Zhou Chengan refused. The girl blocked Zhou Chengan several times and failed. Zhou Chengan made it clear.Zhou Chengan: I met you after that.Lu Zhi: Why don't you like her?Zhou Chengan: If I don't like you, I just don't like it. There is no reason. Just like when I first saw you, I liked you. When I thought about marrying you, I couldn't sleep.Lu Zhi: Smooth-tongued.Zhou Chengan became serious. What I said was true.Lu Zhi: They are all sincere. After he finished speaking, he asked again: Why are you acting so weird all day today? Just because I didn't ask you.Zhou Chengan replied: It's not my business.Lu Zhi: Why is that?Zhou Chengan: You are not jealous. He paused and then said: Although you are not jealous now, at least you asked. If you ask, it means you care.In other words, it's not a matter of jealousy, it's a matter of not caring.Lu Zhi understood Zhou Chengan's thoughts. When he was sleeping, Lu Zhi smiled and said to him: Zhou Chengan, I care about you and like you.

After communicating with Zhou Chengan, Lu Zhi also learned that the girl's name was Feng Lan. She felt that this was all Chen Zhima's rotten millet and there was nothing to worry about. What's more, even her ex-girlfriend I don't know, I just liked it.After Lu Zhi felt that he was always being stared at at school, he no longer felt that way.When there were any activities at school, she always felt that there was a vague gaze looking at her. After a few times, she discovered that it was Feng Lan.She is a girl who looks a bit bookish. Read novelsLu Zhi met her eyes, and the two looked at each other for a long time.While eating in the school cafeteria at noon, Feng Lan came to see Lu Zhi.Feng Lan sat down opposite Lu Zhi. I just couldn't figure out why it wasn't me but you. I don't think I'm inferior to you.Lu Zhi felt that she was probably over the top.Lu Zhi: I like this thing. It makes no sense. Just like you may like cabbage dumplings among all the fillings, while others like sauerkraut.Feng Lan: I don't like eating cabbage.Lu Zhi: Just giving an example. She added: There is nothing to compare between people. Anyway, I am the best in my heart, and you should be the best in your heart. Everyone has their own strengths and weaknesses.Feng Lan: I don't mean that.Lu Zhi: I don't mean that. Why are you staring at me?Feng Lan: MeLu Zhi: In the future, you will meet people who think you are good at everything.

Chapter 33The weather is getting colder, and Lu Zhi is already looking forward to the winter vacation. It is really difficult to get up and go to work every morning.Zhou Jun also had the same idea as Lu Zhi. The two of them wanted to have the same expression when they got up and came out of the room every day.When Lu Zhi finally persisted until the winter vacation was only three days away, his whole person was in a state of excitement.The Lu family called Lu Zhi and told Lu Zhi that Chutong and Li Yu were getting divorced.Lu Zhi also didn't expect that without her as a female partner to act as a control group for the male and female protagonists, they would actually reach the stage of divorce.Li Lan: The two of them were arguing every day. One day in the middle of the night, they got into a fight and got violent. Several people in our yard ran over to break up the fight.Whether he was trying to break up the fight or just watching the fun, I couldn't tell.Li Lan continued, and after that the two of them stopped for a while, and then they were about to divorce.Lu Zhi was not very surprised when Xiao Shuo's plot collapsed. After all, after she became the female supporting role, Xiao Shuo's plot was different from before. She would not follow the original female supporting plot. Come on, in this novel, many things between the male and female protagonists are promoted by her, and the plots of the male and female protagonists must have changed.Li Lan talked to Lu Zhi about some family matters. Their family is now motivated and active. Even Lu Anan knows that he should study hard.Lu Anan had a new dream recently, saying that when she grows up, she will be a teacher like Lu Zhi.Li Lan was sighing, it would be great if An An could really be a teacher like you in the future.Thinking of the changes in the future, Lu Zhi felt that it was still too early to say this, and Lu Anan might not want to continue to be a teacher in the future.

On the day of the final exam, before Lu Zhi went to work, he told Zhou Chengan not to forget to buy groceries and to celebrate tonight.Over at the vegetable station, if Lu Zhi waits until he gets off work to buy food, he probably won't be able to buy anything.Zhou Cheng'an: I understand, I understand. I will tell them later about the second sister's side, and about sister-in-law Chunni. I told Li Changyuan yesterday.Lu Zhi and Zhou Jun faced the sunlight together and set foot on the road to school.Big hands holding small hands, Zhou Jun jumped up and down.Zhou Jun: Sister-in-law, sister-in-lawLu Zhi: What's wrong?Zhou Jun: Sister-in-law, when can I be an uncle?Lu Zhi was stunned for a moment, and then realized that Zhou Jun would be her uncle only if she and Zhou Chengan had children.Lu Zhi asked and found out that it was when Zhou Jun went to play with Tuan

Tuan that Lu Yue told Zhou Jun that he could still be an uncle in the future.Lu Zhi: You want to be an uncle?Zhou Jun, like an adult, said sadly: Every time I go to play with Tuan Tuan, I have to wait until school is over or on the weekend. If I become an uncle, I can always play with my nephew or niece. We played together.Lu Zhi asked again, do you really like it?Zhou Jun nodded.Lu Zhi: But aren't you also a child?Zhou Jun: Is it because of me that my sister-in-law doesn't have a baby now?Lu Zhi touched Zhou Jun's hair, "No, I'm just asking, do you think the baby is annoying?"Zhou Jun: Why are you annoyed? It's so fun.Zhou Jun's eyes sparkled when he said it.

The Lu family was particularly lively at night.Lu Zhi was on winter vacation and was in a good mood. When he was cooking in the kitchen, he cooked a few more vegetables.Li Changyuan was waiting for the meal to start. When Chen Chunni helped bring out the dishes, she couldn't stand it anymore and gave Li Changyuan a slight squeeze.Li Changyuan: Tell me, why did you marry such a capable daughter-in-law so quietly?Chen Chunni: Why, are you dissing my cooking?Li Changyuan quickly said: How dare you?Everyone laughed.We had a very sumptuous meal in the evening. Of course, the most popular thing on the table was seafood, which Lu Yue brought over after going to sea.Lu Zhi and Zhou Chengan sat at the main seats and toasted everyone. The meal officially started.

In the evening, Lu Zhi finished taking a shower and

doing skin care. Zhou Chengan cleaned the kitchen again downstairs. When he came back, he hugged Lu Zhi from behind.Lu Zhi: Well, I smell a bit drunk.Zhou Chengan quickly let go and I went to take a bath.Lu Zhi: Wait, let me tell you something.Lu Zhi: Just forget about drinking today. You don't need to use birth control next time.Zhou Chengan was stunned for a moment, and then he looked excited. He was pacing on the spot, no, no, we still have to wait.Lu Zhi used contraception because he didn't want to have children for the time being, which was partly because of Zhou Jun. In addition, Lu Zhi wanted her and Zhou Chengan to get along, but now these are no longer problems.It's even possible that she and Zhou Cheng'an need to get along, which wasn't a problem in the first place.Zhou Cheng'an: It's January now. If I get pregnant, I can give birth around November because the weather is too cold.Lu Zhi didn't even expect this. Zhou Cheng'an knew this because Li Changyuan was worried about this matter when Li Chuni gave birth to her child.Lu Zhi and Zhou Chengan discussed it. It was best to have confinement when the weather was warm but not hot. However, it was uncertain whether it would be successful, but at least give it a try.Therefore, the two of them still have to continue using contraception for the time being.

During Lu Zhi's winter vacation, it was not troublesome to go home, and he could just go back with the army's car smoothly.Lu Yue was also moved when she found out, but it was cold and she didn't want to bother with it, so she gave up in the end, but prepared a lot of things for the family.Zhou Chengan sent Lu Zhi to the dock. If anything happens, please call me.The driver, Xiao Chen, smiled and said: Sister-in-law, I've been over there all the time. If there's anything I can do, just come to me.Zhou Chengan nodded, then I'll trouble you.Lu Zhi didn't go back by himself this time. He also took Zhou Jun with him, planning to take Zhou Jun to show his grandparents.Lu Zhi and Zhou Jun got into the car. The car started for a long time. Zhou Jun smiled and said: Sister-in-law, my eldest brother is still standing there.Lu Zhi touched his hair and said, "Okay, sit down."

The Lu family knew Lu Zhi was back, but they couldn't be happier and had already been waiting outside the yard.Lu Zhi was hugged by Li Lan as soon as he got out of the car. When he was about to go in, Xiao Chen had already helped to get the things out of the car.Li Lan: Why did you bring so many things?Lu Zhi: I brought some, and the second sister brought some. The second sister even went to catch the sea, and she also asked her to bring out some dry goods at home.Everyone was talking and going back.When Lu Zhi entered the yard, he saw He Li. He Li looked unhappy and snorted coldly when she saw Lu Zhi.Everyone knew that Lu Zhi was a teacher, so they kept asking questions, and Lu Zhi answered in a good temper.When he was about to go back, Lu Zhi looked at He Li and asked: Aunt He, I heard that Chu Tong and Li Yu divorcedHe Li turned around angrily and went home.

After Lu Zhi returned to the Lu family, she was really busy. She was busy taking Zhou Jun back to the countryside to see her grandparents, busy shopping, and talking to her family. She felt that she was just busy all day long. It's the same as a top, but this feeling is very fulfilling.When Lu Zhi met Chu Tong in the department store that day, neither of them expected it.Chu Tong took the initiative to say hello and sneered, I knew the problem was all with you. Are you the same as me?Lu Zhi was stunned for a moment, knowing what Chu Tong meant.Lu Zhi found it strange that Chu Tong's character was willing to divorce so neatly, but she didn't find a way to grit her teeth to compete with Lu Zhi, or find a way to tell everyone that she had done nothing wrong.It's just that Lu Zhi doesn't know whether Chu Tong was reborn or passed through the book.Lu Zhi was calm, I don't know what you are talking about.Chu Tong: I am the heroine, I am the heroine, don't you know?

Chapter 34Lu Zhi couldn't just rely on Chu Tong's words, "I am the heroine, do you know? Do you know whether she traveled through books or was reborn?"Chu Tong: I could be more beautiful than you in my previous life, and I will definitely be able to do so in this life.Lu Zhi:Lu Zhi knew that she was reborn, or that she was the reborn heroine in a novel.Lu Zhi: I don't know what you are talking about. But I want to say, I think you are quite pathetic. Life is so long and beautiful, but you actually want to compare yourself with me.Lu Zhi is not able to understand people like Chu Tong, and he doesn't want to have too much interaction with Chu Tong.

Lu Zhi went back after staying in the Lu family for a week. He brought a lot of things with him when he came here, and even more things when he went back.Although the Lu family was reluctant to part with him, they didn't show it. They just kept telling Lu Zhi to come back when he was free.When Lu Zhi and Zhou Jun arrived at the pier, Zhou Chengan was already waiting for them.Lu Zhi saw Zhou Chengan with a smile on his face. Before he asked him if he missed him, Zhou Chengan said: I miss you.Lu Zhi looked a little embarrassed.

Lu Zhi spent the entire winter vacation very leisurely. He went to see Lu Yue whenever he had nothing to do, prepared New Year's goods, played with Zhou Jun, and even attended Chen Ting's wedding next door.Under Chen He's introduction, Chen Ting found a man who seemed very down-to-earth.Chen Ting also complained to Lu Zhi, saying that men are too ignorant of styles, but she looked a little embarrassed when she spoke. It could be seen that Chen Ting was still satisfied.After attending the wedding, Chen He drank too much and wanted to give Lu Zhi a red envelope, but fortunately Zhou Chengan stopped him.If it weren't for Lu Zhi, I guess Chen Ting would still be in trouble. She might be quarreling with her family because of love, or she might have married that scumbag.

Lu Zhi didn't understand Chu Tong's plan to come to the island to be a stepmother. He didn't know what she was thinking.Li Lan is complaining to Lu Zhi, do you think her brain is broken? Chu Tong is divorced. There are many people who want to marry her, and they don't mind her being married for the second time. Why can't she think about it and do it for others? Stepmother, how could it be so easy for a stepmother to do this?Lu Zhi: Probably, he wants to compare with meLi Lan: You're crazy.Let alone Li Lan when mentioning this matter, even the Lu family felt that there was something wrong with Chu Tong, and they could see that she did it on purpose.

Lu Yue was speechless for a while, so just to be better than you, she came to the island to be a stepmother.Lu Yue spent much more time on the island than Lu Zhi. After asking about it, she found out what was going on.Or it can be said that Lu Yue would know just by asking Li Cuihua next door.While Lu Zhi and Lu Yue were talking, Li Cuihua came over with melon seeds, looking a little excited.Li Cuihua: What's going on? What's going on?Lu Zhi:Lu Zhi: That's right, a neighbor in my hometown got divorced, and her wife came over to marry Deputy Battalion Commander Han.Li Cuihua: Oh, he has three children. These three children are not easy to take care of.Lu Zhi knew that two of the three children, whom Lu Zhi had taught, were a bit naughty and not easy to take care of.Li Cuihua is eating melon seeds. You are talking to me. Come on, let's eat melon seeds together.Lu Zhi didn't want to say anything, but Lu Yue said a few words. Li Cuihua also looked shocked when she heard it, and then went back satisfied.Lu Yue smiled, do you think I said too much?Lu Zhi: Not bad.Lu Yue nodded Lu Zhi's head, you idiot, don't you think about it, why did Chu Tong become the stepmother of three children? Just to compare with you, if I don't say it now, wait a minute. When she comes over, you will become everyone's joke.Lu Yue: I know what she can say. I must say that the husband she married before is the one you like. Maybe she can even add a few words to exaggerate her divorce and make it your fault. When the time comes for you to explain, how troublesome it is, you might as well say it directly, since I didn't tell lies anyway, are you right?Lu Yue: I don't know if she is stirring up trouble.The two people were talking, and Tuantuan was giggling on the side.Lu Zhi hugged Tuantuan and gave him a kiss.

After Zhou Chengan found out, he comforted Lu Zhi and said: It's okay.Lu Zhi:Lu Zhi: I definitely know it's okay, but what do you think? She's been married, so she must have a lot to say.Zhou Chengan: Who said anything about you? I'll go find them at your door and ask them to tell you in person.Lu Zhi: Forget it, just be sure that my wife is right.Zhou Jun came in and didn't know what the two of them were talking about. He quickly said: Yes, yes, my sister-in-law is right.Lu Zhi was amused by Zhou Jun, but couldn't help it, and later he lay on Zhou Chengan's shoulder and smiled.

When Chen Ting came to see Lu Zhi, Lu Zhi knew that Chen Ting and Chu Tong had become neighbors.Chen Ting rolled her eyes. She saw me asking about you. When I asked her, she smiled and looked indifferent. When I asked her again, she hesitated to speak. Isn't it? I want to say something bad about you .Lu Zhi was also a little curious, and then what.Chen Ting: I just said, I know everything about you. After that, her face became a little ugly. After finishing speaking, she said again: I think I heard it. On the first day she came here, she had a quarrel with her mother-in-law.It stands to reason that Chen Ting knows the future development. She knows the content of the novel, so there is really no need to do this. Why bother?

When the New Year was approaching, Lu Zhi got busy. She was going to the city to buy new year goods. This time, Zhou Chengan accompanied Lu Zhi, who happened to have a holiday.The two of them went back to visit the Lu family and Zhou Chengan's grandparents. They gave away many New Year's goods, and then they hurried to buy New Year's goods.He was so busy that he returned to the island before Zhou Chengan had to go to work.Lu Zhi met Chu Tong on the boat. Although Lu Zhi was surprised, he thought it was normal. After all, the island was not big.Chu Tong looked very tired with three children. The three children were very naughty. Chu Tong didn't know how many words he said to them, but they didn't calm down.As a result, when two children saw Lu Zhi, they immediately called Teacher Lu respectfully, and then sat down very obediently. The older one also sat down after seeing his younger brother and sister like this. .Chu Tong:Chu Tong called Lu Zhi out, but Lu Zhi remembered what he said to Chu Tong on the ship, just outside the cabin.Lu Zhi: Do you think it's worth it?Chu Tong: You know what? He is about to be promoted. After he finished speaking, he said: You didn't say you don't care. Since you don't care, what are you talking about?Lu Zhi:Lu Zhi: I don't care, but I'm not stupid, and I'm not letting you throw dirty water on me.Chu Tong: I'm pregnant.Chu Tong: Lu Zhi, you haven't been pregnant. It's because you can't have children or because your man can't have children.Lu Zhi doesn't know what to say anymore. You should calm down.

Chapter 35Lu Zhi's New Year was particularly lively. She thought it was probably because Lu Yue was also on the island.In addition, Li Changyuan's family and Chen He's family had a lot of contact with them.After the New Year, Lu Zhi was still a little disappointed about what he had to do.But actually, I'm not tired at all.Zhou Jun: I don't want to go to school.Lu Zhi: I don't want to go to work.Finally, when the first day of school arrived, Lu Zhi and Zhou Jun were more active than anyone else because they couldn't be late, they really couldn't be late.For this reason, the two of them were laughed at by Zhou Chengan.Lu Zhi and Zhou Jun discussed it together and were too lazy to talk to him. In the end, it was Zhou Chengan who brought back a big lobster for them when they went out to sea in order to acquit themselves, and that was the end.

Chen Ting's husband was promoted, and she was overjoyed when she returned to Chen He. Lu Zhi also learned from Chen Ting that because Deputy Battalion Commander Han was not promoted, Chu Tong and Chu Tong were pregnant. He had a row.Chen Ting: I heard them arguing. Chu Tong said you didn't mean you would be the regiment leader soon. Deputy Battalion Commander Han said he didn't say such a thing, it was probably the introducer who said that. I don't know what the introducer said about Deputy Battalion Commander Han. Stepmother of three children.After listening to what Chen Ting said, Lu Zhi felt that Chu Tong would probably get divorced. If Deputy Battalion Commander Han could not give Chu Tong the life he wanted, how could Chu Tong be willing to be here? It sounded like she was worse than herself. own wordsWhat's more, Chu Tong now always feels that she is the heroine and knows the future development.Lu Zhi talked to Chen Ting for a while, and then went to make a phone call. She wanted to call the Zhou family. Lu Zhi was very fair. Every time he called the Lu family, he would not forget about himself. My mother-in-law's place, the same goes for shopping.Lu Zhi didn't expect that when he was on the phone, Lu Zhi heard Chu Tong talking on the phone with someone.Chu Tong lowered his voice. What did you say at the beginning? What did you say when you introduced him? You said that his future future would be better than that of Zhou Chengan.The matchmaker introduced over the phone was also embarrassed. She didn't know who Zhou Chengan was, but Chu Tong had given him too much. Besides, she thought Deputy Battalion Commander Han's conditions were pretty good.

Chu Tong stopped.Anyway, Lu Zhi has never seen Chu Tong deliberately compete with him since then.Lu Zhi lived his life leisurely.On Children's Day, June 1, in order to satisfy Zhou Jun's request, Lu Zhi and the others had hot pot.When eating hot pot at this time, the ingredients are definitely not as rich as later, but fortunately there is a lot of seafood. The various meatballs made by Lu Zhi are really high in seafood content, pure fish balls, pure shrimp balls, pure fish tofu, Zhou Jun likes it very much.Lu Zhi made some sausages during the winter and had some left over. Zhou Chengan's grandparents also gave them some as gifts from the Lu family, but they hadn't even finished them yet. Lu Zhi also took some to eat. Eating it during hot pot, not to mention it tastes good.When Lu Zhi found that he felt like vomiting, his first reaction was to wonder if he was pregnant.Lu Yue had the same idea, and was even a little surprised. Was she pregnant?Lu Yue didn't know about their previous contraception. He was just anxious for Lu Zhi to have a baby, but he didn't dare to rush it.Lu Zhi: Let＇s eat first. After we finish eating, I＇ll take a look.While eating, Zhou Chengan quietly held Lu Zhi's hand.

The doctor smiled and said: Congratulations, it＇s been more than a month.Lu Zhi and Lu Huaian stopped using contraception some time ago. After calculation, this seems to be the first time they conceived a child without using contraception.According to the two people's ideas, the weather would be suitable when Lu Zhi was in confinement.The two of them went back hand in hand. Lu Zhi looked at Zhou Chengan's cautious look and felt that he was too nervous.After arriving home, Lu Zhi looked at Zhou Jun and realized what was more nervous.Zhou Jun: Sister-in-law, can this pregnant woman eat it?Zhou Jun: Sister-in-law, don＇t do the work, I＇ll do it.Zhou Jun: Sister-in-law, sister-in-lawOh my God, Zhou Jun, when did you become a repeater?

In the evening, Lu Zhi and Zhou Chengan discussed taking care of the child. Lu Zhi definitely didn't have time to take care of the child after she gave birth. She had to go to work. Lu Yue already had a bunch of people with her, and Lu Yue had two more to go. It means having a fetus, so I can＇t trouble Lu Yue.In addition, there is another thing, that is, Lu Zhi will definitely not have a second child. Zhou Chengan has no objection and is even willing to cooperate with the sterilization.When Lu Zhi heard Zhou Chengan take the initiative to say that he wanted to get a sterilization, he held his face and realized that he was indeed married to the right person.Zhou Chengan: If I had known earlier, I would have told you earlier.Lu Zhi:As a result, when Lu Zhi didn't expect it, Lu Yue offered to help take it with him the next day.Lu Yue: Bring one with you, bring two with you. When you go to work, I will help you carry them together.Lu Zhi: It's so tiring. Besides, you're going to have a second child.Lu Yue: It's okay. My parents said that they will come over to help when they retire. I'll help you take care of you first. What does one family say when it comes to two families?Lu Zhi hugged Lu Yue's arm, and the two of them were affectionate. The matter was settled like this.The two sisters were talking. When Lu Zhi heard Lu Yue say that the age difference between the children should not be too big, Lu Zhi quickly stopped Lu Yue's thoughts.Lu Zhi: I only plan to have one child.Lu Yue: AhLu Zhi: Second sister, have you heard?

Lu Zhi spent many days but could not change Lu Yue's mind. Lu Yue did not want to have one child, but Lu Yue felt that at least a second child was necessary. Lu Zhi thought it was okay, so he did not continue to force it.While Lu Yue was still worried that Zhou Chengan didn't agree with Lu Zhi's idea, Zhou Chengan had already performed the sterilization himself.Why does Lu Zhi look at Zhou Chengan and find him pleasing to the eye?I feel better than before.

When Chu Tong gave birth to the child, Lu Zhi's child was not yet born, but his belly was getting bigger, and Lu Zhi's temper was getting worse and worse. There was nothing he could do, and sometimes it was really uncomfortable.Zhou Chengan and Zhou Jun tried their best to make her happy.Chu Tong came to see Lu Zhi after her confinement. She looked at Lu Zhi's face, looked at Lu Zhi's yard, and finally said, I want a divorce.Lu Zhi:Chu Tong: I am the heroine of this novel. One day, I will live a better life than you.Lu Zhi paused, where is the child?Chu Tong: Child, of course I will take the child away, otherwise why should I stay and let that old woman bully me? But I have to pay child support.After hearing what Chu Tong said, Lu Zhi knew that Chu Tong's behavior must be caused by something, but Lu Zhi didn't think that this incident was caused by himself, nor did he think that Chu Tong was really living better than himself. Once you are well, this problem will be solved.Looking at Chu Tong, Lu Zhi thought about her behavior of taking care of the child, and couldn't help but said: Chu Tong, your enemy has never been me, but yourself. You will also encounter many in the future. There are many people, they will be better than you, there will be someone prettier than you, maybe if she takes a step forward, your child will meet many friends, and they will meet people who are better than her, who are better than you. She is excellent, do you want her to be like you?Chu Tong's eyes became sharp.Lu Zhi: You don't have to do this. I'm just telling you a fact.When Chu Tong went back, Lu Zhi felt that Chu Tong's strength seemed to have been relieved, and he was not even willing to continue to argue with Lu Zhi.

When Lu Zhi was about to give birth, Li Lan came over. She asked for leave and came to take care of Lu Zhi.Lu Zhi and Lu Yue took Li Lan around the island, and Li Lan liked the life on the island very much.Li Lan: Come here when your dad and I retire.The three of them were sitting on the beach and talking when Lu Zhi suddenly felt uncomfortable, and both Lu Yue and Li Lan changed their expressions.

When Lu Zhi gave birth to a child, he had one thought in his mind: If he didn't want to have another child, he really wouldn't have another child, this one was really enough.When Lu Zhi heard the child's cry, he fainted.When Lu Zhi woke up again, he saw that everyone was here. When Zhou Chengan saw that he was awake, he quickly asked her if she was feeling uncomfortable and gave her some water.Lu Zhi: No more babies, really no more babies.Zhou Chengan nodded hurriedly, OK, OK, I won't have any more babies, I won't have any more babies now, if I had known earlier, I shouldn't have had any babies in the first place.Lu Zhi:Lu Zhi: Where is the child?Only then did Zhou Chengan think of the child. Li Lan had already held the child in his arms and showed it to Lu Zhi.It's a son, he looks a bit ugly.UmLu Zhi comforted himself that it was okay. The newborn baby looked very good like this.

Lu Zhi had been in confinement for a month, and the most uncomfortable thing was washing her hair because she was a child. Lu Zhi spent a lot of effort to talk through Zhou Chengan, but was finally stopped by Li Lan.It wasn't until after confinement that Lu Zhi washed her hair. She also found that she had gained weight.No way, she ate too much during the confinement period, and now she has to start to control her diet.Lu Zhi: Tell me, how much fat have I gained?Zhou Chengan: No matter how fat you are, you still look good.Lu Zhi: Real or fakeZhou Chengan: Of course it's true. He added: You and I will never tell lies.Lu Zhixiao, I believe you.

On the day Li Lan was going back, Lu Zhi, Zhou Chengan, and Lu Yue went to the pier to see Li Lan back. Lu Zhi thought about it and asked everyone to take the boat to the pier with Li Lan, and then Came back by boat again.It was also a sunny day, otherwise Li Lan would have wished Lu Zhi had insisted on not even blowing the wind.Lu Zhi and Zhou Chengan walked side by side, holding hands.Lu Zhi: By the way, we haven't decided on the child's name yet. Have you thought about what to call it?Zhou Chengan: Zhou Yu.Zhou Chengan smiled and said: I just thought of it.Lu Zhi: Why is it called Zhou Yu?Zhou Chengan: Because it's so nice to meet you.Lu Zhi:While the two were talking,

Lu Zhi heard Lu Yue and her brother-in-law laughing out loud from behind.Lu Yue: Okay, okay, Lu Yu, that sounds good.Zhou Chengan: I think it sounds good too. After he finished speaking, he asked Lu Zhi: What do you think?Lu Zhi looked at him, "It's great to meet you."——End of text

Chapter 36When Lu Yu was two years old, Lu Yue became pregnant with her second child. Li Lan considered retiring directly, otherwise Lu Zhi and Lu Yue would definitely be too busy with their two children.Because Li Lan came over, the house became lively. Lu Xiangde was also thinking about Li Lan, so he even retired early and came to the island together.The two of them really like this side of the island. Sometimes when they are free, Lu Xiangde will go fishing. For this reason, Lu Zhi and the others have so many fish that they can't finish them all. They really can't finish them.Lu Zhi found that Zhou Chengan had become more and more clingy in the past two years, almost more clingy than Lu Yu.And a kiss good morning and a kiss good night.Lu Zhi felt that he shouldn't tell her about the good morning kiss and the late kiss.When Lu Zhi received the letter from Chu Tong, she was a little surprised. She took the letter and read it over. It was Chu Tong who told Lu Zhi about her current situation. She did not continue to compete with Lu Zhi, but in her heart It's better to tell Lu Zhi that he will definitely live better in the future and live better than before.It's very interesting that I'm living better than before, which is very interesting.However, Lu Zhi and Chu Tong probably wouldn't have many opportunities to interact with each other anymore, and Lu Zhi didn't take it to heart.

When Lu Zhi heard the cute voice, her eyes lit up, and they were coming over.Woooooooooooooooooooooooooooooooooooooo ooooooooooooooooooooo cute.Tuantuan: aunt, aunt.Lu Zhi: Come on, come on.Lu Zhi hugged Tuantuan and kissed Tuantuan's little face, making Tuantuan giggle.Lu Yue: I like girls so much, why don't I give birth to one?Lu Zhi: It doesn't matter. Tuantuan is enough.Lu Yue looked at Lu Zhi and shook his head with a smile: "I finally know why I like you. You see, there is no difference between such a grown-up person and a child."Lu Zhi: I am Mr. Lu, okay?Lu Yue: Okay, okay, Teacher Lu.Tuantuan yelled in Lu Yue's milky voice: "Teacher Lu."Lu Zhi: Don't call me Teacher Lu. I won't teach you when you go to school.Anyway, she doesn't teach Lu Jun, she doesn't teach Tuan Tuan, and she doesn't teach her own son either. This kind of teaching is too tiring.Tuantuan: Aunt~Lu Zhi: Yes, I call her Auntie, not Teacher Lu.Their family was lively. Lu Zhi asked Lu Yue about her pregnancy. Lu Yue had been feeling nauseous recently. Lu Zhi also had hawthorns there and told him to give them to Lu Yue later.They were talking and laughing.

Lu Zhi and the others couldn't let Li Lan and Lu Xiangde live apart, so they all lived at Lu Yue's place. Lu Zhi always sent Lu Yu to Lu Yue's place before going to work, so Their family usually eats at Lu Yue's place in the evening.When Lu Zhi got off work, he went to Lu Yue's house with Zhou Chengan and Zhou Jun.Zhou Jun talked about school and friends, and Lu Zhi and Zhou Chengan listened carefully.When someone greeted them, Lu Zhi always looked gentle.When they were passing by the seaside, Lu Zhi looked at the sea and listened to the sound of the waves, and suddenly felt a sense of tranquility over time.At this time, Lu Zhi felt that the name of her and Zhou Chengan's son was Lu Yu, which was really good.It seems that he also knows why Zhou Chengan thought of this name that day.Lu Zhi: Lao Zhou.Zhou Chengan: What's wrong, wife?Lu Zhi: Let's call our son Lu Yu.The two people looked at each other and then laughed.It's great to meet Zhou Chengan.

Printed in Great Britain
by Amazon

40446065R00139